THE LOST MISSION
OF SANTA ISABEL

by
JOAN CANDLER

Baja Press

"Joan Candler has penned a swift moving tale of treasure hunting and greed, of love and deceit, of adventure and suspense. Evoking memories of The Treasure of the Sierra Madre, the story reveals the deadly effect on those seeking hidden riches. MJ Steele is a smart, beautiful, strong minded woman caught up in the search for legendary treasure. Friends and foes surround her, but which is which? Is her husband, Ricardo, dead or alive? Is anything as it seems? You'll find out by reading this highly enjoyable story."

—*Steven P. Marini, award winning author*

"Joanie Candler has turned the historical story of the infamous missing Santa Isabel treasure into an action adventure tale, a quest jumping from the beautiful, wild Baja California of 1786 to today. There is murder and deception and a sweeping landscape swirling around one of the strongest women characters to emerge from Baja literature, a woman you can't help but root for from beginning to end. *The Lost Mission of Santa Isabel* is well worth your time."

—*Holly Lorincz, editing and publishing consultant*

THE LOST MISSION OF SANTA ISABEL

Joan Candler

Baja Press
First Edition: November 2014
All rights reserved.

ISBN: 978-0-9909422-1-4

Some towns have been architecturally embellished and geographically relocated for the sake of storytelling.

To Bill Candler

A tough act to follow

PROLOGUE

1768, Lower Baja California

Buzzards circled overhead creating moving shadows on the scorching mesa below the Sierra de Camalli Mountains. Jose Garcia knew the birds were following him but he no longer cared. He was hot, tired, and without hope. The heavy cotton shirt stuck to his back, the sleeves were in tatters. He stumbled along lava rocks dripping blood through his goatskin sandals. His lips were parched and he could barely swallow, thirst would soon overcome him.

He squinted through ripples of heat toward the horizon and the mountain beyond. Something green caught his eye. Nopali? He must be dreaming. It was not possible.

He pulled the knife from his pocket and ran toward the bush. Jose, now only ten feet away, knew the cactus was not an illusion. He plunged his knife through a broad leaf, tore away the thorns, lifted a slice to his mouth, and hungrily chewed through the pulp. The scent of melon and lemon filled his nose. Jose started to gag, took a deep breath, and rubbed the wet cactus over his face, arms, and bloody feet. He dropped the leaf and looked around. The sun cast a golden shadow on the mountain creating a patchwork of yellow and green. It would be dark in not more than an hour.

When Jose left his wife and children a week ago, he thought that the map of the Mission of Santa Isabel was the key to his fortune. He left his home on a stolen burro with ample supplies for the journey. Yesterday, the animal foamed at the mouth, fell to its knees, gave one shrill bray, and died. Now he walked along the trail with a lap desk containing a map, a small box, and a jewel-encrusted gold necklace.

Everyone at Tres Cruces knew Jose was a kind and gentle man, above suspicion, the trusted servant to Don Miguel. A member of the Garcia family had been the personal servant to the Cortez dynasty since the 1600s when the king of Spain gave two thousand hectares to Luis and he built Tres Cruces.

Each day Jose arrived at dawn, prepared breakfast, and carried a tray up the stairs to the private quarters of Don Miguel. Later, when his master went to the library, Jose changed the linens, removed the empty wine bottles, mopped the floor, and took Don Miguel's clothing downstairs to be washed and ironed.

Occasionally the job presented small opportunities. Any leftover food went back to Jose's family, a coin or two found under the bed or bureau went into his pocket. Most importantly, Jose had access to family secrets. He knew where Don Miguel kept his jewels and family papers, and he knew when Don Miguel and his wife fought over his mistresses or about his cruelty to servants.

But it was by accident that Jose overheard a conversation between Padre Tomas and Don Miguel as he approached the library carrying a tray of tea and biscuits. The door was partially ajar and Jose paused.

The men were discussing the Jesuits' departure from the Baja peninsula in one week. King Charles III of Spain, influenced by the twisted stories of religious enemies, believed the Jesuits were exploiting the Baja peninsula for personal gain.

"Take this for safe keeping," Padre Tomas said, handing a scroll to Don Miguel. "One parchment contains the map of the treasure and the other has drawings of the most valuable pieces. I have made two copies. One will remain with you, the other I will take to Spain."

Padre Tomas's eyes were heavy with sadness and concern. The journey is long and arduous," he said. "I fear I may not return."

"God willing you shall, Father," Don Miguel said.

"Even if I survive I may be sequestered in a monastery," Padre Tomas continued. "Should something happen, another Jesuit will return next year. The contents of this box will decipher the map that leads to the Mission of Santa Isabel. You will form a convoy to the mountains beyond Santa Maria," Padre Tomas said. "The treasure is buried under a landslide."

"It is an honor for the Cortez family to accept responsibility for the safety of the map," Don Miguel said.

"In recognition of our faith in the family, I have a small gift," Padre Tomas said as he placed a black velvet bag on the desk.

"Open it carefully," he said.

Don Miguel untied the ribbon and its contents slid onto his desk. He paused in awe then touched the gold necklace encrusted with emeralds and pearls.

"It was made for the Aztec queen Chimati in 1521," Padre Tomas said. "The matching earrings are at the

Mission of Santa Isabel and will be a gift to your family when we unearth the treasure."

"Thank you for your faith in the Cortez family," Don Miguel said. "We shall not disappoint you. Tomorrow I will take everything to the dungeon for safekeeping. Now, let us drink a toast to your safe return to Spain."

Jose knocked on the door.

"I have your tea, Don Miguel," he said entering with the tray.

"Leave everything on the table by the door. I will not need your services again tonight," Don Miguel said.

Jose partially closed the door and listened to the voices fade as the men departed from the library. Then he entered the room and approached the desk. His fingers touched the necklace. He would never have an opportunity like this again to avenge the generations of servitude his family had endured. He took the small sealed box, the necklace, and the parchment containing the map and placed them in Don Miguel's lap desk. He would not notice anything was missing until tomorrow morning. By then Jose would be in La Paz. He knew every rancho, watering hole, and impassable road to the mountains beyond Santa Maria and the treasure.

Now, five days later, Jose was exhausted and thirsty. Finding Santa Isabel was not as important as staying alive. He was a fool to place his family at risk. If only he could get to the mountain on the horizon. He needed to hide the box. But where? He paused and looked around. Why not the Nopali? Jose knelt and began to chip away at the sand with his knife. Thirty minutes later he placed the box inside the hole and sighed with relief. By the time he heard the diamondback rattlesnake it was too late. The snake struck his neck and its venom killed him instantly.

Padre Tomas stood on the bridge of the ship and peered at the evening sky. The red sunset was a good omen. He let the cold salty sea moisten his lips, pulled the cassock tight to his chest, and placed his arms inside. The old priest reflected on the events of the past month. He accomplished his goal: The vast wealth the Jesuits had accumulated was safely hidden in the side of a mountain. Only he and Don Miguel had the map. Yet, he alone had the final piece of the puzzle. In the sealed box he left at Tres Cruces was a Piedra Iman, the lodestone used by curanderos for witchcraft and direction. Padre Tomas smiled as his fingers touched the old leather book. Without the leather book the map was worthless. No one would ever find the treasure.

CHAPTER 1

2002, Los Santos, Baja California Sur, Mexico

MJ Steele maneuvered her SUV around mud and holes as she headed for Hacienda Azul. A full moon lit the winding road. Tall coconut palms cast fingers of light on the black shadows of the water. She was tired and disappointed by the lack of progress at the town hall meeting. She wanted to put her feet up and have a glass of wine. MJ vowed she would be better prepared next week. Drama was something she could do without. Period.

Fifteen minutes earlier, MJ Steele, summa cum laude from UCLA, an author, and former curator of Mayan jewelry, was sandbagged by a resident of Los Santos who did not understand why the town needed a new museum and library. Never mind that Los Santos had the most complete collection of artifacts in Baja California thanks to her father-in-law Oliver Marshall.

When MJ finished her presentation to the crowded audience at the Los Santos Town Hall she planted a smile on her face and said, "Thank you for the opportunity to present the plans for the Oliver Marshall Museum and Biblioteca." Then she stacked her drawings, slid them into a case, and headed for the exit.

In the path between her and the door, Johnny Thompson leaned against the wall with his legs casually crossed. Johnny, in his early forties, sported a western hat, sideburns, cowboy boots, and a leather belt laden with silver ornaments. Short and wiry, he had been a country and western disc jockey from Lubbock, Texas before he reinvented himself in Los Santos like so many other expats. He now worked for the radio station in La Paz and provided local news to the gringos.

Johnny smirked on his face. He extended his hand.

"Congratulations, MJ," he said. "Nice job."

"You think?" she answered. "I'm not so sure."

"What you need to remember is it's nothing personal," he said. "Besides, you got off easy because you are a woman—and Rick Delgado's wife."

"Excuse me?" she said, her eyes flaring.

"Loosen up," he continued. "Your plan is sound. The town would be well served with a bilingual library and Oliver Marshall's collection of memorabilia."

"It didn't look that way to me," she said. "Mr. Gonzalez questioned everything I said."

"Don't pay any attention to Gonzalez," Johnny said. "He's chewed up every new idea in town."

MJ looked past Johnny to see her friend Ginger waving and pointing at the car.

"Thanks Johnny, but I've got to go," she said. "I promised Ginger a ride home and I'm really tired. Let's catch up soon."

MJ was hardly in the car when Ginger asked, "What's that all about?"

"Johnny was giving me tips for success in Los Santos," she said. "I'm really discouraged. When it comes to new ideas, living here is like pushing water upstream. It's almost impossible to get anything accomplished."

"Well, you are a gringa," Ginger said.

"That's what Johnny just said."

"You know that Mexicans are wary of American projects," Ginger said. "They come with big ideas about adding to the local economy with jobs, benefits, and support for our schools, but most of the promises don't trickle down to the locals who need it the most."

"But my husband is a local," MJ said. "He was born and raised here."

Rick's mother, Lupita Delgado, was the daughter of a prominent local family who met Oliver Marshall when he led a group of students from the University of California, San Diego to the cave paintings near San Ignacio.

"You know what?" Ginger said. "Don't make this into a bigger deal than it is. You're the woman who never takes no for an answer."

MJ's cell phone rang. "Speak of the devil," MJ said, knowing Rick was due to call.

"Do you want me to fish the phone out of this garbage pail you call a purse?" Ginger asked.

"No. Let it ring. I'll call him when I get home."

MJ pulled up to a small house in the barrio of Colonia del Rio, where Ginger lived happily among her Mexican neighbors.

Given the choice, she had no interest in being surrounded by expats. She left that behind in the States. The cottage had a pitched palapa roof held up with posts that extended past the house. The design created a deep veranda covering the frame like an umbrella. Multicolored Christmas lights flashed in the window.

"Why don't you turn those off?" MJ said. "It's June."

"Number one, everyone can find my house; two, the lights are a beacon for me after two margaritas; and three, it keeps the occasional thief from my door." With that, Ginger leaned over, gave MJ a hug, flipped the backpack on her shoulder and got out of the truck. She turned to MJ. "There isn't enough money in the world for me to live where you do. The wind howls, the waves sound like thunder, and you need a compass to find the place." She blew a kiss to MJ and walked toward the house.

MJ drove away deep in thought. In the six years since they'd arrived in Los Santos, Ginger waited on tables, started her own catering business, crewed on sailboats, and learned to speak Spanish. MJ wished Ginger would find someone to love again. But the truth was, she never got over Johnny.

MJ gripped the wheel in frustration thinking of what Rick would say about the town meeting. He'd tell her it's just a bump in the road, that she'd never take no for an answer anyway. All true. After all, she practically chewed his head off the first time they met.

Six years earlier, MJ drove down the Baja with Ginger in an old Toyota 4Runner with no air conditioning. Both women, on a quest for adventure, thought Baja California would be the perfect place. Ginger owned a catering service and crewed around the Catalina islands on weekends. MJ planned to interview Baja women on the trip. Ten days after leaving the States, the women drove into Los Santos hot, tired, hungry, and dirty. MJ literally ran into Rick Delgado as she walked down the street reading a guidebook.

"Excuse me, don't you look where you're going," Rick said grinning at the tall blond woman wearing a baseball cap and a faded orange golf shirt.

MJ looked up and frowned. She was in no mood for someone with an attitude. She pursed her lips, stuck her jaw out, and put one hand on her hip. "Since you saw I was reading you should have stepped out of my way."

"Can we talk about it over coffee?" Rick asked.

MJ turned to Ginger. "Do you want some coffee?"

"No thanks," Ginger said. "I'm going to check out the Eco Tour office we passed a few minutes ago."

Rick held out his hand.

"I'm Rick Delgado, and you are?"

"Martha Jane Steele, but everybody calls me MJ," she said.

"Well, MJ, there is a great little restaurant a block from here called Miguelitos. They have the best chile rellenos in Baja. You can have coffee, but the margaritas are a whole lot better."

As Rick entered the restaurant, Miguelito came running from behind the counter wiping his hands on a salsa-covered apron. "Rick," he said, looking up at his friend and giving him a bear hug. "Good to see you again."

"Miguelito, I would like you to meet MJ," Rick said.

MJ looked down at this barrel-chested man wearing a six-inch pastry hat.

"Mucho gusto, senorita. Come, sit over here," he said heading toward a small table with flowered ladder-back chairs. "We seldom see Rick and never in the company of a beautiful woman. I will be right back with margaritas."

Over lunch, MJ baited and bemused Rick with her quick wit and barbed comments. He smiled and answered her in kind. An hour later they agreed it was a draw and made plans for dinner. MJ was instantly attracted, but guarded. By midnight she knew that she'd be staying in Los Santos for a while. A year later they were married. After Rick's father, Oliver Marshall, died, they moved into the family home, Hacienda Azul. The idea for a bilingual library and museum came from Oliver's extensive collection of Baja books and artifacts. As MJ neared home she reflected on her frustration at the town meeting. Damn it. Why couldn't she overcome the barrier of distrust among the locals.

The SUV maneuvered through a thicket of palo de arco at the last bend of the road and Hacienda Azul appeared in silhouette on the bluff. The ocean was dotted with silver sparkles of light from Japanese shrimp boats anchored in the bay for the evening. Fishermen trolled throughout the night, then at dawn they loaded the fish on a larger vessel and shipped the bounty back to Asia. MJ stepped from the truck. Cool, moist ocean air sent a chill through her body. The incoming fog edged over the horizon. She closed the gate, wet with mist, and stepped into rivulets of water spilling in every direction. The gardener had left the watering system on again. She walked toward the house and realized Chiquita wasn't there to greet her. Her neighbor, Alberto, was always leaving food scraps for the dog.

MJ put the key in the door. It was unlocked. She entered the kitchen, let her eyes adjust to the light of the living room, and reached for the switch. Then MJ noticed books scattered on the living room floor.

A hand clasped her mouth and a husky voice said, "Silencio, señora, silencio."

MJ reacted instinctively from her years of training. Bending her knees, she grabbed the man's arms with both hands, and flipped him over her back. He careened across the floor and landed with a thud against the kitchen cabinet. Gasping for air and shaking violently, MJ approached the sprawling man. He was lying on his back, one arm over his head, the other on his chest. Blood oozed from his curly black hair and formed a puddle on the polito floor. A layer of fat above his belt exposed his heaving stomach. He was alive.

MJ walked to the wall. Her hand shook as she dialed the number to call the police and listened to it ring. Then everything went black.

CHAPTER 2

Long before Rick Delgado stood in front of the attentive audience at the La Princess Hotel in Cabo San Lucas, he imagined a moment like this. Since childhood, Rick wanted to please his father, Oliver Marshall. Whether wandering through Jesuit ruins, scaling Baja peaks, or chipping at rock formations, Oliver Marshall was the most important person in his life.

Rick tapped the mike once. "Good afternoon," he said. "My name is Rick Delgado." He looked around the packed room.

"Thank you for coming to Cabo San Lucas, even though there isn't much in the way of entertainment here."

The men chuckled.

Rick was right at home. He was a natural salesman, dressed for the occasion: short sleeve shirt open at the collar, khakis, penny loafers, thick brown hair that fell into cobalt blue eyes, a rugged square jaw, and athletic shoulders. He was one of the guys and on his own turf. He smiled at the audience of engineers from the California Mining Consortium. They had the financial means to make his years of preparation and hard work pay off and decide the future of the El Triunfo Mine.

"Today I am going to present a plan that will make your trip worthwhile." He paused. "And I can assure you there will be ample time for at least one round of golf when I'm through."

He lifted a folder from the podium. "On the table you will find a synopsis of my presentation," he said. "Feel free to take notes but please save your questions until the end." Rick placed his hands on the podium.

"I am going to begin with a brief history of the Baja peninsula, starting with the development of the Jesuit mission system."

Rick continued with information on the history of Baja California: the limited supply of water, diseases the Spanish brought to the native population, the discovery of gold, silver, copper, and black pearls. He enticed them with The Legend of Santa Isabel, the rumored treasure hidden by the Jesuits before their hasty departure in 1768.

"According to local folklore, the treasure is buried under a mountain landslide north of Loreto," he said. "An intriguing idea, no?" Rick nodded to a man in the back of the room. Lights dimmed and a screen was lowered from the ceiling. "Here we can see the rapid development of the Baja peninsula during the past twenty years," he said pointing to a blue dot on a bar chart.

"Now let's get to the reason you are all here, The El Triunfo Mine." Rick spent the next half hour outlining the cost of manpower, utilities, equipment, and infrastructure. He ended with a chart of projected profits for the next five years. With a nod to the back, the lights went on.

Any questions?"

"What is the possible backlash to reopening the mine?" asked a man in the second row.

"Good question," Rick said. "We have taken steps to mitigate any issues in Addendum C in the back of your folder." Rick scanned the room for more questions. "Okay, let's wrap it up."

He stepped in front of the podium and looked at the audience. "In two years we will have our feet on the ground and in three years we will be profitable. Then we can face a greater challenge, the search for The Lost Mission of Santa Isabel." The audience gave him a round of applause, took their folders, and left the room.

Jim Coste, the manager of corporate development, made his way to the front. "Great job," he said. "Come up to our headquarters in a couple of weeks." He handed Rick a business card. "Send your material ahead of time. I'll soften the board for final approval before you arrive."

Rick was elated. No more impact studies on traffic, housing, and environment—or worry about money borrowed at ridiculous interest rates. His determination and hard work were going to pay off. The next challenge would be town meetings. Angry gringos, who were concerned about saving the environment, would inevitably fight with Mexicans who needed jobs.

Rick walked into the lobby and stopped to call MJ. She didn't answer. Typical for his wife, who didn't let a cell phone dictate her life. Said it was part of her charm. MJ, or rather, Martha Jane Steele, certainly lived up to her name. She was a handful: sassy, determined, and bright. He recalled how she bedazzled him with a tale about a book she was writing called Women of Baja California. The yarn was partially true. She was on leave from her job as a curator of Mayan artifacts and planned to travel and write in the Baja. But until she and Ginger came to Los Santos, all they did was hike, bike, kayak, drink Mexican beer and tequila, and leave a trail of unhappy men in their wake. Rick was thankful she finally settled down, finished the book, and was focused on a library and museum to house his dad's collection.

Rick put down the phone. He would try her again later from El Triunfo. Near the exit he waved at two Mexican senoritas. They giggled with embarrassment. Women always noticed the good-looking guy. His cell phone buzzed. Rick didn't recognize the number. "Bueno," he said as he walked through the lobby fishing for his parking ticket.

"This is Anita. Federico wants to know what time you are coming."

He looked at his watch. "Tell him I'll be there in an hour." Rick handed the ticket to the valet and leaned against the column of the Princessa Hotel. A blanket of grass overlooked the eighteenth hole. Beyond, a hazy pink sky sat above grey clouds on the horizon. Two cruise ships were hunkered down in the harbor. Tourism was the lifeblood of Cabo San Lucas, a place for fishing, boating, sightseeing, golfing and shopping. Every day thousands of Americans and Europeans tore through stores and restaurants in a frenzy searching for silver, jewelry, tequila, and T-shirts. By early evening they were back onboard the cruise ship, drinking margaritas and discussing their next stop, Mazatlan, as they watched Cabo slowly disappear with the sunset.

Tires squealed as the Toyota rounded the circular drive and came to an abrupt stop. Rick handed the valet twenty pesos.

"Thanks," the young Mexican man said.

The corridor between San Jose and Cabo San Lucas was busy with traffic. Rick passed a city bus and noticed a woman fanning herself with a newspaper. Next to her, an old man wearing a stained sombrero slept, his head bobbing up and down. A Mexican cabbie weaved dangerously through traffic, headed for the airport. He barely missed a beat-up truck hugging the curb. Children, oblivious to any danger, waved at everyone from the open bed in the back. Rick exited at San Jose and found a parking place near the center. He reached into the back seat for a bandana and cowboy boots and topped it off with a white sombrero. Magnolia Street was just around the corner.

San Jose had the same character as a typical silver city on the mainland. The town focus was a mission church surrounded by colonial buildings of pink, yellow, green, and blue shaded by towering ficus trees. Rick cut through the park and entered a narrow street. Everything deteriorated quickly. Plastic bags, paper cups, candy wrappers, and a Coke bottle littered the sidewalk. The stench of rotten food wafted up his nose. The two-story building he was looking for was dead ahead, flanked by an abandoned adobe warehouse and a tortilla store. A faded sign read Dulces y Periódicos. Laundry hung from the upstairs balcony. On the fire escape, a child waved the paw of a cat. The scene brought back memories of a childhood trip to Santiago to visit his cousin. He lay awake all night listening to dogs barking, trucks honking, and loud music blaring from the restaurant below.

At the entrance Rick brushed by a Mexican woman holding the hand of a small girl who was pulling on a dragon piñata. He made his way inside and glanced at the counter. An American tourist was dressed in white shorts and a T-shirt that said I'm kind of a Big Deal.

"Do you have any copies of the New York Times?" she asked.

Behind the counter, Consuelo continued to count change until she deposited the coins into the register. Finally she looked up. "Finished," she said. "Mañana. Plane comes late tomorrow. Maybe two o'clock."

He nodded at Consuelo and headed down the hall toward the sign that said Baños, moved the curtain aside, and opened the door. A Casablanca fan pushed heavy, hot air around a smoky room. It smelled like stale beer and Lysol. He squinted, closed his mouth and tried not to breathe deeply. Six men were seated at a table playing poker. They tossed plastic chips toward the center and never looked up. No one entered the room without an invitation. In the corner three teenage boys sat on the floor. One read a magazine while the others played jacks.

Rick looked to the large picture window across the room. Inside, a man sat behind a 1950s rounded, steel desk talking on the phone. Federico Ramirez could talk on the phone, bark at his assistant, and keep tabs on the adjacent room without moving his head. If there was a problem, a small door hidden behind a map of Mexico opened to the basement. A tunnel led across the street to a vacant building and a quick escape. The police were paid plenty to look the other way and would call if they saw trouble. Nearby, Anita, Federico's paramour, deftly maneuvered colored magnets on a wall calendar while talking on a phone cradled on her shoulder. Ten names were sorted by colors with matching magnets. Anita knew the phone number of every woman, her availability, cost for services, and her problems with boyfriends or children.

Yesterday, Rick made an appointment with Federico, anticipating a successful meeting with investors. He looked at his watch. Seven o'clock, right on time. He wiped his hands on his pants, ran his fingers through his hair, took a deep breath, and knocked on the door.

"Come in," Federico said.

Rick stood waiting for instructions. Federico motioned to the only chair in the room. He continued to talk on the phone.

"Tell Oscar he has one more day to come up with the money. I want at least $10,000. You know how to convince him." Federico slammed the phone and looked up at Rick. "And what do you have for me?" he asked.

"Great news," Rick answered.

CHAPTER 3

Alberto Sanchez sat in his living room watching the World Cup finals. He was completely riveted. The game was tied, two-two, and Mexico had the ball with less than a minute to play. "Come on, Raoul, give the ball to Oscar, yeah, good," he shouted. The phone rang. "Lousy timing," he said, walking to the phone.

"Bueno."

"Hola," Feruza said. "Sorry to bother you but I just finished the report you need for the eight o'clock meeting tomorrow. Fortunately the Mexico office had a copy of the map and all of the correspondence you requested."

Alberto walked to the refrigerator, opened the door, and took out a Negra Modelo. "I really appreciate it."

"Not a problem," she said. "See you tomorrow."

Alberto hung up and turned to the TV just in time to see Oscar being carried off the field by his teammates. The final score: Mexico 3, Ecuador 2. As he reached for the remote control Chiquita began to bark. He opened the screen door and stepped outside. Two men were running down the path from the Delgado house toward the arroyo. Chiquita had one man by the leg and wouldn't let go. The other man disappeared behind some cholla. Within seconds an engine started and a truck pulled up. The driver reached over and opened the passenger door. The man who on foot pulled himself into the truck, gave Chiquita a kick, and slammed the door. The truck squealed as it tore up dirt and disappeared into the fog rising over the dunes.

Alberto grabbed his keys and bolted for Hacienda Azul. In two minutes he was at the kitchen door. He knocked, turned the handle.

"Hello, MJ? Is anyone here?" He walked across the floor and stopped. There was something sticky on his shoe. He stepped back and looked at the dark colored stain. Blood? Alberto quickly headed for the living room. Books were thrown around the room. An overturned lamp sat on the floor near the fireplace. Alberto's eyes scanned everything until his eyes settled on MJ, who was tucked behind the coffee table near the sofa. He walked over, knelt down, and felt her pulse. It had a slow, steady beat. He squeezed her hand. Her eyes fluttered. Gradually, he pulled her toward the sofa, found a pillow, and propped her head. She sighed. Alberto headed down the hall toward the bathroom. He returned with a glass of water and a cold washcloth. The cold wet towel on MJ's forehead startled her. She bolted upright, grabbed his hand, and screamed. "MJ, it's all right, it's me, Alberto."

She opened her eyes, looked at him for a moment, and began to cry. He placed his hands on her shoulders. "It's okay. You are going to be fine," he said.

MJ looked bewildered. She touched the lump on her forehead, and winced.

"What happened?" he asked.

"I don't remember," she answered.

"You have one nasty gash at your hairline. It may need stitches; you lost a lot of blood in the kitchen. Don't move. I'll get a clean washcloth."

MJ nodded.

Alberto returned with a washcloth and a mirror. "Here take a look," he said. "Does anything else hurt? Should I call an ambulance?"

MJ closed her eyes and breathed deeply. "No, please don't call anyone. I'm okay. Just give me a couple of minutes." She looked around. A leather manuscript was lying under the table. The bookcase was in total disarray. She shuddered and shook her head. "I should have known better," she said.

"What do you mean?" Alberto said.

"Well, the kitchen door was unlocked. But Rick sometimes forgets to lock it. I wasn't paying attention." MJ pursed her lips in disgust. "And I was preoccupied with what happened at the town meeting," she said, taking a sip of water. "I didn't notice anything until I went in the living room and there were books everywhere. I stopped and looked around. The room was in shambles. I went back to the kitchen to call the police. When I picked up the phone I heard a sound. I turned around to see what it was. I don't remember anything else." MJ paused and looked down at her hands.

"You were lucky," said Alberto. "I saw men running from your house, and Chiquita was chasing them."

"Chiquita? Where is she? Is she all right?"

"She was heading toward the dunes after the truck the last time I saw her," he said. "I'm sure she's fine." Alberto knelt down next to MJ. "You're the one I am worried about. Are you sure you're okay? You may have a concussion. I think we should go to the clinic."

"No," MJ said. "Please. Give me just a few more minutes, okay?"

Alberto looked around at the mess. "Looks like you came back during a robbery. There have been several around town recently."

"Rick and I don't have anything valuable," she said. "Just a little cash and some jewelry my mom left me." MJ reached for the table and tried to sit up. A sharp pain went across her forehead. She winced. "My computer is in the bedroom on the desk," she said. "The jewelry is in the top drawer of the nightstand."

"I'll look," he said. "Just try to relax."

MJ glanced around the room. This was way too much for her to absorb and remember. She put her hands to her mouth and gasped. "Oh my God, where's my computer?"

Alberto walked into the living room with a satin bag and MJ's computer. "I guess you're right, nothing's missing. It doesn't even look like they went into the bedroom." He placed the items on the table and looked at MJ with a serious expression. "There's something I need to say. As an attorney, my advice for you is to call the police. They have the experience to deal with the situation."

MJ looked at Alberto and frowned. "You must be kidding," she said. "Why call the police? What good would it do? We'd have to go downtown and file a report. Besides, nobody's there, it's after hours. Unless there's a dead body, they won't come to the house. Thankfully, there isn't. The fewer people who know, the better." She looked down at the wedding ring on her hand and began to turn it in circles. Finally she said, "The person to call is Ginger. She might think of something I've overlooked."

CHAPTER 4

Thirty minutes after he left San Jose, Rick was still brooding over his meeting with Federico. The guy was edgy and expected his money soon. He hoped there was enough time to get out of this mess. Rick reached for his cigarettes, tapped the pack against the wheel, put one in his mouth, and lit it. MJ hated the fact he smoked but it eased his tension.

He was frustrated about everything that had gone wrong during the past several months. His secure world was beginning to unravel. He knew MJ was suspicious, but didn't want to involve her. She'd be out there front and center, second-guessing his every move.

Everything changed after he visited Mama Estrada six months ago. Mama shared a long-held secret about the Mission of Santa Isabel and asked for his help. He spent the next two months leafing through property deeds in Loreto. How could he say no? She had been a family friend since he was a boy and his dad took him trekking up the Sierra Lagunas, swimming with grey whales, and fishing in the Pacific. Her home was filled with all his childhood memories of an unspoiled Baja.

Ten years later, Rick went off to UC San Diego knowing he would return home as often as possible and eventually make Baja his home. So it was no surprise that he invited Don Higgins to visit his home after class one day. "How about coming down to Los Santos during spring break," he said. "We can surf, or rock hound."

Don jumped at the chance. He really liked Rick and knew he'd be a terrific guide since he grew up in Mexico and his father, Oliver Marshall, was Chairman Emeritus of the Geology Department at San Diego. Two weeks later they met at the airport in Los Angeles and boarded a plane for Cabo. During the flight, Rick talked about his father.

"Dad fell in love with the Baja peninsula during the 1950s when he took students to the cave paintings near San Ignacio," Rick said. "It was an annual event. One year, after the students went back to the States, dad decided to check out southern Baja and flew to Cabo San Lucas. Back then Cabo was a small fishing village with a dirt runway. He hired a guide, packed enough supplies for a week, and headed north. He stopped in Los Santos and never went any further." Rick took a sip of the Coke on his tray. "Am I boring you?"

"Hell no," Don answered. "You're giving me a history lesson and a tour at the same time."

"Dad fell in love with the town," Rick said. "He bought a piece of land, built a casita, and spent the next ten summers there." Rick sighed and lowered his seat back. "Los Santos wasn't without problems," he said. "When the aquifer from the Sierra de Lagunas dried up, the townspeople lost their income from growing and harvesting sugar cane."

Don turned toward Rick. "What made your dad decide to stay?" he asked.

"My dad was the most eligible bachelor in town," Rick said. "That is, until he met Lupita Delgado. They fell in love, married, and a couple of years later I was born. He retired from San Diego about the same time Los Santos got back on its feet. The water started to flow from the mountains again, and the farmers decided to grow chili peppers which required less water."

"So what was so special about growing up in Mexico?" Don asked.

"My dad," Rick answered with a grin. "He collected anything to do with Baja: wooden bowls, rocks, beaded dolls, jewelry, arrows, books, maps. He'd sit me down on the floor, point to something, and ask me what it was. I loved the game and I learned a lot. I was fascinated by the stories of the missions the Jesuits built."

Rick looked at his watch. "We're going to be landing in a few minutes. Remind me to tell you about the Lost Mission of Santa Isabel, the one Erle Stanley Gardner spent so much time and money trying to find."

Rick was jolted back from his college days into reality when he looked in the rear view mirror. The bright headlights from a truck he had noticed earlier, near the airport, were still behind him. The clock on the dash said 8:15 p.m. El Triunfo was an hour away. Tall, dark shadows from the mountains loomed against the sagebrush. There were curved roads ahead, and no shoulders. The drop was precipitous. Rick felt very alone.

Five minutes later he passed the sign for Cardon National Preserve. There would be no more homes and little traffic. He glanced in the rear mirror: same lights. They were closer and brighter. Could someone be following him? Ahead, an arrow reflector alerted late night visitors to the entrance of the preserve.

He rounded the next curve and was greeted by two men who stood in the road and motioned for him to stop. He lifted his foot from the accelerator, and caught a glint of metal as a hand came up. Rick pushed the gas pedal to the floor and swerved the truck away from the men. He heard a thump and a sharp crack as he swept by. His rear window shattered with a boom. Hot needles from glass shards pierced his neck and arms, bouncing off of the dashboard onto his hands, which were dripping with blood. Rick clutched the wheel. The road ahead was ten miles of desolation. When he glanced back again the same headlights came over the rise.

Rick was desperate. He had to find a place off road. But where? He wracked his brain. Then he remembered El Mármol, the place he and Doc Wiley visited last year when they were headed for El Triunfo. El Mármol was located near the cliffs on the Sea of Cortez. Seventy-five years earlier, the largest quarry in Mexico shipped onyx around the Sea of Cortez to San Francisco. By the 1950s, the invention of plastics and the cost of shipping changed everything. Wiley was curious to know if anything remained of the old dock and marble quarry. Rick and Doc forged their way into the site and found the path from the storage area to the harbor two-hundred feet below. Nothing remained except planks on pilings covered with barnacles.

Rick realized El Mármol couldn't be too far away. He crawled down the hill looking for the turnoff. Old Doc Wiley insisted they leave a small red reflector on a mesquite tree near the road to make the cutoff easier to find next time. Rick began looking for the marker just past a large arroyo. He squinted and shifted the truck into low gear; his headlights caught something red in the brush. He stopped and ran his flashlight across the undergrowth. Success.

Rick made a wide swing into the thick scrub as bright lights appeared at the crest of the hill. He turned off his headlights and the full moon disappeared under a canopy of trees and everything went black. Parking lights were barely enough to see anything as he weaved through the impassable road. Branches reached out, clipped the side mirrors, and smacked defiantly against the hood. The summer rains had made havoc of the road. The truck bounced over mud and rocks. Ahead, specks of blue sky appeared between the treetops and the road widened. He was almost there.

Without warning the truck lurched, and Rick careened into the dashboard. He threw the Toyota into reverse. A boulder the size of his tire sat in the road. He slammed his foot to the floor, jerked the wheel to the left, and sped past, clipping the fender with a loud crunch. The reflection of light on his mirror told him the men were right behind.

Rick panicked. What was he thinking coming down this road? There was no way out. But he had one huge advantage: he had been here before. He sped toward the Sea of Cortez. On his right, blocks of onyx, left behind fifty years ago, were stacked near the road. He was nearing the quarry. Pale cream marble walls, solemn and erect, gleamed in the moonlight. The onyx schoolhouse was the only building still standing. The upper walls had been carted away, but the buttresses were still in place and gave credence to the once thriving town. Cemetery headstones, enclosed with a low marble wall, reminded him that El Mármol was a thriving town fifty years ago, not the desolate place he now passed.

Rick continued down the thirty-foot slope that edged to the Sea of Cortez. The moon on the ink black ocean cast a golden sliver of light toward the cliff. He opened the door. Angry waves crashed against the rocks below. He took a deep breath and put the car in neutral. The Toyota slowly rolled toward the water. Rick secured his sombrero, buttoned his jacket, and jumped out. He stumbled, quickly recovered, and ran toward the small warehouse near the cliff. He was almost there when someone shouted,

"Stop, now!"

Rick took another step. A shot rang out. He turned around and looked back at the headlights. Then he tumbled over the edge of the cliff.

Helen and Jack Hayes left the seaport town of Topolobampo on mainland Mexico mid-afternoon, expecting to arrive at Cabo San Lucas before sunset. The 40 Bristol was sailing on the Sea of Cortez toward Cabo San Lucas guided by a full moon. The couple would arrive later than expected, detained by playful humpback whales following the boat.

Helen gazed at the thick black line of cliffs on the horizon. Cardon cacti perched on the edge reaching toward the sky. The scene reminded her of a chocolate cake with candles on top. Helen stood on the deck with a glass of wine savoring the memory of the humpback whales. Jack checked the map against the depth reading for shoals and set the compass for S/SW, bringing them to their final destination, Cabo San Lucas. Just before the boat rounded the bluff, an orange glow appeared on the water. As they turned Helen could see a fireball of flames licking up the edge of the cliff.

"Jack, grab the binoculars on the seat. What do you see?"

Jack focused on the fiery scene. "Looks like a truck, or what's left of it, at the bottom of the cliff burning on the rocks." He moved the binoculars up the side of the cliff. "I see lights up top," he said. "To the left. Small ones, probably flashlights."

Helen brought the map over to a lamp. "I think we're at El Mármol." She walked over to Jack and showed him the place. "We should call ship to shore and give them our reading," she said. "They'll send somebody."

"I hope nobody was in that truck when it went over," he   said.

CHAPTER 5

MJ dozed off on the sofa with an ice pack on her head. Her stomach was in knots. Alberto leafed through a Baja 1000 magazine. They both heard the squeal of tires followed by the loud blare of a horn. Then dogs began to bark. MJ frowned.

"Guess who," she said.

A door slammed against the kitchen counter and two German shepherds bounded into the living room, sniffing at everything in sight. "Hello, MJ?"

MJ looked up with exasperation at her best friend.

Ginger stood six feet tall, wore a red tank top with white formfitting shorts. Her red hair cascaded over her head and tangled her shell earrings in an unruly mess. Ginger's eyes were ablaze. "What's going on? Someone broke in? When? How? Where's Chiquita?"

Ginger stopped, put her hands on her hips, and looked at MJ. "You look like hell. You're going to have a first class shiner. How did it happen? Are you okay? Why is your arm wrapped?"

"Ahem," Alberto said.

"Oh, hi Alberto. Nice to see you."

"Can I get you something to drink? Something to calm you down?" he asked.

"Sure. Three fingers of a scotch, hold the water, and two ice cubes. Thanks." Ginger reached into the leather purse hanging from her shoulder, pulled out a hair tie, and began to braid her hair. "Where's Rick? He should be home from Cabo by now."

"He decided to-" MJ began.

"That's right, I forgot. He's spending the night. How'd the lecture go?"

MJ tossed the washcloth aside. "Ginger, stop please. You are making me crazy. How can I tell you anything if you don't shut up." MJ tried to sit up and winced in pain. "I asked you to come over because I thought you could help. Now I wish I hadn't bothered. If you don't stop right now I'll need another ice pack on my head."

Alberto returned with the Scotch and handed it to Ginger. Then he walked over to the sofa, kissed MJ on the forehead, and said, "I think I'll leave the two of you alone. If you have any problems or hear strange noises give me a call. I'll stop by tomorrow."

Alberto turned to Ginger. "Nice to see you again. I had forgotten how stimulating you are. Goodnight."

MJ looked at Ginger and put her finger over her lips. "Shish."

They heard the kitchen door close, looked at each other, and burst out laughing.

"You sure know how to turn a guy on Ginger. Glad you haven't lost your touch."

Ginger grinned. "Hell, MJ. He takes life way too seriously. He's such a good-looking guy. Too bad he's so inaccessible. I wouldn't mind being first in line to help him with whatever he needs when he realizes what it is." Ginger fell into a chair.

"Before you tell me what happened, I want you to know that I'm spending the night."

MJ opened her mouth to protest.

"Don't even think about arguing with me. No way am I leaving you here alone. My dogs won't let anyone near this house. And I brought my gun."

MJ shook her head no and said, "You know how I feel about guns."

"So what," Ginger said taking a gulp of her Scotch.

"Thanks, you're just what the doctor ordered," MJ said.

Ginger shook her empty glass and headed for the kitchen. "I want to know everything that happened and I promise I won't interrupt. But first I'm getting another drink."

It was 2 a.m. before MJ finished her story. Ginger gave her a sleeping pill, two ibuprofen, a half a glass of port, and put her to bed. Then she whistled for the dogs.

"Hanz, you stay here," she said walking over to the front door. "Fritz, come with me." She walked toward the guest bedroom without much enthusiasm, opened the door, and flipped the light. Old pots, carved death masks, and a large photo of the cannibalistic Sari Indians standing with Rick's father, stared back at her. The man was either very brave or very stupid.

Ginger brushed her teeth, washed her face, and was sound asleep as soon as her head hit the pillow. Fritz' barking woke her up. She rolled over, lifted her head and looked at the time: Six a.m. The doorbell was ringing and someone was banging on the front door. Fritz followed her down the hall barking all the way. Hanz growled at the intruder on the other side of the door.

"Hanz, Fritz. Sit." They sat at attention.

"Who is it?" she asked.

"Police. Open the door."

Ginger opened the door a couple of inches and stared into the faces of two Mexican Federales and a local policeman.

"Are you Mrs. Delgado?" asked a Federale.

"No, she's asleep. I'll get her." Ginger turned to see MJ walking down the hall.

"What's wrong? Who's here?"

"The police."

The policemen waited for Ginger to step aside. MJ brushed past her and stared at the grim faces of three men in uniform. But it was the fourth person who made her gasp. Father Gomez.

"Oh my God. Something's happened to Rick."

CHAPTER 6

Don Hernando Cortez stood on the patio of the three hundred and fifty year old hacienda watching the sunset. A bulldog of a man, he was thick bodied with surprisingly short arms and legs. Brown bushy eyebrows extended across his forehead over hooded dark eyes, making him look angry unless he smiled. The event did not occur often. He felt a chill through his jacket as he watched the flat hand of fog descend over the stone lighthouse. Waves crashed on the jetty below. A candle glow from the last light of the day peeked through the horizon on the Sea of Cortez.

Hacienda Tres Cruces perched on a cliff at the end of a crescent beach. When Cortez landed near La Paz bay in 1535 his men placed a cross in the ground, built a campsite, and named the property Tres Cruces. The first building was a supply shed they built from the stones near the beach. The foundation of the present hacienda was built from the same stones.

Tres Cruces sat on a land grant from King Carlos II and included four hundred hectares stretching from Punta Coyote to Punta La Gordo. Sir Francis Drake was rumored to have buried bounty from the Manila Galleon on the islands nearby.

Don Hernando was the oldest surviving male heir to a fortune he would inherit upon the death of his mother Antigua, eighty-eight, and in remarkable health.

But Don Hernando was a patient man. This evening, he hoped his years of planning would pay off. He would find the map of the Lost Mission of Santa Isabel, stolen by a servant of his great grandfather, Don Miguel, in 1768, shortly before the Jesuits were expelled from Baja California.

He was close, very close. For several years, Don Hernando had paid a clerk in Loreto to be alert to requests for survey maps or corporation papers pertaining to the Cortez family. He knew someone would ask for a map of the land adjacent to Santa Maria, the last mission built by the Jesuits, in 1767. According to local legend, the Jesuits constructed Santa Isabel to the north in 1768.

An important breakthrough came two months ago when the town clerk in Loreto called. He told Don Hernando that Ricardo Delgado came to the office and requested survey maps of the land adjacent to Santa Maria. If Rick Delgado was snooping, he must know something. Don Hernando should have suspected the son of the scion of Baja history, Oliver Marshall, would be the one. Did he have the map? There was only one way to find out.

Don Hernando opened the desk drawer and fondled the skeleton key that led to the vault where the second parchment was located. It contained a complete list of jewels, coins, pearls, and other treasures the Jesuits accumulated, with ink drawings of the most valuable items. The parchment that was stolen contained the map of the Mission of Santa Isabel.

As Don Hernando closed the balcony door the phone rang. He walked to his desk across the room. "Bueno," he said. In the background he could hear men shouting. "Bueno," he said again more loudly.

"Boss, we have a problem," Martin said. He explained the details of the past hour.

"When we went back to the roadblock we found out that Francisco has a broken arm and maybe a couple of broken ribs," he said. "We're going to bring him out to your place. We don't want anybody asking questions at the hospital in La Paz."

"Are you crazy?" Don Hernando screamed into the phone. "I'll send my doctor out to YOU. Get your head screwed on straight. Tell me where you are and I'll send Doctor Amelio." Don Hernando paced back and forth in front of the desk. "And tomorrow morning go back to El Mármol. Check the place out. Look for anything and everything. Clean up your tracks. And don't make any more stupid mistakes."

Don Hernando slammed the phone on the desk. What a mess. Rick Delgado was a damn fool. The guys were told to rough him up. Tell him something might happen to his wife if he didn't level with them. Now Rick was dead and took the information about the lost mission with him.

He picked up the phone to make another call when his mother walked into the room.

"Mother, what a nice surprise."

Don Hernando kissed her on both cheeks, then stood back and admired her elegant attire. Antigua wore black patent leather heels, a plum suit with black piping on the collar and cuffs, and had a black cashmere shawl draped over her shoulders. Her red hair was the same color he remembered from childhood.

"Is something wrong?" Antigua asked.

"No, why?"

"I could hear you shouting as I came in. Has somebody been hurt at the copper mine again?"

"Francisco broke his arm in a car accident. I'm sending Dr. Amelio to treat him. There's nothing to worry about."

Antigua handed her son a program.

"You missed a wonderful recital this evening, the Osborne String Quartet, from Chicago. Tomorrow night Rachael Carrera, the lyric soprano, will be here. I hope that business will not keep you away again."

"I'm looking forward to tomorrow evening. We had a last minute scheduling change and the project had to be completed today."

Antigua picked a piece of lint off Don Hernando's jacket.

"The music festival is held the same week every year and people make quite an effort to attend. I am concerned that our landing strip is outdated and will have to be enlarged before next year."

Don Hernando felt the rage growing inside him. He lowered his hand to his waist pocket and balled his fist.

"Perhaps we should consider having the festival at Palmetto. The San Jose airport can easily handle small jets."

Antigua's eyes grew cold.

"As long as I am alive the festival will be held at Tres Cruces."

Don Hernando kissed his mother on the forehead.

"Of course. Why don't I meet you in the library in five minutes for a glass of port wine. I need to make a quick call."

Don Hernando waited until the door closed. He lit a Cuban cigar and dialed.

"Did you find anything at the house?" He took a long puff on the cigar. "She did what? Are you sure he didn't trip on something?"

Don Hernando leaned back in the chair, closed his eyes, and listened. Finally he said, "Listen to me carefully. She is our only link to the map. Her husband ran his truck over a cliff an hour ago. The guys will tell you what happened. Don't let her out of your sight. Do you hear me?"

Don Hernando slammed the phone on the receiver, cleared his throat, and spit phlegm into a spittoon. The goal of his men was to find information about the Lost Mission. Don Hernando pondered the more elusive question. But why do I really want to find the map in the first place?

"Damn you, Mother. Damn you to hell," he whispered. "I have spent my whole life trying to win your favor."

Nothing Don Hernando had ever done made Antigua happy. He graduated from Yale with honors, married the daughter of his mother's best friend, and accumulated a fortune developing property. His squeezed his eyes closed and recalled that unforgettable event when he was twelve. Don Hernando and his brother Don Miguel were swimming in the saltwater pool hidden behind elephant trees and cactus. Miguel was younger but was always a tease.

"Hey, Donny Banana. I know what nobody else knows. All of you looks like a banana, a skinny little banana."

Don Hernando lost his cool, grabbed Miguel by the hair, and held his head under water. Every few seconds, he pulled up his brother gasping for air and thrashing his hands around.

"What did you call me, Miguel? Want to call me that again?"

Suddenly he heard the stern voice of Antigua.

"What are you doing, Hernando? Stop it. Let Miguel go."

Miguel swam to the edge of the stairs, ran up, clutched his mother's legs, and cried hysterically. She took him into her arms and hugged him. She turned to Don Hernando.

"Do not ever mistreat your brother again. You will not bring shame on our family, do you hear me?"

"Yes, mother."

How Don Hernando hated his brother that day and hated him still today. He stubbed his cigar into the ashtray with such force, red ashes scattered over the bottom. Then he stabbed the cigar until the bottom was black with ashes. On his way to the library he stopped at the French gilded mirror, checked his jacket, straightened his tie, and tucked a loose hair behind his ear. Would he ever be perfect enough for his mother?

CHAPTER 7

The sky was a cloudless Matisse blue. Hot winds blew up the hillside, throwing layers of dust around the frayed tar pan covering the old Jeep. Wiley Crookson braced himself against the fender and lifted his weary body from under the hood. He groaned, looked at his watch, and sighed. He was an hour late for the scheduled weekly geology tour with his drinking buddies. Today they were visiting the waterfall at Agave Pass. Not to worry. By now the guys were on their second round of drinks at Noisy Harry and fighting over the best baseball team this coming season.

Wiley, the resident guru of geology in Los Santos, looked every bit the part of a crotchety retired professor from the Northwest, wearing broken glasses and a faded University of Oregon hat to cover his crinkled face, ragged beard, and mustache which was held in place with dried saliva. He wore a wide hand-tooled leather belt with a silver buckle and jeans with gaping holes at the knees. Wiley climbed in the car and turned on the ignition. The engine coughed, paused, and roared.

"It's about time, you miserable piece of junk." He whistled, and yelled, "Cindy, Buster."

Two dogs, a standard poodle and Doberman Pinscher, leaped over the chollo bush and raced toward the Jeep, each determined to have the front seat. The truck shook as Cindy flew over the door and landed with a whop on Wiley, her paws digging into his leg and her nose an inch away from his head. She was the most aggressive dog he'd ever owned. Wiley cupped his mouth and shouted, "Hey Frieda, Frieda." He laid on the horn for ten seconds before Frieda, wearing a flowered muslin apron and heavy black work shoes, came to the door. She tucked a loose strand of hair into her bun and scowled.

"Send Heriberto to pick up Jesse at the airport. I haven't got time."

"But you haven't seen your son for a year."

"I promised the guys I'd take them to Agave Falls for some real good rock hounding. This is OUR day, and I'm not going to spoil it for a kid who never gave a damn about me in the first place." Wiley threw the Jeep into gear, pressed the pedal to the floor, and flew out the driveway. Frieda looked at the trail of dust and flying rocks and shook her head.

Wiley headed toward Los Santos with a vengeance, sweeping past Washingtonian palms, cholla, desert thorn, and barely rounding the curve in front of the Sanchez farm. Chickens flew, but the goats munching on the grass hardly lifted their heads. He waved at Mrs. Sanchez, who was watering the dirt to keep the dust down in front of the crumbling adobe. She shook her head with annoyance. Wiley pushed the lighter button on the dash, reached for a Marlboro, and lit it. He took a deep breath and began to relax. The radio reception tower came into view. He hit a switch and music blared from the radio station in La Paz. Mexicans listened to such happy, lyrical, enthusiastic songs. When the news came on he reached to turn down the volume.

"Ricardo Delgado . . . muerte . . ." Wiley stopped and listened, straining to understand what the announcer said.

After a few minutes, and an interview with the Federal police, he pieced together what had happened.

Wiley knew Rick had given a presentation in Cabo yesterday, then headed to El Triunfo. Apparently, his truck went over the cliff at El Mármol, burst into flames, and burned beyond recognition. What the hell was he doing at El Mármol? Wiley pulled over to the side of the road, stunned. He and Rick were buddies. And they had a common interest. Over the last five years they scoured countless abandoned silver mines and old missions hoping to find a key to their fortune. They would choose a site, research the location, and spend a couple of nights each month on the back roads of Baja. Everything was a kick; they were a pretty good team. Wiley was an authority on rock formations, the mechanics of old mining sites, and how to find gold and silver deposits. He enjoyed sharing the information with the son of a fellow geologist, Oliver Marshall. Rick, in turn, provided his dad's research papers on Mexican land rights and the location of watering holes and ranches. An added bonus for Wiley was the treasure trove of old books and manuscripts Rick had in his home that included obscure information on Santa Isabel.

During the past year, their relationship got more complicated. Wiley loaned Rick money. Rick gave him a small stake in the El Triunfo mine. Then Wiley made a discovery he would keep to himself. It happened last fall during their visit to San Andras, the mining camp located south of Sierra Pintada where $75,000 worth of placer gold was mined in the 1890s.

The trip began like so many others. He and Rick left at the crack of dawn for San Ignacio, a village untouched by time. They drove into town past the old Dominican mission located on the town square. Children played in the streets, an old man sat in front of his ice cream cart waiting for their parents, and dogs basked under the jacaranda tree. Hikers with backpacks at their feet sat under the shade, hoping the Eco Tour Center would open soon. San Ignacio was the jumping off point to see gray whales in Ignacio Bay or the cave paintings in the San Francisco Mountains.

Wiley and Rick found Fischer's Hotel, a landmark, where twenty years earlier Herb Fisher ran a one-man operation taking tourists up the San Francisco Mountains to view the cave paintings in an old Dodge van that barely skirted the edge of the road. When Harry Crosby published The Cave Paintings of Baja California, the Mexican government realized the five-thousand year old paintings should be registered as a historic site.

By 6 a.m. the following morning Wiley and Rick were on their way. An hour later they turned off Mexico Highway 1 and headed north. When they reached the San Andres Ranch, they rented horses, gear, and mining equipment. Rick thought they should separate to cover more territory, so they agreed to meet at the campsite midday. Rick chose a large black stallion and headed out. Wiley thought mules were more reliable and had better footing. With the help of a ranch hand, he saddled one, climbed aboard, gave it a whack, and took off carrying mining gear, tortillas, and plenty of water. Cindy and Buster were right behind, wagging their tails and yelping.

The lower terrain looked more comfortable, so Wiley headed up with caution. He opened his satchel, checked the map and compass, and noted the breathtaking vistas across the volcanic mesas of the Desierto de Vizcaino.

Everything reminded him of Lawrence of Arabia's beige desert glistening in the sun. He stopped and photographed the volcanic plug domes of the Sierra Santa Clara.

After two hours his back ached from bouncing on the mule and he was getting hotter by the minute. The gold mine was nowhere in sight. Buster and Cindy were easily entertained, sniffing every tree and chasing rabbits. Wiley pulled a handkerchief from his pocket and wiped his forehead. A few minutes later the dogs began to bark. He rounded a bend and stopped. Whatever he was looking at was dead. Very dead.

White bones were scattered on a hillside surrounded by a single, massive cardon cactus. Beautiful contrast, ugly scene. Wiley called the dogs. Cindy approached with a large bone that could be anything. It looked dry and sun-washed. She wouldn't want it for long, the taste would be horrible. He rode closer. No sign of clothing, nothing but the bones of a person, probably a man. Women were seldom alone in the mountains. But why would anyone be in this area? He noticed something peculiar about the skull. It lay at a right angle from the spine.

Then he saw the mound. He walked over and kicked the dirt. It was as hard as a rock. But Wiley knew better. He went back to the mule, unbridled a pickaxe, and began to whack. Slowly. Drops of sweat fell from his brow and hit his tongue. He pulled his hat down, rolled up his shirtsleeves, and continued. Fifteen minutes later the axe came down with a thud on something hollow. Two whacks later he hit wood. Wiley pulled a knife from his pocket and loosened the dirt, exposing a black, hand carved, ancient Spanish box. He used his knife to loosen the dirt, pried open the corroded brass lock, and lifted the cover.

The box was empty. There was nothing inside but shreds of purple velvet clinging to the corners. He carefully inspected the brass detailing that was etched with a family crest and stared in disbelief. The coat of arms belonged to the Cortez family. Why would a hand carved lap top box with the Cortez family crest be buried under a cardon cactus in the middle of nowhere? And what happened to the contents?

Wiley looked at his watch. He was late. Rick would start to worry and head in his direction. He took out his camera, photographed the site and the box. He quickly reburied the box, gathered his gear, and headed back down the mountain, leaving discreet trail markers along the way. He smiled about his little secret. He wouldn't tell Rick. Wiley remembered the obstacle to his getting rich years earlier when Oliver was involved. Over the next few months, Wiley investigated the design of the Spanish box, determined its age, and researched the Cortez family history during that time. His hard work paid off. He knew a great deal about the Cortez family and the history of the box.

Wiley was jolted into reality when Cindy dove across the steering wheel and started barking at an approaching truck. A minute later, his plumber, Ricardo, pulled alongside. The man rolled his window down and gave Wiley a quizzical look. "Are you all right?"

"Yeah. I dropped my glasses so I stopped for a minute to find them. They were under the seat."

"Okay." Ricardo waved and the truck disappeared over the hill.

Wiley's train of thought went back to his research on the Cortez family. He was missing an important book that he thought was in Oliver Marshall's original collection. With Rick dead, he had the perfect excuse to get it. He'd call MJ, express his condolences, and mention the book that Rick promised him. He had to be careful. MJ was a smart cookie. She might get suspicious. But then again, she was distracted by Rick's death. The book was related to his search for the Mission of Santa Isabel and the secret he and Oliver Marshall shared. No one knew what happened all those years ago. No one, that is, except Oliver and Wiley.

CHAPTER 8

MJ stood in the living room of Hacienda Azul. She was deep in thought and heading into dangerous territory. For the past two days she tried to understand what went wrong. Why would Rick drive onto a lonely road and go over a cliff? Then there was the matter of timing. She was mugged the same evening.

Earlier MJ dug out Rick's journals. They didn't reveal much. But he'd been acting strange, quick tempered and evasive, for several months. She recalled a particularly bad evening. They were in bed in the playful early stages of lovemaking. Rick squeezed her breast as she ran her fingers through his hair. Then he stopped and sighed.

"Well one of us should do something," MJ said. "Have you fallen asleep down there?"

"Not me." Rick folded a pillow and placed it under his head.

"You seem a bit distracted. Is something wrong?"

"No, I'm just tired I guess."

"You were so quiet at dinner. Then you snapped at Chiquita. Not like you at all."

"I'm sorry."

MJ ran her hand over Rick's arm. "You had a long day dealing with Wiley's old Jeep again," she said trying to change the subject. "Why doesn't he just get another

Jeep? The Bed and Breakfast is doing well. Frieda works so hard running the place. No one ever sees her anymore."

"Stop," he said. "Wiley is Wiley, a crotchety old bastard, but he knows every mine in the Sierras. Besides, he was my dad's best buddy. So I spend a day a week with him. So what?"

"I think he's a bit peculiar. Odd. Maybe even a bit dishonest. Or to be kinder, he sometimes doesn't tell the whole truth. What do you think?"

"I think I don't know where you are heading with this."

"Remember last week when he got here before you? I found him snooping around your office. I've been waiting for the right time to mention it."

"Well this isn't it. Bentley is off limits for discussion right now. I have a lot of preparation for the conference in Cabo next month. I'd hoped we could completely relax and enjoy each other this evening."

But the mood was gone. Rick leaned over and kissed MJ on the cheek. "Goodnight."

Things didn't get any better after that. Rick was quick-tempered, often evasive, and didn't want to talk about what was wrong. They cooked dinner together but laughed less about events of the day. Rick hunkered down in his office gathering material and making phone calls for the El Triunfo project. He was all business: totally focused and not much fun.

But nothing prepared MJ for the shock she felt yesterday at the bank. Inside their safety deposit box she found an insurance policy and stacks of money that she had no idea existed.

The kitchen door slammed and Ginger walked in.

"Hey what's up," she asked. "Have you calmed down since I left?"

MJ looked up with a frown. "What do you think? No." She shook her head with disbelief. "I'm trying to make some sense of what the police told me. His truck went over a cliff, and he's dead. But Rick would never do anything that stupid." MJ sat down on the sofa and looked at Ginger. Tears welled up in her eyes. She clenched her fist and bit her knuckles in dismay. "He was my husband. A wonderful, honest guy."

After a couple of minutes she calmed down, reached for a sack of bills, and dumped them on the coffee table. "There has to be some explanation for this. Twenty-five thousand dollars in cash," she said. "Where did it come from? How long was it in the safety deposit box? And this."

MJ handed Ginger a manila envelope. "A million dollar life insurance policy with me as the beneficiary. I had no idea. He never mentioned it. Don't you think he could have told me?"

Ginger placed the folder on the table. "He probably never thought it would come to this."

"The only clue I have so far is this," MJ said, handing a notebook to Ginger. "The W must mean Wiley, and the ME must be Mama Estrada. I haven't had time to check the dates against Rick's calendar."

Ginger ran her thumb through the pages without comment.

"I called Wiley but Frieda answered," MJ said. "She told me he was out. Jesse's in town for a couple of weeks." She walked to the bar and poured herself a glass of water. "Do you want some?"

Ginger frowned. "Not unless you put ice cubes and scotch in it."

MJ ignored her. "There has to be an explanation for all this. What happened to Rick just doesn't add up."

MJ's cell phone rang. She dumped everything from her purse onto the sofa and retrieved the phone. "Hola," she said. MJ rolled her eyes at Ginger and listened.

"Sure Wiley, what books do you need?" she asked, reaching for a pencil and paper. MJ scribbled as she listened. "I think I can find them. Give me a couple of hours. I'll call you back as soon as I do."

Ginger pretended to be busy reading a magazine. She looked up. "And?"

"Wiley needs two books Rick promised him last week for a lecture. I'm going to look for them, then take a nap."

"Good idea. While you're asleep, I'm going downtown to pick up a few groceries."

Two hours later Wiley drove through the gate of Hacienda Azul. He parked the Jeep under coconut palms and headed for the front door. The view was a panorama of the Pacific. Fifteen acres of estuary and farmland overlooked dunes held together with threads of sagebrush. The green chili fields formed a patchwork against the wild daisy and indigo bushes. Lacy creosote danced in the breeze. Wiley's jaw was tight as he approached the door. He was annoyed that MJ asked him to leave Buster and Cindy at home. She didn't want them near the cranes nests in the reeds. He rang the bell.

MJ opened the door wearing Rick's plaid shirt. She had dark circles under her eyes.

"Hello, Wiley," she said.

He shuffled from foot to foot. "I want to tell you again how sorry I am about Rick."

"Thank you." MJ motioned in the direction of the living room. "Let's sit for a minute."

Wiley chose the chair facing the bookcase hoping something might catch his eye. Then he turned serious. "It was quite a shock," he said. "Everyone in town is talking about it. Rick and I were buddies so people ask me what happened."

"Do you have any idea? Did you notice any change in him over the last couple of months?"

"Naw. Nothing unusual. We laughed, told jokes, talked about Los Santos. I'm still trying to figure out what he was doing at El Mármol."

MJ was aware that Wiley avoided looking at her.

"There's more to this than meets the eye. I found the Rick's journal and he mentions you several times, including an entry for El Mármol."

Wiley fidgeted in his chair. "Rick and I went lots of places. I remember El Mármol. I got sick the day we were supposed to go and he went alone."

"Well I've never heard of the place," MJ said. "I found an old Baja travel guide and read about it."

"Yeah. The local barber said his grandfather worked at the mine. His dad went to the onyx schoolhouse they built. It was a self contained little community. Mata Hari had a specially designed bathtub shipped to San Francisco from the dock on the Sea of Cortez." Wiley paused. "Somebody told me that the Federales had a helluva time finding the place. Guess he went right over the edge of a cliff. There were no skid marks. Creepy they said."

Wiley looked at MJ. Tears welled up in her eyes.

57

"Sorry. Guess I wasn't thinking. I'd better be going," Wiley said.

"Let me get the book." MJ returned with a paper bag and handed it to him. "I only found one. The older book must be misfiled or packed somewhere else."

Wiley gritted his teeth and nodded. "Do you think it could be here in the living room?"

"Not likely. The oldest books are boxed and waiting for the new library. Rick knew where everything was. For me it's a guessing game."

"I could come back and help you look for it."

"Good idea. I'd like you to fill in some details about the places you and Rick visited. How's Monday?"

"It won't work. Maybe the following week, after Jesse leaves. I'm spending some quality time with my son. He doesn't come often enough."

"I'll call you in a week," MJ said as she closed the door. She walked to the sofa, put her feet up and closed her eyes. Just thinking about Rick made her ache with sadness and loss. She began to sob.

A few minutes later Ginger walked in carrying two bags of groceries. "I just saw Wiley tearing down the road. He didn't look very happy."

"That man has the sensitivity of a toad," MJ said wiping the tears from her eyes. "I have no idea how Frieda puts up with him."

"There's something about the men in this town. Maybe it's what they eat." Ginger opened the pantry door and began placing the groceries on the shelf. "I'm putting the extra bag of coffee in here along with the soap."

Ginger sang "Whistle While You Work" as she made herself busy. Then she stopped and poked her head out the door, holding a tube of Colgate and some paper towels. "Hey, by the way, I had a terrific idea as I was searching for the toothpaste in the market."

MJ opened her eyes and sighed. "Why do I think I'm going to need a drink to hear this. Did you buy aspirin too?"

Ginger finished unloading and returned with two Cokes. "I have a thought," she said. "I want you to visit Elisea Torres."

"Who?"

"The curandera who lives in the Sierra Lagunas."

"I don't need a folk healer, I need facts. No thanks."

"MJ, listen to me. The woman is famous for healing and she's a mystic. What you don't know is Elisea was a Godsend two years ago when Kevin cut my leg open. The knife left an ugly purple scar and the pain wouldn't quit."

Ginger pointed to her leg. "Look."

MJ peered at Ginger's scar unimpressed.

"All those stitches and you can hardly see the scar. Elisea is amazing. And she he speaks through the dead."

"Next I suppose you are going to tell me she can communicate with Rick."

"Exactly. You know Maria Lopez, from Las Barriles? She visited Elisea after her father died because the old man hid money on his property and no one could find it. Elisea solved the problem. Maria's father spoke through Elisea and told her where it was. Sure enough, when she got home they found a metal box buried under the fender of the truck in the backyard. The locals swear by her."

"I appreciate your help but . . ."

"Please, just think about it. You have nothing to lose and you might just learn something. Okay?"

MJ was exhausted and her head was spinning. "I'm going to take a nap."

The kitchen phone rang. "Let me get it," Ginger said, heading for the phone. "If it's important I'll let you know."

"Bueno. Ginger aquí. Oh, hi, Johnny." Ginger crinkled her nose as she listened. "Yes, she's here. Just a minute I'll see if I can find her."

Ginger walked toward MJ with her hand cupped over the receiver. "It is Johnathan Clay Thompson," she said facetiously. "He has a very important message."

Ginger shrugged her shoulders and gave MJ a quizzical look.

"Everything is always very important to Johnny. In his own mind." She handed the phone to MJ.

"Hello?" MJ leaned against the door and listened. Finally she said, "Thank you, Johnny. It really was a shock, but I'm doing okay. Fortunately Ginger keeps me laughing and is cooking up a storm."

Ginger motioned for MJ to sit down but she shrugged it off.

"I don't know, Johnny. You know how I feel about sharing personal information. Let me think about it and get back to you. And thank you for calling." MJ hung up the phone. "That was weird."

"Why?"

"Johnny asked me if I wanted to appear on his radio program Friday and talk about Rick's interest in reopening the mine. Thought I should keep the momentum going. Good for local jobs, etcetera. According to his sources, the California group might still be interested."

MJ tapped her fingers on the coffee table. "I have my doubts. His final pitch was that I could mention everything that Rick's family has done for Los Santos and talk about the new library and museum."

Ginger shook her head. "Well I'm not exactly objective. Since he is a former lover, if not a very stimulating one, he must be up to something."

"Don't be such a cynic."

"I just don't trust him," Ginger said. "He slept with everyone in town."

———

Jonathan Clay Thompson hung up the phone and tapped the three-inch heels of his cowboy boots quietly on the floor. He glanced at the silver cufflinks on his white shirt and folded his hands on the table. Finally he surveyed the two men seated across from him. "I don't know if she'll go for it. And even if she agrees, I'll have to lead her into a conversation about Rick. It won't be easy. MJ can be a loose cannon."

"That's not what we want to hear," one of the man said.

Johnny stared at the three hundred pound wrestler sitting in his Chippendale chair. One wrong move and the antique would be kindling. The man's bowling ball head was pink and shiny and complimented the silver crowns of his teeth. The silk Tommy Bahama shirt was a montage of color across his large chest. The muscles in his thighs clung to his black silk worsted pants.

"We chose you, Johnny, because we know you can do the job," he said.

The second man was small and very still except for the sound of his knuckles cracking. A sound that reminded Johnny of childhood Thanksgivings when he and his brother broke the wishbone. He wondered how long it would take the man to break his arm. Or neck? The little guy was dressed totally in white: shirt, tie, pants, and belt. He wore white buckskin shoes with his heels and toes pressed together like a mannequin in a window display.

"We want our money," the bald man continued. "That woman MJ is the key. Find a way to expose her."

Johnny could feel the perspiration under his arms dripping inside his shirt and the bandana around his neck getting sticky.

"You haven't given me much time," he said.

The smaller man spoke. "We know that you supplied Rick with old photos of the El Triunfo mine last month. He must have said something about what he was doing."

Johnny noticed a fly on the handle of his letter opener. It moved to his sweaty hand, then from finger to finger. Johnny didn't flinch. "What if I can't get her to come on the radio show?"

The smaller man opened his briefcase and placed a manila envelope on the desk. "It would be a shame to ruin your reputation. The local paper would sell lots of copies with your photo on the front page. Think about it."

The men stood. "We're going on a three day trip. Have some answers when we return."

They turned and walked out. Johnny opened the envelope and winced. He had always been so careful, but not this time. Inside were explicit photos of him in bed with Maria Lopez Garcia. Every detail of that night was in glossy black and white.

Johnny was being blackmailed and there was nothing he could do about it. Maria wasn't some woman he met at a party and slept with. This was a much bigger problem. Maria was the wife of the Governor. In the best-case scenario he would lose his job. In the worst case, they would find his body floating in the Sea of Cortez.

CHAPTER 9

They left before dawn. MJ walked down the path to the SUV with a flashlight guiding their way. She and Ginger carried backpacks with food supplies, a first-aid kit, and clothing. MJ opened the door, placed her backpack behind her, started the engine, and switched on the defroster. Ginger kept the backpack with snacks and water at her feet. The ride to Aquaja would be a seventy mile trip through the Sierra Lagunas over a rutted road and would take at least three hours.

Yesterday, Ginger phoned Juanita at the village store and asked her to contact Elisea regarding their visit. Juanita confirmed the visit last night. The curandera was expecting the two Americanos by midday.

The women were quiet on the ride through town. MJ wore a navy all weather jacket that belonged to Rick, jeans, a wool cap, and hiking boots. Her face was sad and brooding and her eyes were focused on the foggy road. They passed the oldest theatre in Baja, a white columned building on the plaza, built in 1918. They turned onto Calle Militar. The darkened windows of historic homes reflected the wrought iron lanterns hanging near the carved shuttered doors. Soon shopkeepers would emerge to sweep the sidewalks and hose down the buildings. Many of the old homes were now coffee shops, galleries, or artisan stores. Busloads of tourists arrived daily, shopped for two hours, and returned to Cabo San Lucas, charmed by the small colonial town. At the bottom of Militar the only light in town was red. The park on the corner, usually alive with children playing on brightly colored swings, gym bars, a slippery slide, was dark and empty.

Ginger unscrewed a thermos and reached for a mug. "Would you like some coffee?" she asked.

"No thanks," MJ said. She was thinking about the book on curanderas she read last night. She pushed a button and "Schubert's D-Major Symphony" began to play. Ten minutes later they passed the sandy beach of Las Palmas, a privately-owned estuary protected by cliffs. It was a favorite spot for Los Santos residents to fish and swim.

Ginger reached into her purse for a notebook.

"We turn left a mile past the old gabled brick ruin ahead. Look for an arroyo and a stand of mesquite trees on the right just before we get there."

Fog sitting in the underbrush licked its way toward the center of the road. MJ turned on the windshield wipers. They squeaked from dryness and atrophy.

MJ took the left past the ruin and said, "Okay, now what?"

Ginger looked at her directions. "Juanita told us to be sure to close the gate after we go through. The goats somehow always know when it's open. It takes hours to herd them back in." After closing the gate they continued in silence again.

"Let's see if it's warm enough to open a window and get some fresh air," MJ said. "How much longer is the drive?"

"Who knows," Ginger said. "The road is a mess from the storm last night. I'm glad we have a shovel in the back. The ideal solution would be a man, six foot two, with curly black hair and muscles everywhere."

"You have a one-track mind," MJ said. "I just hope we don't run into wild boars or a mountain lion. They aren't fussy. They'll eat anything."

MJ put a CD into the player on the dashboard. "Here's your favorite song," she said.

Paul Simon began to quietly sing "Fifty Ways to Leave Your Lover."

———

Elisea awoke to the sound of a woodpecker tapping on her window. It was such a wonderful daily ritual. Tap tap tap. She opened her eyes. It was 6:30 a.m. Morning light cast shadows across the wall of the old pueblo.

Elisea, a fourth generation curandera, learned her skills from her mother Sophia, who died five years earlier. She stepped on the cold floor, stretched, and gazed at the beautiful blue hand-carved shutters, a gift to her mother in exchange for healing Don Miguel Cortez. Elisea was only ten when it happened, but she would never forget the day.

Antigua Cortez, matriarch of one of the oldest families in Baja California, brought her younger son to Elisea's mother, Sophia, after every doctor in Mexico couldn't find a cure for his illness. "Please see what you can do," Antigua said clutching the child.

The professional opinion was that Miguel suffered brain damage when he nearly drowned at the family swimming pool at Tres Cruces. The child slipped on the diving board and hit his head. Fortunately, his brother Don Hernando was nearby and saved his life.

By the time Sophia saw Miguel, his speech was slurred and his eyes glazed. He screamed at the sight of water and kicked anyone who came near him. Antigua was unable to bathe him and finally resorted to putting sleeping pills in his food. Servants washed him and changed his clothing while he slept.

Sophia asked Antigua several questions while she took notes. She watched the interaction between Antigua and the child. Finally she turned to Antigua and said, "The child has mal de ojo, the evil eye."

Antigua seemed perplexed.

"The disease is treatable if you follow my instructions," said Sophia. "Take Miguel home, calm him down, and massage his body from head to toe with the shell of an uncooked egg. When you finish, make the sign of the cross all over his body and recite the Apostles Creed three times." Sophia made a cross on her arm. "Then break the egg in a glass of water and return it to me," she said.

The next day Antigua returned to Sophia's house with the glass. The white of the egg rose to the surface. The yolk sank to the bottom and assumed the shape of an eye.

"Good," Sophia said handing the glass back to Antigua. "Take the egg home and bury it in your backyard." She walked across the room, chose a single bunch of dried herbs, and threw a large handful into a steaming kettle. Ten minutes later she handed Antigua a glass jar. "This is borrage tea, Give Miguel a cup when you get home. Do this every hour until he begins to sweat.

The liquid will purge his body of evil fluids. By sunset Miguel will feel better."

After Antigua departed, Sophia explained her treatment to Elisea. "The cure for malo de ojo comes from the Spaniards who learned the ritual from the Moors," she said. "A child who is admired for his beauty or intelligence often get the sickness from the person who admires him the most. Antigua loves this boy so much she is the reason for his mal de ojo."

The event happened thirty years ago. When Sophia cured Miguel Cortez she became the most powerful curandera in Baja California.

A month later, an old lumber truck drove into town.

Two men stopped at the tienda and asked for directions to the casita of the curandera. They told Sophia they worked for Antigua Cortez and had a gift for her. Over the next week the men cut wood and made templates of animals, birds, fish and stars. They painted the shutters blue, and hung the exquisite designs on Sophia's house. Everyone who came to visit the curandera knew where to find the house.

Little had changed over the years since the blue shutters were added to the house. Elisea, like her mother, would soon have patients at the front door. She washed, dressed, and knelt before the shrine of the Virgin of Guadalupe praying for guidance with her decisions on this day.

Elisea peeked through the shutters. Five people were waiting outside. Señora Lopez, dressed in black and clutching rosary beads was first in line. She came weekly with a new ache, blister, bite, scraped knee, or anything that would reassure her of continued health. Elisea did not recognize anyone else. The Americans would arrive midday. Before they arrived, she needed to gather special herbs and make poultice. Over the next two hours Elisea prescribed various medications and remedies. At ten o'clock she hung a sign that said "Closed," found a basket, and headed across town where she would choose leaves, stems, and blossoms, grind them with mortar and pestle, and create life saving combinations.

Elisea, a petite but imposing woman, wore her hair braided into a crown like the women before her. She was aware of the respect she commanded from local residents. The village was fortunate to have a curandera. At times she was overwhelmed with the sense of responsibility that came from the gifts of healing her family had possessed for generations.

When she passed the village store, the men tipped their hats and said, "Buenas Dias, Señora."

Elisea nodded and continued up the road.

The sun was high by the time MJ and Ginger arrived in Aguaje. They made a quick stop at the village store for directions and headed toward Elisea's home. MJ navigated the SUV around sleeping dogs, children playing soccer, broken toys and a wheelbarrow. Every casita considered the road an extension of its yard. Two turns later MJ and Ginger arrived at the small palapa casita. A white cat looked up and quickly scooted under the front steps.

"Wow, look at those shutters," MJ said." "I wonder who made them?"

"I don't know, but they're terrific."

"Oh. The sign on the door says cerrado. I thought she was expecting us."

"Not to worry, she's home. There's smoke coming from the chimney and I smell tortillas."

They climbed the steps and before MJ could knock, the door opened. A petite woman in a black dress embroidered with herbs, bees, and flowers stared at them. Her necklace was festooned with silver amulets and large hoop earrings covered with bird feathers. Hooded black eyes and were almost lost behind the lines on her forehead and in the smile on her face. "Hello," she said. "I am Elisea Campeche."

Ginger extended her hand. "I am Señora Doyle and I have brought my friend Señora Steele to visit you."

"Mucho gusto. I have been expecting you. Come in please."

MJ and Ginger followed Elisea through the tiny hallway toward the back of the house. They passed a small bedroom with candles flickering around the Virgin of Guadalupe. MJ paused at the door. The Virgin's presence radiating through the room mesmerized her. She looked down the hall and hurried to catch up with the women. The large kitchen they entered was a potpourri of visual and aromatic delights. An edged chrome cast iron stove sat like a Goddess at the center with an enamel pot that filled the room with the aroma of cinnamon and clove. The bookcase covered an entire wall and was filled with multicolored glass jars: each one labeled with the ingredients. Herbs hung on strings from the palapa roof and covered half of the room with oregano, rosemary, jasmine, and rose hips, all fighting to dominate the senses.

MJ stared in amazement at the array. Elisea walked toward a long pine table, stained with age. She nodded at a bowl filled with grapes, apples, and tomatoes. "Please take a piece of fruit," she said. "You must be hungry after your long journey."

MJ took an apple and surveyed the room. Something was missing. But what? There were no books. Elisea learned her healing techniques from her mother. Reference guides and recipes were unnecessary. MJ thought the kitchen looked the same a hundred years earlier, except for a small light bulb hanging from the ceiling.

Elisea turned to Ginger. "Thank you for bringing MJ. There is a pitcher of tea and a dish of anise cookies under the mango tree outside along with a week old Spanish newspaper." She smiled. "But the news rarely changes."

"Thank you," Ginger said. She looked at MJ and nodded, then closed the door.

Elisea continued past the ficus tree to a small round table with two rawhide chairs. "Sit down please. Before I begin, do you have any questions?"

MJ looked thoughtfully at Elisea before she answered. "Yes." She folded her hands on the table. "Last night I read a book about curanderas and I'm curious. Why did you decide to become one?"

"It is in my blood. Every woman in my family has practiced the craft for generations. It is a gift from God, the spirits, or the Virgin of Guadalupe. Or perhaps my Mayan ancestors."

"I must tell you that I . . ." MJ began.

"I know what you are going to say. You have doubts about my powers. You are a scholar, a historian of Mexican jewelry brought to Baja California by Spanish noblewomen. You consider yourself a realist, and knowledgeable about what is documented rather than surmised. You are a skeptic about mysticism."

Elisea took MJ's hand. Her long fingers curled around an amulet that dangled on the silver chain. MJ felt the coolness of the necklace against her palm. When Elisea opened her hand she held a heart with a blue sapphire, MJ's birthstone, the month of September.

Elisea placed both hands over MJ's. "Your husband Rick is in this room. Shortly he will speak to me. Close your eyes and listen to what he says."

———————

Ginger was leaning against the truck smoking a cigarette when MJ came out of the casita.

"Hey, is everything okay?" Ginger asked.

"Yeah sure. It wasn't at all what I expected."

"What do you mean?"

"Elisea told me several things about Rick I didn't know. I closed my eyes and she spoke through Rick."

"That's what happened when Maria Lopez saw her."

MJ took a cookie and walked toward the truck. "Let's go where we have some privacy. I'll give you the short version on the way."

MJ turned back and took one last look at the blue shutters. When she asked Elisea about their history she was told they were a gift to her mother as well as the story that surrounded them. Amazing. It could even make a skeptic like MJ a believer.

Once they were settled in the car, MJ found a Coke and took a sip. "That's better," she said turning to Ginger. "This is what she told me Her first words were, 'Things are not what they seem.' followed by, 'Stay calm and confide in Ginger but nobody else. Someone you trust will betray you.' "

Ginger put her hands to her mouth. "Did she really say that?"

"Yes. I opened my eyes because I was startled. Elisea put her fingers to her lips and said 'shish.' Then she shook her head no and I closed my eyes. After that I just listened."

"This is pretty amazing stuff," Ginger said.

"Next she said, 'listen carefully to what people say. One door will lead to another until you discover what happened to Rick.' She told me to visit his oldest friend who had the information I needed, and then to go to the home of Rick's childhood. I'm thinking she meant visit Mama Estrada and to go to Rick's summer home in Santa Juanica."

MJ took a bite of a cookie. "Her scariest words were, 'You are afraid of dark spaces, but soon you will have to visit one. It is very important.' That confused me. What could it mean?"

"Maybe you have to visit the El Triunfo mine," Ginger said.

"I get nervous in my bedroom closet. Elisea's final words from Rick were, 'I will be with you again.' Then she told me to open my eyes. I asked her what Rick's words meant. She looked at me with soulful eyes and said, 'All I can tell you is that Rick's voice is very strong.'"

MJ paused. Then her eyes widened. "Do you think it means Rick is alive? Why would she say these things if he wasn't alive." MJ put her hands over her eyes to cover the tears inching their way down her cheeks.

Ginger put her arms around MJ and said, "God, I hope so. You need to believe he's alive."

Ginger found a Kleenex and handed it to MJ. "Elisea gave you a lot to take in. Based on what she said, what you are going to do next?"

MJ wiped her eyes and blew her nose. "For starters, I'm calling Johnny from the general store. If I go on his radio show, I'll find out why he really invited me."

She turned on the ignition. "Sunday I'm leaving for Santa Juanico. But first I'll visit Mama Estrada. Rick mentioned her a couple of times in his journal."

They drove into town and MJ maneuvered the truck between two vehicles at the village store.

"One other thing," MJ said. "I'd like Alberto to come to Loreto. Rick went to the town clerk's office more than once recently according to his journal. Why? What was he looking for?" MJ tapped her fingers on the wheel, then turned to Ginger and smiled. "Will you ride up with him?"

"Sure. Why not?"

MJ got out, locked the car, and took a hard look at the general store. The tienda was showing its age. A faded Pemex sign hung from two rusted hooks under the sagging palapa roof and the gas pump had gaping holes where the hose used to be.

Two men quickly made their way to the truck. "Petrol, señora?" one asked.

The second man lifted the windshield wipers and sloshed water onto the window from a galvanized can. He smeared dirt with an old cloth, making it impossible to see. Ginger looked at MJ who suppressed a laugh.

"They're the only game in town." MJ said. Do we need gas?"

"It wouldn't hurt."

"Solamente quatro galones, por favor." MJ held up four fingers.

The men quickly finished and MJ handed them the money.

"Muchas gracias," they replied.

The women walked up the steps and through the front door where they were overwhelmed by the selection of items. There was something for everyone in the store. Children's shoes, canned goods, balloons, and candy were prominently displayed. Pens, paper, and scissors sat on shelves between multicolored piñatas, jeans and blouses, kitchen goods, and electrical appliances. The place even sold tacos and tamales inside an igloo chest on the counter. Ginger nodded at the wall where several people waited patiently in a queue for the phone.

"It's the only phone in town," she said. "I think we'll be here for a while." Half an hour later, they finished their calls and headed for the truck.

"Damn," Ginger said climbing into the truck. "I really don't want to crew this weekend. What I have in mind is going to bed with a good book. Unless I get lucky," she giggled.

"At least we just ate the best tamales in Mexico," MJ said. "Let's go home." She opened the door and threw her purse on the back seat. "In a week, I'll have a much better idea of what happened to Rick. Nothing makes sense now. But it will."

CHAPTER 10

Rick opened his eyes. The room was black and smelled of hay and manure. Cold seeped through his chest from the heavy blanket on top of him and the clothing he wore. He tried to roll on his side, but something covering his arm was in the way. He felt a kick against his leg followed by the voice of a child.

"Mama, mama," cried the boy. "Como esta'?"

There was a rustle of fabric and a woman with long hair wearing a flowing nightgown approached carrying a lantern. It cast a circle of light that grew larger until it covered the wall. "Jaime, come and sleep with me," she said.

Who were these people? Where was he?

The boy took his mother's hand and left the room. Rick lay in the stillness, closed his eyes, and wondered where he was. Memories returned in random order like photo images. First there was a shot and he was falling down the side of the cliff. Warm blood seeped from his arm to his knuckles. Then nothing, until he heard men shouting. They left and there was silence. A day passed. When he woke again, sun warmed his face. Later, the moon and stars shined above him. He remembered being lifted on a horse. A man was holding him. Then everything was quiet until today.

The woman was ripping cloth and wrapping the bloody leg of the screaming child lying next to him. She told Rick he was recovering from a bullet wound and lucky to be alive. The memories clung to the edges of his mind until they gradually faded and the blackness of night enveloped him. He fell asleep.

When Rick opened his eyes again he heard the woman singing. Her long hair was twisted into a braid on top of her head. She wore a simple blue dress with a fringed apron tied at the front that covered most of her skirt. She was barefoot. Thick black eyebrows created a dark line across her forehead above her radiant smile.

She turned toward the door. "Oxiard, ven pronto," she said. "Senior Ricardo esta' despierto."

Rick heard a cane banging against the wooden steps followed by the rhythm of the slow shuffle of feet. An old man with a familiar craggy face entered the room. It was Oxiard, a friend of Rick's father and the brother of his caretaker in Santa Juanica. Slowly, he made his way across the room and placed his hand on Rick's head. Rick knew he was safe at their rancho in the Sierra Laguna Mountains.

Three boys dressed in jeans and plaid shirts peeked into the room and began to giggle. They continued laughing until the woman raised her hand. "Go get your father in the barn," she said. "Tell him Ricardo is awake."

Rick now remembered the woman's name was Ruita. She was Oxiard's daughter-in-law. He watched her fold blankets and prop them against the wall. Then she slowly eased him into a sitting position. When she finished, she pulled the only chair in the room over to her father-in-law. "Sit here, papa."

A door slammed. Heavy footsteps climbed the stairs and a middle-aged man with the energy of a twenty year old bounded into the room with a big grin. "Thank God you're alive," he said. "We were very worried." Chayo gave his injured friend a bear hug. "You look much better than when we found you."

Rick grinned at the curly black haired man who was the size of Goliath. But how did he get here? Chayo, wearing jeans tucked into leather cowboy boots and the same cougar silver belt, stood back and put his arms on his hips. "You need a good breakfast," he said turning to the boys. "Go help your mother in the kitchen. We're going to celebrate." A cascade of feet and laughter faded down the stairs.

Chayo took his father's arm. "Dad, you start downstairs. Go slowly." He walked his father to the top of the stairs. "We're right behind you. Tell Ruita we'll be there soon."

Chayo helped Rick to his feet and led him toward the stairs. Rick struggled down the narrow staircase with Chayo's assistance. He felt the warmth of the cast iron stove before he entered the kitchen. Bacon seared as eggs cracked against a bowl. The smell of homemade tortillas and strong coffee made him very hungry. The men walked toward the small sitting area of the room. Two upholstered chairs with threadbare arms were covered with patchwork quilts. Oxiard sat on a ladder-back rocker and put his legs on a footstool. Chayo poured coffee from the pot that was sitting on a wooden crate and handed a cup to Rick.

"Thank you," Rick said looking around the room. He took a sip of his coffee. "Tell me, how did I get here?"

"We brought you here on horseback two days ago from El Mármol," Chayo said. "You were in terrible shape. We thought you'd die on the way. But thank God, you didn't." He grinned, then his face turned serious. "Why were you at El Mármol?"

Rick took another sip of coffee. "I'll tell you what I remember." He began the story of what happened at El Mármol. After a few minutes he paused.

Chayo sensed how exhausting the ordeal was for him. He held his hand up for Rick to stop. "Ruita, can we have some tortillas? I think Rick needs something to eat."

Rick shook his head no.

"It's fine," Chayo said reassuringly.

Rick's voice was tense when he continued. "As I ran toward the cliff I heard a shot. I dove to the edge, reached down, and grabbed a rope. Then I fell over the side and dropped to a small cave ten feet below."

The men looked at each other with confusion. Finally the old man said, "A rope? I don't understand?"

"I had been there before. Wiley and I made a side trip to El Mármol last month. He told me that I had to see the old onyx factory and mine. He was curious to know if anything was left of the original dock at the bottom of the cliff." Rick rubbed his eyes. God he was tired. "It's a pretty amazing place," he continued. "All that marble lying around for anyone to cart off. Have you ever been there?"

"I was there years ago," Oxiard said. "When there was an onyx schoolhouse."

"It's only a shell now," Rick said. "Anyway, we were trying to figure out how the workers got the onyx to the bottom of the cliff, so I rappelled over the side. On my way down I found the cave ten feet below." Rick took a bite of his tortilla. "Wiley and I wanted to be sure we could find the cave again so we placed a boulder near the edge, drove a u-bar two feet below, and tied a rope around it. It was sheer luck that I found the rope when I put my hand down." Rick heard his stomach growling.

"I knew I was shot when I landed on the ledge. A few minutes later I heard voices above so I waited. I had to get out of there. I was bleeding pretty badly."

"When I found you, you were barely breathing," Chayo said. "How did you get to the top?"

"I wrapped the rope around my waist, tied it over my weak shoulder, and used the natural footholds in the rocks to lift myself."

The men looked at each other in amazement.

"How did you pull yourself over?" Chayo asked.

"I don't know. But I must have somehow because the last thing I remember was looking at the moon over my head."

The three men sat quietly sipping coffee.

A voice from the kitchen said, "Breakfast."

The three boys appeared out of nowhere. The oldest one eased his grandfather out of the rocker while the middle boy carried his blanket. The youngest boy was in charge of Rick. He wrapped his hand around Rick's thumb and led him to the kitchen table. Oxiard sat between Rick and Chayo at the head of the table. The old man said a prayer of thanksgiving and the celebration began. Ruita cooked a special meal that included berries and pinon nuts. She passed around hand-churned butter and goat cheese. The boys sat at a mesquite bench across the room with a cloth over their knees and plates on their laps. The only sound in the room was utensils scraping against plates.

When breakfast was finished Ruita stood and began to gather the dishes. "Would you like more coffee?" she asked. All three men said yes. Rick was sleepy. The heat from the wooden stove along with the first food he had eaten in days made him groggy. His arm began to ache. Rick turned to Chayo.

"How did you know where to find me?"

"News travels fast in the mountains. I got a call from my neighbor Jamos on the shortwave radio. He was in Santiago buying boots and everybody was talking about the car that went over the cliff at the old marble factory. Someone mentioned your name so he called me." Rick heard the clang of pans being washed nearby.

"Ruita is the reason you are alive," said Chayo.

"How so?"

"She read the stars."

Rick looked over to where Ruita was washing dishes. She smiled.

"After she read the stars she told me to call Jamos and go to the place where you died. But she said I could tell no one. We packed our horses and left that day."

Rick understood how lucky he was. Ruita was the local curandera; Farmers consulted her when they wanted to plant crops, visit other family members, or have other children. He was humbled. He was alive because a ranchero, a cowboy living in the Sierra Laguna Mountains without electricity or a phone, listened to his wife, a curandera. Ruita practiced ancient traditions and had a basic faith and values that did not exist in his world.

The men spent the rest of the day discussing their alternatives. Rick was very weak. Both men thought he should wait a couple of days before he left the rancho.

Rick would not be deterred from going as soon as possible. He was worried about MJ. Would the men who almost killed him harm her? Why did they follow him from Cabo San Jose? What was their motivation?

It was midnight before they made a final decision. Tomorrow they would journey a hundred miles over the mountains to the coast. That night, Rick lay in bed under a moonlit sky and marveled at the honor of the family who found him. He owed them his life. He would not forget.

CHAPTER 11

Ginger was late. Harry wanted her on the boat by 7 a.m. that morning. "Can't you find anyone else?" she asked when he called.

"I'm desperate Ginger," he said. "I tried everyone, honest."

Well at least it was a short run. They would leave Cabo San Lucas on Friday morning, spend some time in Mazatlan, and arrive back Sunday afternoon. And the food was already on board. But Kevin was first mate. Damn.

She told Harry after the debacle on their last trip that she'd never work with Kevin again. And she wouldn't, except Harry was desperate and agreed to pay her double to come.

"Listen, I talked to him," Harry said. "He knows this is his last chance. No one will ever work with him again if he screws up this time."

Ginger had a run-in with Kevin two years earlier on a trip to Acapulco aboard a beautiful two-masted Drummond owned by a Brit who flew special friends to the Baja twice a year. The friends didn't change, but the women were always different. That year, Lawrence brought a beautiful young blond. Kevin made a provocative comment when he took a glass of wine to her table. She called him out on the spot. He turned beet red, bolted into the kitchen, and threw a knife across the counter. It glanced off the hood of the stove and hit Ginger's leg tearing a gash that needed stitches.

Even with stitches in her leg, Ginger was in high demand and worked a full schedule. The roll of a cook on a charter is critical. It was a known fact that if Ginger was on board, the kitchen was in good hands. She came with quite a resume. Ginger learned her trade washing dishes in her dad's Italian kitchen in Toledo, Ohio then she became a short order cook in an Asian restaurant. Long before she went to college, Ginger promised herself she would get as far away from Ohio as possible. The University of California in Los Angeles looked appealing so she applied, was accepted, majored in oceanography, and graduated cum laude. During her college years she made cakes on special occasions and developed quite a business. And the rest was history. The only time she used her knowledge of oceanography was to identify fish and marine life from the side of a sailboat. Ginger parked her car at the dockyard and ran toward the pier. The guests would be on board by eight o'clock and they would sail within an hour.

They left Cabo just past nine. The sky was clear, the waves calm, the ocean turquoise against the shore. Men on paragliders lazily made their way past the sailboat and steered toward the crystal sand of the Palmilla Golf Course. They were a patchwork of color against the Sierra Laguna Mountains.

Ginger had planned the evening meal and everything she needed was on board. She would serve sierra, a whitefish, stuffed with herbs of oregano, thyme, parsley, and cilantro. Also baked potato, and asparagus brought by truck from Ciudad Constitution. Twenty years ago no one in Baja California grew asparagus. Now there were vast fields in Ciudad Constitution, a hundred miles north of Cabo San Lucas.

Ginger's piece de resistance was her dessert: strawberry shortcake. The captain provided luscious strawberries from his farm in Santiago. She would make a simple Irish shortbread from her mother's secret recipe, add whipped cream, and, viola, the perfect dessert. She was happily adding eggs to the shortcake when she realized she didn't have enough butter. The storage refrigerator was below deck. Ginger wiped her hands on her apron and headed below. As she passed the largest stateroom, she heard voices, and stopped. Did someone say MJ? She stood outside the door and listened.

"If Johnny comes through like he promised we can leave on Tuesday," said a man. "Otherwise things could get messy."

"Don't get excited over nothing," said the other man. "Let's enjoy the trip and deal with things when we get back."

Who were these men? She looked at the number on the door. They were the replacements for a European couple that missed their connecting flight and would sail next week. Ginger remembered them: two American men from the welcoming party earlier in the day. They said very little and basically kept to themselves. Not exactly an ideal situation for a small sailboat. The only way she could find out more about them would be to check the roster. It was risky. If Harry found out, he'd fire her. The idea would have to wait until later. Dinner preparations were her first priority.

There were compliments all around for Ginger's fabulous meal. Mrs. Sampson, dressed in white linen pants, black patent leather sandals, and a red cashmere sweater flung over her shoulders, positively gushed with enthusiasm.

"My dear, where did you learn to cook? Masterful! The sierra was so moist and flavorful, and the shortcake! Please share your recipe. If you ever decide to return to the States let me know. You'd be a wonderful addition to any restaurant."

After dinner, Ginger wrapped up the galley, organized everything for breakfast, and waved goodnight to the Canadian couple drinking scotch on board. She could hear them laughing from her room below the galley. Everyone else had gone to town. It was nine o'clock and Ginger was exhausted. The sailboat rocked gently and the sails clanged against the mast as she made her way to her bedroom. The soothing sounds usually put her to sleep.

Ginger flicked off her sandals, dropped her clothing on the bathroom floor, and turned on the shower. She hoped the water would be hot. MY God, she smelled like fish. No wonder she slept alone every night. Five minutes later she threw a nightgown over her head, and crawled into bed with a nagging question. Should she tell MJ about the conversation she overheard earlier? She really didn't have enough information. Besides, it would upset MJ. However, the nagging comment about Johnny unsettled her. She'd sleep on it. She was too tired to think. Within seconds after the light went out, there was a knock at the door.

"Ginger, you have a ship-to-shore message marked important," said the porter. "I'll slide it under the door."

Ginger flipped on the light, put her feet on the floor, and with a long stretch of her arm picked up the envelope. It was from MJ.

"Ginger. Please come to my house straightaway when you return tomorrow."

Ginger tossed the telegram on the floor. It told her absolutely nothing.

She rolled over and went to sleep.

CHAPTER 12

La Paz was home to the seat of government for Baja California Sur. Every official document had to be signed and notarized in the city before it could be entered into the official book. Each document had its own book and department: property deeds, marriage certificates, bank loans, wills, building leases, and death certificates. Mexicans hated the process. It often took weeks, if not months, to maneuver the minefields of corruption, bribery, or documents that were mysteriously lost between departments. For most Baja residents the more efficient way to do business was through a handshake, a scribble on a sheet of paper, or a slap on the shoulder at the local bar.

It was Saturday and MJ had a dual mission in La Paz. She was meeting Johnny at the radio station, but first she would drop off Rick's death certificate at the notary office. She found a spot for the truck behind the building and entered the waiting room. It was Friday and the place was packed. She gave her name to the receptionist and took the only available seat. She placed the manila envelope on her lap that contained the sum total of Ricardo Marshall Delgado's life: his name, date of birth, parents' names, marital status, the date he died, and the cause of death. Everything about Rick that really mattered to MJ was unimportant to the state of Baja California Sur.

MJ sighed and closed her eyes. She thought about the circumstances of his death, how sudden and unexpected it was. The whole episode was unreal. And unbelievable. MJ's heart quickened when she remembered Elisea's words, 'Things are not what they seem.' Why was she here? The paperwork didn't have to be filed today. She could do it tomorrow, or next week. Resolute, she stood up and approached the receptionist. "I've changed my mind." MJ walked out the door and headed for the truck. The morning was sun was warm and radiated positive thoughts as she continued toward the central city.

La Paz was a bustling city and it suffered from growing pains. Construction crews worked on the old roads pushing boulders and dirt around the arroyos as she drove by. Huge pipes lay in trenches on the side of the road waiting for water from the Sierra Lagunas to subside from the rainstorm earlier in the week. Sailboats peeked between low plastered buildings, their masts rising above the tops of the buildings. Ahead the crescent beach and Malecon came into view. The vista was lined with palm trees; the mile wide harbor filled with shoals, a long stone jetty served as a breakwater. Most boats entered through a nine-foot channel off Prieta Point, but the depth varied according to the tide, and the winds could be treacherous.

John Steinbeck had a genuine fascination for the city of La Paz in his book, The Log from the Sea of Cortez. It contains a day-by-day account of his visit around the Baja peninsula at the beginning of the Second World War. His bird's-eye view of Baja California — which captured a time before the flood of tourists forever changed the tiny obscure fishing villages of Cabo San Lucas and La Paz — fascinated MJ.

Driving toward town, MJ passed tall square colonial homes with brick walls, shuttered windows, and lush palm trees untouched by time. As she got closer to the heart of the city she noticed empty lots with Se Vende signs. Several stately homes had Se Renta signs with neglected yards, torn shutters, missing roof tiles, and peeling paint. Many homes needed repair.

MJ continued to the radio station and her meeting with Johnny. His show ran for an hour from 10 a.m. to 11 a.m. He asked her to be at the studio an hour before airtime. Johnny had hosted a program called "Baja Happenings" for the past ten years. It was popular with Americans and was the only radio show in English. MJ rarely listened since she could find the information in "The Gringo Guardian" or "The Cabo San Lucas Weekly."

It was a short block from the Malecon to the radio station; a three story building wedged between the Arcos Hotel and The Antigua Café. The restaurant was a shabby building with a palapa roof, the familiar large Tecate sign, and the best shrimp tacos in town. The place was already in full swing with families waiting for tables on benches outside. Children tossed beach balls and wove between the benches, a Mexican dog bit at his stomach for fleas.

MJ smiled. God, she really loved this place.

She made the quick walk up the steps, entered the main office of the radio station, and approached the main desk. The nameplate on top said Mariposa Guilliarte. A stunning young Mexican woman with black flowing hair and silver hoop earrings looked up.

"May I help you?" she asked in flawless English.

"My name is MJ Steele and I'm here to see Johnny Thompson." The woman, momentarily startled by the informal reference, made a quick recovery.

"I'll tell him you are here," she answered and headed down the hallway. Her hair and hips swung in perfect rhythm and she disappeared around a corner.

Within seconds Johnny appeared.

"MJ, great to see you," he said. "Give me a hug."

Before MJ could react, Johnny threw his arms around her and kissed her on the forehead. He took a step back.

"You know how sorry I am about Rick," he said looking into her eyes with genuine sadness. "Can I get you a Coke or a glass of water?" he asked. "Or a cappuccino from the restaurant next door. Anything you want."

"A glass of water would be fine, thank you," said MJ.

Johnny motioned toward the hall. "Let's get some water then go to my studio where you can adjust to the mike. The baffle affects how we sound. We'll go over questions I might ask on the show."

They continued down the hall to Studio B.

Johnny's studio was eight by ten foot room with a large window that looked into the next room. It had fabric walls, a small table, two patched upholstered chairs, and a large clock set to international time. Johnny's chair faced the control room where the show was coordinated. MJ could see a long table banked with control switches. A row of televisions hung from metal arms on the ceiling, each one showing a different channel. At the table the control man was typing on a computer, oblivious to the activity around him.

Johnny smiled and folded his hands on the table. "MJ, first, let me ask you, would you be willing to take calls from outside listeners? It is your decision, but audience participation is more meaningful."

"I don't know. What's the difference?"

"Listeners feel they get more honest information if they can ask questions," he said. "Just in case you have concerns, two people in the next room answer the phone and screen potential people. Then a light flashes here, and I take the next call."

Johnny pointed to a small button near the mike. "There is a five second time lag between the question you hear and what is heard by our listeners. All you have to do is nod and I can interrupt a call in mid stream."

"So tell me about how you'll structure this interview." MJ asked.

"Okay, let's go over some ideas," he said.

Forty-five minutes later, Johnny looked at the clock, nodded to MJ and began.

"Good morning and welcome to Baja Happenings," said Johnny. "We are privileged to have as our guest today MJ Steele, an authority on pre-Colombian artifacts and jewelry, and the wife of Richard Marshall Delgado who died mysteriously in a car crash at El Mármol on Tuesday. MJ has agreed to accept questions over the phone so please call 612-157-1991."

MJ was immediately on the defensive. What did Johnny mean by died mysteriously?

Johnny looked up from his notes and said,

"Thank you for being here today, MJ. Our audience is aware of how much the Marshall Delgado family has done to increase our knowledge of Baja history."

"Thank you for having me," MJ said.

Johnny sipped some water and continued, "Rick's father, Oliver Marshall, spent much of his life collecting Baja memorabilia. Many of these items are currently on display at the History Museum here in La Paz. Let me ask you, what made your husband decide to fund a controversial mine project in El Triunfo that was so vastly different from anything else the Delgado family has pursued?"

The microphone was six inches away. MJ began to speak just as she had been instructed. "Rick thought the mine would be an opportunity to give something back to the community. The silver mine would employ local Mexicans, encourage tourism to the East Cape, and create new businesses. And it is fully supported by the Mexican government."

"So what went wrong?"

"Other Americans who came to lower Baja for the beauty and tranquility, as we did, began to fabricate information about the downside of mining development. Much of the information we read in the paper is untrue."

"Now that Rick has died do you think the project will continue?"

"That will depend upon the California consortium. They provide the funding. We will need a local person to coordinate the money and on site activities. Nothing has been decided yet."

"I recently spoke with Wiley Crookson, Rick's good friend. He expressed an interest in continuing Rick's work. He is a geologist and could be a good choice to handle the project. What do you think?"

MJ glared at Johnny. She'd been blindsided.

She drummed her fingers on the table. "Wiley will have to submit his application to the consortium like everyone else. They will make the decision."

"One final question before we open the phones up to callers, okay?"

"Sure."

"Because of the mining issue, Rick had become a somewhat controversial figure in lower Baja. Do you have any reason to believe that Rick's death might not be an accident?"

"Why do you ask?" The question hadn't come up during their rehearsal.

"There have been rumors about the money Rick used for the initial investigation of the mine. Do you know if Rick had difficulty with funding?"

MJ opened her mouth to speak, then paused. She bristled at Johnny. "Of course not. There were no secrets between Rick and me," said MJ glaring into Johnny's eyes.

During the next fifteen minutes MJ fielded questions that Johnny suggested audience members might ask. Three minutes before the end of the program, Johnny took a call from a woman.

"Hello, you are on the air."

"Yes, I have a question for Mrs. Delgado."

MJ thought the voice sounded familiar.

"My name is Anna and I would like Mrs. Delgado to verify some information."

Johnny's jaw dropped. Was the caller who he thought it was?

"A few months ago my son, who works for the department of records, registered a large insurance policy to Ricardo Marshall Delgado and listed you, Mrs. Delgado, as the beneficiary. Do you know anything about it?"

MJ waved across the table for Johnny to cut the call.

Johnny interjected, "I'm sorry but the station does not allow our guests to comment on documents of a personal nature without prior consent. If you wish to submit your request in writing we will be happy to forward the information to Mrs. Delgado. Thank you for your call."

MJ breathed a sigh of relief.

"Well, that's all for now," Johnny said. "Tune in next week when Carl Clifton will tell you about the international surfing competition at Riggers Surf Club in July."

Johnny switched off the mike and looked at a very shaken MJ seated across the table. "We're off the air," he said. "You just dodged a bullet. Care to talk about what's going on?"

MJ stared at crack in the laminate on the table. She ran her finger over the ridge. Then she looked at Johnny. "Maybe. But you have to tell me about Rick's problem with funding for the mine. You didn't level with me. Why?"

MJ took a sip of water. Johnny rose from the chair, rubbed his chin, and walked across the room and back again.

"Everybody tells me things," he said. "My job is to flush out what's true. And I never write or say anything that doesn't have at least two sources I can trust."

"Are you going to tell me what you know or not?" she asked.

Johnny paused once more and looked straight into MJ's eyes.

"Could it be possible Rick was hiding information from you?"

"What kind of information?"

"There's talk around town that Rick had invested money in something other than the mine and the library."

MJ stood and faced Johnny. "There's always been gossip about Rick and his family. It's mainly distrust and jealousy because his dad bought land when it was cheap and married the daughter of a wealthy Mexican family. What new piece of information do you have?"

"Okay, this is what I found out," Johnny said.

There was a knock and the door opened. Johnny's secretary Mariposa poked her head in. "I'm sorry to bother you Mr. Thompson, but you have a call from Mr. Amigo. He said it was urgent. Shall I tell him you'll call him back?"

Johnny blanched. "No, I'll take it in my office. Thank you, Mariposa."

Johnny started toward the door then stopped and reached over for his notes on the table. He looked at MJ. "This phone call may take a while," he said glancing at the clock on the wall. "I have an appointment in half an hour. Can we meet later today or this evening in Los Santos?"

"Call me later," MJ said.

Johnny looked into MJ's eyes. "Rick was a friend and so are you. I'll tell you everything I know later." Then he closed the door. When Johnny reached his office he threw the papers on his desk. The agreement had been to talk on Monday, not now. He picked up the phone.

"Hello, Johnny here."

"So what do you know about a woman named Ginger?" asked a voice on the other end.

CHAPTER 13

The marketplace in La Paz is an institution. It hugs the Malecon for ten city blocks. Vendors sell toys, kitchen supplies, meat and fish, shoes from Leon, clothing, candy and anything you can carry. Farmers bring fresh vegetables daily from farms. Rabbits and chickens are sold live. Over a hundred stalls are assembled Friday morning and hauled off at sunset on Sunday. The metal-framed plastic tarps, decorated with colored umbrellas and batik, are a visual feast of red, blue, yellow, stripes and flowers.

Piñatas danced in the wind as MJ wove between the aisles toward her destination, a vendor who etched hand carved crosses in silver filigree. He completed the design by adding Mexican semiprecious stones or black pearls that were plentiful in La Paz bay a hundred years ago but now almost unattainable. MJ hurried past vendors who shouted,

"Hola señora. Una momento. Muy barrato. Señora, mira, mira."

Two children with ice cream cones ran by, barely missing MJ's skirt. The boy had a ring of chocolate dripping down his chin, and was followed by small dog wagging his tail and barking.

"Where are the parents?" she wondered.

MJ she could see the cotton candy and piñatas and knew the crosses were nearby. She paused to get her bearings because a wrong turn could create chaos in her mind.

"Señora Delgado," a man's voice behind her said, "Señora Delgado, por favor."

MJ turned and saw a tall, dark-haired man with very green eyes. He smiled, bemused by her confusion.

He was dressed in casual expensive clothing. A loose fitting beige silk shirt that hung to his hips, jeans, and black leather tasseled loafers. He walked toward her.

"Señora, I would like to speak with you," he said. "It concerns your husband Ricardo."

MJ looked to her right and left to determine if he was alone. She left the radio station a few minutes ago and her decision to visit the marketplace was an impulse. She regained her composure and said, "And you are?"

"Ramon Diaz," he said. "I am a friend of your husband. We have been friends since childhood."

MJ took a bold step forward and looked into the man's eyes.

"That's impossible," she said. "Rick and I have been married for five years and I know his friends. I have never seen you before in my life."

"Señora Delgado, we can both see the market is crowded," he said. "Will you come with me to a nearby restaurant? We can have lunch. I will explain everything."

He smiled reassuringly, extended his arm in an overview motion, and said, "We are surrounded by people. Should you choose to walk away, I will not follow you."

Ramon brushed past the woman selling piñatas toward the back of the booth. He opened the curtain leading to the next street, looked at MJ, and said,

"Come please, Señora Delgado."

MJ noticed the street was busy with shoppers. She recognized the façade of the local bank. She followed Ramon to a well-known restaurant named Mario's. It was centrally located. She could leave quickly if necessary.

Fresh flowers sat in miniature pitchers made by local artists and painted with a Baja mission scene, the name Mario's painted on the back. Tourists loved them.

A waiter appeared and led Ramon and MJ to a quiet table at a back wall lined with photos of Mario and various movie stars who had dined there. Everyone from Steinbeck in the 1940s to John Travolta was photographed standing and smiling next to Mario.

According to local legend, Mario was on an Italian freighter heading for Mazatlan in 1940. He jumped ship, made his way to La Paz, married a local Mexican woman, had ten children, and never left.

"I had eight boys and a couple of girls. They kept me busy," was his favorite quote.

Mario bought the land on La Paz bay sixty years earlier, built an adobe restaurant, added outside dining and a palapa roof, and still came in regularly to greet people.

MJ and Ramon sat quietly observing each other as the waiter brought water, a bottle of wine, and menus. Ramon tipped the bottle toward her glass.

"May I?" he asked.

MJ paused trying to size up the situation. When she did not answer he poured wine into her glass and another for himself. His green eyes held her gaze.

"And how do you know my husband?" she asked.

Ramon smiled with assurance. He seemed to be nonplussed by her question.

"Ricardo and I have been friends since childhood," he said. Rick's mother Lupita and my father are cousins. Their parents are brother and sister."

MJ folded her hands on the table. Why should she believe him? She needed more proof.

"Why hasn't Rick ever mentioned you?"

"I don't know. Until this year I had no idea what happened to Ricardo. My father told me his cousin Lupita and her husband moved to the United States from Mexico and he didn't know where they were."

He paused and took a sip of wine.

"There are many things about your husband you are not aware of." he said. "I am only one of them."

MJ tensed and looked down. Ramon was the second man to suggest that Rick did not tell her everything.

"Tell me how you found me in the market," MJ said. "Were you following me?"

"Yes," he answered.

"Why?"

"It was the easiest way to meet you."

He signaled to the waiter. "The radio station announced that you would be a guest. When you left I followed you."

Ramon folded his hands on the table.

"There are several people who know what you do and where you go. I care. Others mean to harm you."

Over the next hour MJ asked Ramon many questions. He told her that his father sent him to visit Oliver and Rick each summer until he was twelve. Then his mother became ill and needed constant attention. Over the following years when Ramon asked about Ricardo, his father said the family had moved from Baja California. He did not know how to contact them.

"Then my father died a year ago," Ramon said. "I was executor of the estate. My sister died five years earlier in a car accident."

"I am sorry," MJ said.

Ramon paused, took a deep breath, and continued, "When I finally went through the papers in my father's safe I found clippings of Ricardo from the time he played football at UCSD. There were articles about Oliver, the Baja collection, and correspondence between my father and him."

Ramon paused, as if unsure of what to say next. He reached for his wine and drank the rest.

"They actually met again a couple of years before Oliver died, when he came to the University of Seville to give a symposium on the Jesuits in Baja California."

Ramon stared at the empty wine glass on the table. His eyes were downcast. "Before Oliver was married, he spent several months doing research on old records and manuscripts that the University of Seville kept in the archives."

The restaurant began to fill. Two couples were seated at a nearby table. Ramon leaned toward MJ.

"It has taken me a year to find Ricardo," Ramon said. "Three months ago I contacted him. We were supposed to meet the day he died."

What should have been an easy ride for MJ back to Los Santos was filled with mental replay of her conversation over the last hour with Ramon.

She passed an American man running down the highway. No Mexican in his right mind would be running in the heat in the middle of the day. She concentrated on the beautiful purple Sierra Lagunas. They never lost their appeal; the majestic mountains sat on a lush green blanket of cardon cacti.

She crested a winding hill where the Pacific Ocean sparkled in the distance against blue sky. A momentary calmness entered her body. MJ looked at the clock on the dash. Four o'clock. She'd be home in five minutes. Then she remembered that she hadn't called Johnny. Cell service was nonexistent on this stretch of the road so she'd have to call when she reached Hacienda Azul.

Ramon Diaz watched MJ disappear through the maze of people at the bazaar. The meeting was productive. He was unsure how she would react, but she handled the new information like a professional. She was bright and would remember everything. It was a quick walk back to the hotel room. He had to make a call. He found the business card and dialed. On the third ring a man answered.

"Bueno."

"Hi, it's Ramon. I followed her from the radio station as you suggested, and we had lunch."

"How did it go?"

"She listened, but I am not sure she believes the story. You may need to intercede on my behalf."

"Let's wait a few days," he said. "Mrs. Delgado has to process everything that has happened recently, including what you just told her. Since you have waited this long, a few more days will not matter."

"I would like to discuss this," said Ramon. "Can we meet tomorrow?"

CHAPTER 14

Johnny hung up the phone with fire and anger in his eyes. Bastards. It was one thing to blackmail him but another thing to use his friends for leverage.

There was a time, a few years ago, when the two couples, Rick and MJ, and Ginger and Johnny, were inseparable. How could he forget their summers at Los Cerritos after the expats left for the States? The four of them would meet at the Pemex station and head for the beach. Rick would maneuver the old pickup truck through sand, ruts, goats, and chickens as loud Mexican music blared on the radio. Finally they'd come over the ridge to Cerritos, the most beautiful beach in all of Baja California.

Johnny brought steaks, Rick carried a case of beer, MJ made potato salad, and Ginger wowed them with chocolate cake and strawberries. They played tick-tack-toe on the frosting until the berries were all gone.

From July through September the beach was deserted Monday through Friday. Then, during the weekend, Mexican families between Los Santos to Cabo would flock to Los Cerritos with children, parents, fishing poles, and dogs. The children would paddle around for hours in surf that only reached their knees.

MJ and Ginger would spread a blanket, lie down, take in the sun's rays, and talk for hours. They never seemed to run out of things to say. Johnny and Rick would leave the girls and drive a couple of miles south to and surf in the high waves.

After Johnny and Ginger split up, the tension was so high that the four of them never got together again. Rick and Johnny continued to meet for the first few months. Over time, they saw each other less. Then Johnny moved to La Paz and they rarely ran into each other. He thought Rick's idea to reopen the El Triunfo Mine was a dumb idea, fraught with problems. And now that Rick was dead, it was unlikely to happen.

But Johnny's deep ties to MJ and Rick gnawed at his psyche. He had to tell MJ about his recent discovery. He certainly wouldn't hold out on her for a couple of thugs who were trying to intimidate him. He called, got her voicemail, and left a message.

"Hey MJ, sorry about the interruption earlier. Listen, I want to talk to you about Rick. I can be in Los Santos anytime this afternoon. Just let me know when."

Johnny locked his office and headed out the door. A blast of hot humid air hit him in the face. La Paz might be beautiful, but it was unbearable in the summer. He found his sunglasses and walked to the parking lot. The car started easily and he flipped the air to full blast. He drove along the Malecon vaguely aware of his surrounding, trying to figure out when his life went off course. Wasn't he at the top of his game? He owned an expensive automobile, a new home on La Paz bay, attended every party worth going to, and made tons of money. Then why was he so scared?

Johnny knew the answer. It was Maria Lopez Garcia. He pushed in the lighter, found a cigarette, lit it, and took a deep puff. He had overstepped his bounds. It was one thing to have an affair, but not with the wife of the governor. He had become too busy with the beautiful people, the movers and shakers of Baja.

Less than twenty four hours after the hatchet men sat in his office, he had the information they wanted about Rick. It was easy. Rumors were already on the street. A source in San Jose told him that Rick was running bets with the mafia. That was strange. His father Oliver had left a small fortune in Mexican property. Couldn't he mortgage it? Johnny also verified Rick's insurance policy for a million dollars. Did MJ know? She reacted very quickly to the question on the radio. He'd ask her later today. The thugs had several pressing questions.

"Find out why Rick was checking on property around Loreto. What was he looking for? Does his wife know anything about it?"

For all Johnny knew Rick could have been searching for another mining site. Yesterday, he called an old friend at the town clerk's office in Loreto. Oscar responded immediately. The fax was sitting on his desk at home. He went to a party last night in Los Barilles and still hadn't looked at it. Five minutes from home he pulled off the road and called MJ. Still no answer. He left another message.

"Johnny again, with important information," he said. "Rick was at the town clerk's office in Loreto last month. I have copies of the papers he requested. Also, Rick made a stop in San Jose the evening he died. I can be at your house in two hours. Call me."

Johnny looked at his watch. It was 3:15. He rounded the last curve before his home in Las Playitas. The compound overlooked an estuary where two sand hill cranes were pecking in the reeds looking for crabs. A parade of small sailboats were heading east for the annual race at the yacht club. He had missed it again this year.

Johnny eased the SUV over the recently graded washboard road. Ah, the charm of Mexico. Mr. Ortega waved and continued pruning his roses. Johnny tooted his horn and pulled into the driveway. He was out of the car before the garage door closed.

Five minutes later he was sitting at the pool drinking a Johnny Walker Red with one hand and smoking a cigarette with the other. He wondered if he had time for a quick swim. The folder from Loreto was sitting on the table. He reached over, picked it up, and read it. The top page showed a parcel of land thirty miles northwest of Santa Rosario surrounded by government property. It had no roads or water. To the north the land was flanked by an impassable mountain range, the Santiago Mountains.

Johnny turned to the second page. It listed the name and date of anyone who requested the document since the mid-1960s. Strange. The third page had the phrase FYI penciled at the top. The page revealed that the Mexican government owned the land until a quitclaim deed was issued for mining rights in 1957. A corporation in Mexico City purchased the land from the original owner in 1975. The name and phone number of the corporation was included. Was this the information Rick was looking for?

Johnny tossed the ice cubes around his glass. How serious were these men? Was his life in danger if he didn't contact MJ? Was she at risk too? He finished his drink, put the papers in the folder, and headed for the garage. His watch said four o'clock.

When Johnny hit the remote door opener, he knew something was wrong. The gun he felt against his neck confirmed his fears. He looked at the man behind him through the rear view mirror. He was a dark-skinned man partially hidden by a Mexican sombrero.

"You're going to back out nice and easy and listen carefully to my directions. Got it?"

Johnny nodded his head. He put the truck in reverse, mentally plotting what options he might have, while trying to ignore the gun. They drove out of the Las Playitas compound unnoticed. Everyone had gone inside for siesta. When he reached the main road and stopped the man said,

"Turn left."

Johnny slowly eased the truck south, away from La Paz. He gripped the wheel. They drove in silence. The only sound he heard was the man's heavy rasping. His clothing smelled of acrid cigars.

Johnny turned toward the back seat. "How much longer before we can stop. I gotta take a leak."

"Shut up and keep driving."

The smell of garlic from the man's breath was overpowering. The guy could be a walking advertisement for Listerine. Johnny heard the crunching of paper, a match sizzle, and within seconds a puff of cigar smoke hit his nose. Johnny flipped the air to full blast.

"I'm allergic to smoke," he said.

The man ignored him. Maybe he had orders to keep quiet. They rode in silence and Johnny wondered where he was going. He didn't think the man would shoot him. Not yet anyway. Not before he beat the crap out of him for information about Rick and MJ. The intruder's silence required a new plan. Johnny worried they'd pull off the main road before he could make his move. After another mile he eased the truck to the side of the road.

"What're you doing?" he asked.

"I told you I'm going to take a leak," Johnny said opening the door. "Follow me if you want, but I've got to go." Johnny walked toward a mesquite tree and disappeared behind some bushes. He heard the door of the Land Rover open and close.

"I'm right behind you," the man said. "Don't make any foolish moves."

Johnny stood in the sun and unzipped his pants. When he finished he turned and got a look at his assailant. The man's hat still covered much of his clean-shaven face. A white shirt, open at the neck, revealed a gold cross that was twisted among the curly black hair on his chest. His large stomach hung over the black pants and hid his belt. A gun, pointed squarely on Johnny, quivered in his hand. The man was nervous. Johnny took a step forward, tripped over a rock, and fell into a creosote bush. He waved a hand into the air.

"I'm okay," he said. "Give me a second. I think I've twisted my arm."

Johnny slowly got to his feet and limped toward the man, rubbing his elbow in pain.

"I many have sprained it, look here," he said raising his hand toward the man.

"Don't come any further," the man said.

The sound of a shot rang through the air.

CHAPTER 15

The midday sun was hot and the Pacific was calm, dark blue, and inviting. Wiley headed down the deserted beach toward Hacienda Azul. He pushed a stained sombrero lower on his head and smiled about his timing. MJ was in La Paz doing an interview and wouldn't be home for a couple of hours.

Somehow Johnny conned her into going on his radio show. That man sure was an operator, but he was predictable. If Johnny saw Wiley at the local bar, he made a beeline across the room like they were best friends. Then Johnny started in with the questions. Did Wiley know about the recently discovered gold near San Ignacio? Were he and Rick still wandering around old missions? Would Wiley like to appear on his show? Wiley sniggered. He knew the real question Johnny wanted to ask was, had they found the Mission of Santa Isabel?

Wiley would never tell anyone that through sheer determination and a bit of luck, he was getting close. There were a couple of loose ends. And maybe Oliver's collection had the answers.

His most important link came from the box with the Cortez family seal he found in the mountains six months ago. He searched the Cortez family records in the La Paz library and traced the initials on the box to Don Miguel Cortez, the heir of Tres Cruces when the Jesuits departed in 1768. The section on Don Miguel Cortez contained a paragraph written by Father Javier, the Dominican priest who arrived immediately after the Jesuits left.

Father Javier wrote, "A parishioner told me a distressing story about Padre Tomas, the Jesuit priest who returned to Spain last month. Shortly before the Padre left, he visited Don Miguel Cortez II at Los Cruces. Padre Tomas' had requested a heavy box be carried to the family library. It is rumored that precious jewels, gold, and a map to the treasure named Santa Isabel were inside. The following day, the personal servant of Don Miguel disappeared. A handyman said he left the hacienda with a wooden box strapped to a mule and enough supplies to last a week. The servant has not returned. Everyone believes he is dead."

Wiley wondered if there was a connection between Don Miguel's servant and the box he found in the mountains. Were there jewels and a map inside? Who took the contents and reburied the box? And if there was the map of the Mission of Santa Isabel, where is it now?

Wiley knew Oliver had a copy of the diary of Father Javier that contained the same information he found at the library in La Paz. MJ verified the book was in his collection, but when Wiley asked for it, she said it was misfiled. Could the book be in the bodega of Hacienda Azul? Or was MJ lying? His eyes grew tight and angry at the thought.

Wiley's second breakthrough came from a notation in a ledger the Jesuits made of items they took back to Spain that Oliver owned. Wiley borrowed it from Rick a few months ago. Oliver made a pencil notation in the margin next to the item The Journal of Padre Tomas that said,

"A copy in La Paz?"

Wiley's attempt to find the book was a merry-go-round. He drove to La Paz the day after he found Oliver's notation. The building was across the park from the oldest church in the city. He parked the car in front of the museum and went up the granite stairs two at a time. He opened the hand carved oak doors. Inside was a grand old room with a cove ceiling flanked by Corinthian pilasters. Curled paint hung from the molding that reminded Wiley of his mother's gnarled fingers.

An attractive young woman sitting behind the reception desk looked up and said,

"May I help you?"

The old geologist was pleasantly surprised to hear English. He handed her a piece of paper, and gave a brief description of the item. "Can you please tell me where I can find it?" he asked.

She scrutinized the paper. "Well it's not on the shelves because of its age." She turned to a file cabinet, opened the drawer, and leafed through some folders.

"I'm afraid we'll have to search the basement. The books was heavily damaged during the flood ten years ago. Many were damaged beyond repair. Books with pages stuck together were set outside on tables to dry. The process took almost two weeks."

Wiley shifted from one foot to the other as she continued.

"For the oldest books, written on parchment, a specialist from Mexico came to oversee the project."

Wiley coughed and asked her for a Kleenex. "Do you have any records of the books that survived?"

"Someone did write down the information. We have it in a locked cabinet upstairs."

Knowing the very logical and precise way the Mexican mind worked, Wiley realized it could take months before he had an answer. "Would it be possible for me to search through the records?"

"No, that is impossible. Government regulations do not allow anyone except employees of the library to conduct a search."

She smiled with enthusiasm. "I'll be happy to present your request to my supervisor, Mrs. Gonzalez, when she returns from her vacation at the end of the month."

Wiley thanked the woman for her time and left. He'd have to come back weekly and ask. The Mexican government was notorious for losing papers and claiming it never received them. A month later Mrs. Gonzalez sent a letter stating his request was not possible at this time. She was sorry.

Wiley had to take matters into his own hands; he decided to visit to the basement today. Wiley knew that MJ and Rick did not have an alarm system. They thought it was an insult to the Mexican people. The problem wasn't people from Los Santos but migrant workers from the mainland who were dirt poor, who lived in tents in the fields, and picked chilies. Their kids didn't go to school and sat in the heat under a tarp all day trying to amuse themselves. Damn shame. On the other hand, if MJ had a security system he wouldn't have the opportunity to make an unannounced visit. Did MJ know about the hidden room in the basement of Hacienda Azul? Oliver showed him the room when he was building the house. Said it was a wine cellar, and maybe it was. But Wiley had to find out.

Wiley walked along the beach. At the bocana, he made a sharp right and skirted a line of palo de arco trees. The area was a jungle. Herbert Pepperman, who owned the property, was a real whacko. The place was so thick with ficus, bogunvilla, palo de arco, and palm trees you couldn't see his house. For Wiley's purposes it was ideal.

He made his way through the brush to the basement door. It was almost one o'clock. He didn't have a clue what he'd find inside. He pulled a small tool from his pocket and smiled about his skill of lock picking. His first practices came from selling copies of final exams to students. They were stolen from the locked drawers in the professors' offices. By the time he graduated, he was fencing computers, watches, and other valuables stolen from wealthy New Yorkers. In Los Santos, he changed tactics and became a local hero by helping Americans get back into their homes and cars.

Wiley maneuvered the lock on the old door. It broke into two pieces and fell on the ground. Not a problem. He reached into his pocket and pulled out a slightly rusted serviceable lock and put the broken one in his pants.

The door opened easily, emitting a creek. He flicked the light of his LED flashlight and peered around. What a sight. The room was a nightmare of boxes on tables against all four walls. Not much was thrown away since the old man died. The light skimmed over broken bowls, old paintings and lithographs against a wall and the tables. He walked over to a stack of boxes. The labels read Scenes of America, the Golden Gate Bridge, The Grand Canyon. Nothing. Then he moved to a long table with stacks of maps with curled edges. The United States of America, Seward's Folly, The Mississippi River, The

Lewis and Clark Trail, California Missions in the United States. Still nothing.

Wiley had no idea that Oliver Marshall was such a hoarder. How could he find anything in this mess? It would take hours. A wave of depression came over him as he looked around. A ray of light shined through the open door he just entered. The stillness unnerved him. He heard nothing except the faint boom of ocean waves.

Wiley shook his head, took a deep breath, and focused on why he came, the bodega. He moved the light across the room to the paneled door between the bookcases. It didn't have a handle, but it wasn't completely closed. He walked to the door, placed the flashlight between his teeth, and pulled the edge with both hands. When the door flew open Wiley knew he was in trouble. He lost his balance, let go of the door, dropped his arm to break the fall, and heard a crack as his hand hit the floor.

The flashlight landed four feet away inside the bodega and was shining directly in his eyes. Cold sweat seeped through his shirt. He shivered. The room began to spin in color. Could he have vertigo after all these years? Wiley laid his head on the floor trying to regain his composure. Something tickled his face. He brushed the edge of his cheek. A cobweb. He hated spiders and Baja California had more varieties of spiders than anywhere else in the world. Could it be poisonous?

This was no time for panic. Wiley took a deep breath and perused his options. He rolled to his side and pushed himself up on his knees with his good hand. He placed his weight against the edge of the table and used his hand and elbow to pull himself upright. When he stood the room began to spin again. He closed his eyes and took deep breaths, counting to five as he breathed in, held his breath, and breathed out. Wiley was soaked with perspiration, and needed to go to the bathroom, but this was hardly the time. It took five minutes before he was able to walk into the bodega. Using the frame of the wine rack for support, he reached over, picked up the flashlight, and shined it around the room. The bodega was empty. He saw nothing except rows of wooden wine stacks covered with dust that smelled of old tannin.

CHAPTER 16

MJ rounded a curve into a valley of green cardon cacti bursting with bonnets of yellow flowers. They gave her a burst of enthusiasm as she approached Los Santos. She crested the hill and peered at the sun reflecting against the white line of the Pacific. Almost home. The clock on the dash said it was nearing five o'clock. She was exhausted from her interview with Johnny and her chance meeting with the mysterious Ramon Diaz. She reached for he aspirin bottle in the bucket between the seats, popped two in her mouth, and doused them with water, hoping it was enough.

Caravans were lined up in front of the candy stores to her left, but she barely noticed until one pulled in front of her. It would be slow going for the next mile toward town. The small tiendas featured signs of cardboard and plywood that said Dulces. The makeshift buildings sold candy and sweets made of nougat, peanuts, and cones of brown sugar wrapped in plastic. They were stuffed by rows into bins, waiting for eager hands to take them home. At first glance, the brown sugar packed cones looked like candles, but they were old-fashioned handmade sugar cane.

Los Santos processed sugar in vast fields below the Sierra Lagunas for a century, until the 1950s. Nowadays when tourists drove through town, the ruins of brick buildings with twenty-foot high chimneys were still visible. There were several ruins scattered throughout the town. During the heyday of sugar processing, the tall green stalks were cut, put through a hand press to extract the juice, and then boiled in large vats until the liquid was thick. Then the brown heavy sugar was cooled in wooden molds and sold in bulk. Mexicans still buy sugar cane stalks in the vegetable markets and use the juice for a variety of things.

MJ crawled behind a silver trailer from New Hampshire with two bicycles tied to the spare tire. A decal on the back window said "Live Free or Die." Her plan was to stop at Santa Café for dinner. Ginger was still making her way back from Mazatlan. Her other option was to eat at home, but the thought of cooking overwhelmed her.

After the Airstream turned left, MJ changed her mind and made a quick decision to stop at Los Santos Restaurant. She'd order two slices of pizza, a piece of chocolate cake to go. She found a parking spot and dashed into the café. The wonderful aroma of tomatoes, bread, fried onions, and sausage enveloped her. Service was fast. Church bells for mass were chiming as MJ headed for the truck. She passed a family walking toward the church. A child, looking very serious, clutched the hand of an old woman dressed in black, as the rest of the family followed.

MJ was pleased with her last minute choice for dinner. If she had any energy later, she'd search through Rick's notes on Wiley and where they traveled during the past year. Then a glass of wine and she'd be in bed by nine.

"MJ hello," said a familiar voice.

MJ turned, hoping she could exchange quick pleasantries and be on her way. But it was not to be.

"Father Leo, what a surprise," she said. Although she was exhausted, she was genuinely pleased to see the priest.

Father Leo approached with open arms. He put his broad hands on MJ's shoulders and looked in her eyes. "I should have called you days ago," he said. "I am so sorry, MJ. How are you?"

"I'm okay," she said. As long as I keep busy." MJ lowered her eyes and sighed. "I never thought." She bit her lower lip and continued, "Oh Father, I just can't understand how it happened" she said. "Or why." Tears welled up in her eyes.

Father Leo took her hand. "Do you have time for a cup of coffee?"

"Of course," MJ said trying to regain her composure. "And I know the perfect place. The bookstore now has an espresso machine." A smile came over her face. "Besides, I'd like to spend the next hour with someone who can make me laugh."

Father's eyes lit up. "It is in the hands of God, but let's see what I can do."

A couple of teenagers dashed by, barely missing them. "Excuse me, Father," one said trying to catch up with his friends.

The coffee shop was packed and the line was through the door, but they barely noticed. They were catching up on old times.

"I'll remember your wedding day until the day I die," said Father Leo. He glanced at the assortment of sweets trying to decide between a scone and a chocolate muffin.

"It was pouring down rain, the huerta was flooded, people in formal attire couldn't make their way across. The bridge was gone. The band decided to entertain everybody while they waited for the water to recede. Didn't Ginger have a problem getting to the church?"

"Yes," MJ said. "She was living at Punto Lobos then and parked her car near the arroyo. They found the car and steering wheel a week later, but the motor had disappeared." MJ laughed. "A fisherman brought her to Los Santos in a panga boat. Ginger carried the bridesmaid dress and shoes in a plastic bag, but didn't have time to shower again and smelled like fish all day."

"But the Lord was on our side," said Father Leo heading for an empty table. "The clouds parted, the sun came out, and it was a beautiful day after all."

"Father, something happened yesterday that I would like to share with you," MJ said in a serious tone. MJ related the story about her visit with Ginger to meet Elisea in Aguaja.

"Father do you believe Elisea could be right? Can I believe Rick is alive?" MJ asked.

Father Leo rubbed the side of his chin. He took several seconds to respond, then said, "The traditional role of a curandera is to heal through the knowledge she has gained from ancient cultures and traditions. Many of the healing rites have a strong basis in faith, the veracity of the healer, and the belief in a higher power."

The screeching of chairs from the group at the next table who were leaving ground their conversation to a halt. Father Leo paused until they were gone.

"Religion has similar roots. It is the belief in a superior being, a belief in God. In the Catholic Church,

God is named Jesus. Other faiths call him Yahweh, or Allah. The common denominator is faith."

Father Leo folded his hands on the table. "I have met Elisea several times. She is a powerful woman. Mexican people sometimes use her when their faith is in question due to a catastrophic event. She practices a healing process steeped in common sense by mixing herbs and plants that only now scientists and physicians are beginning to respect."

MJ looked past Father Leo toward a painting of the Virgin of Guadalupe, the patron saint of Mexico who was first seen by Juan Diego in 1531. After the Spaniards had conquered the Aztecs they treated the indigenous people harshly. Few people were willing to abandon their pagan God until the Virgin of Guadalupe appeared to Juan and left an impression of what she looks like on his tilma. The miraculous appearance of Virgin of Guadalupe to Juan Diego is the foundation of the Catholic Church in Mexico.

"Do you think the message from Elisea came from God?" she asked.

"I think God guides our faith," Father Leo responded. "Until you have a reason to doubt Elisea, listen to her advice. See where it leads you."

Father Leo looked at his watch, "What happened to the time? It's forty minutes past five. I have to meet Sister Agnes in ten minutes."

He pushed back his chair, took one last bite of his muffin, and reached for MJ's hand. "Please call me any time you have questions and stop by the cathedral on your next visit to Loreto." Then he made a mad dash out the door of the café.

MJ stirred the latte in her cup and thought about Father Leo's comments. She sat and perused what he said for a few minutes, then reached for her purse and made her way to the truck. On the drive home Rick continued to roll around in her head. This would never do.

Driving through the gate of Hacienda Azul she made a promise that the ghost of her husband would not intimidate her. She knew that Rick's presence would be everywhere. She marched toward the house with determination and threw the kitchen door open. The first thing to catch her attention was Rick's jacket hanging behind the door. She placed the pizza on the counter and headed toward the living room. The logs he stacked next to the fireplace stared back at her. The books and artifacts on both sides of the mantle belonged to him. So was most of the furniture.

MJ took a deep breath, walked into the bedroom, and threw open the shutters. Next she moved to the bathroom and placed all of his toiletries and medicines in the bottom drawer. She removed a book lying on the bedside table, his glasses, his socks under the bed, anything that caused her stomach to ache, and put them in the bottom drawer. Then she sat on the bed and looked around. His favorite sweater, a V-neck she gave him last Christmas, covered the back of his desk chair. MJ walked over and picked up the blue cashmere, clutched it to her chest, and sobbed. "You are not dead, I will NOT believe you are dead."

No matter what she removed, Rick was still in the room whether she saw his belongings or not. Her stomach growled. Did she have the stomach for cold pizza or was a glass of wine a better choice? The doorbell rang and startled her. Who would come by this late in the day?

Before she had time to react, it rang again. She headed for the door, and it rang a third time. Chiquita, confused by the noise, started barking and ran toward the door. Somebody was very impatient.

The sun loomed just above the horizon as she passed the dining room window. It was almost sun set. When she reached the front door she opened it with determination. MJ looked down at a child, no more than ten years old, wearing worn trousers and a white shirt. He stared at her with dark brown eyes, his lips pursed with determination.

"Are you Señora Delgado?" he asked.

MJ gave him a quizzical look. It was the second time today someone had called her by that name.

"I am Martha Jane Steele, wife of Ricardo Delgado."

The boy pulled an envelope from his pocket and handed it to her. "I was told to deliver this."

Before she could react the boy whistled and a black horse galloped toward him. He mounted the stallion, and with a flick of his whip, galloped toward the beach. She watched him cross the field, pass through the arroyo, and disappear through the boca. MJ blinked in disbelief.

MJ stared at the standard issue envelope with the name Señora Delgado written in blue ink. She ripped it open and began to read.

Friday, May 10

Dear Mrs. Delgado,

I have important information about your husband the day he disappeared. Please meet me Sunday at 3 p.m. in San Jose at the corner of Obregon and Hidalgo, the street across the plaza from Mission San Jose.

At the bottom of the letter a simple map identified the plaza, the surrounding streets and the church.

It was signed, *A*.

MJ pondered who A could be. The person could be a man or woman of any age, Mexican or Anglo. Amazingly, she was caught unaware for the second time that day.

CHAPTER 17

The fog crept into the basil fields before dawn in Los Santos the following morning. It sat resolute along the beach, slithered through the mango trees, then slowly lifted toward the church steeple.

MJ peered out the bedroom window and saw absolutely nothing. It was a typical foggy Saturday morning in May, and a nuisance. She turned on the radio hoping for the nine o'clock weather report for Cabo San Lucas and the Sea of Cortez. Ginger was due to arrive late tonight or worst-case scenario, tomorrow when MJ was meeting A in Cabo San Jose.

MJ's good night sleep was a combination of the heavy moist air, a glass of wine, and a sleeping pill. Chiquita stuck her moist nose on MJ's dangling hand and began to lick it.

"All right," MJ said. "I'll get your breakfast."

MJ put her feet on the floor and immediately retreated. Where were her slippers? The letter from A sat on the bedside table, along with the beginning of a "to do" list. The first entry was Call Wiley re: the book he borrowed. The man was such an annoyance. The second was Call Mama re: the delay in arrival. Mama would have to wait till Monday. MJ was meeting A in San Jose tomorrow. Why rush through a visit to Mama in Santa Rosario. She'd spend the night, eat the best lobster tacos in Baja, and then continue to Santa Juanica.

MJ found her sippers under the bed and padded to the kitchen. She fed the dog, had three cups of coffee, an English muffin, completed her list, and listened to the morning news. Then she made two phone calls.

The first call was to Johnny. He left her two messages yesterday. The second one sounded frantic. She tried his home and cell. No answer. That was odd. Johnny was like a dog on a bone when he wanted something. Finally, she left a message.

"Hey Johnny, what's up? If you have something important to tell me answer the phone."

Her second call to Mama Estrada required some finesse. Mama sounded disappointed until MJ mentioned she was bringing strawberries covered with chocolate. Of course she'd have to convince Ginger to make them.

MJ still hadn't made up her mind about a third call to Ramon Diaz. What would she say? Or why she would call in the first place? Everything she wanted to know sounded like an interrogation.

"Mr. Diaz, I would like to ask you a couple of questions. When was the last time you saw my husband? And would you please explain your relationship with Rick again? Why not just meet him in La Paz and get some direct answers. Maybe that wasn't a smart idea either.

By early afternoon MJ put aside her thoughts about Ramon Diaz and moved on to Wiley Crookson. She compiled a list of every book he borrowed during the past year. They definitely fit a pattern: five books on Baja California missions; two on mining; and one on early Spanish land grants. The most revealing information was the two books on searches for the Lost Mission of Santa Isabel. One was the expedition Nellie Cashman made to the Baja in the 1880s with a group of investors from the mainland to search for gold. The second one involved Erle Stanley Gardner's trips during the 1950s to look for the lost mission. He spent ten years searching almost a million dollars, all in vain.

The other day Wiley asked to borrow The Diary of Father Javier. The rare book was written in 1969. She was sorry she loaned it to him and she wanted it back. Soon.

What was Wiley up to? This year Rick and Wiley changed their focus from the Lost Mission of Isabel, a treasure hunt that MJ thought was more folklore than reality, to the reopening of the mine at El Triunfo. Why was Wiley so interested in the lost mission? Did Rick know about this? Did he care? MJ tapped her fingers on her notepad. She closed her eyes. Something important was missing. But what?

She decided to have something to eat. An apple, a glass of milk, or a cookie would help her focus. She went to the refrigerator, contemplated her choices, and decided on an apple. When she reached for it, a jar of mustard shattered on the polito floor leaving a trail of yellow muck and glass everywhere.

She quickly found some paper napkins and a large spoon, knelt on the floor, and began scooping the mess into the wastebasket. As she crawled around the floor, she remembered the horrible dark room in the basement that she and Rick emptied after his father died. Well, almost emptied. Everything pertaining to Mexico and its history was catalogued and placed in boxes and left there. The wine in the bodega was moved to a small room behind the master closet. Anything else Rick's father collected that was not included in the new library was also down there.

MJ never went back. But she wasn't sure about Rick. Would he hide the important paper Elisea mentioned in the basement? MJ took a deep breath. She opened kitchen the door and called Chiquita. The dog peeked her head out from behind a bush and wandered over.

"It's now or never, girl," MJ said, roughing the dog's head. "We're heading to the dungeon."

Cool wet grass brushed against MJ's legs along the overgrown path. She carried a flashlight and a hammer she found in the kitchen drawer. She needed a third hand for a glass of wine. Though it was too early in the day to be drinking, a glass of wine might fortify her against the dark space ahead. MJ rounded the corner and stopped short when she saw the entry door. The lock was missing and it was partially open. Huh? She paused and called Chiquita.

"I'll kick the door but you go first. Okay, girl?" MJ threw her heel against the door. Splinters flew and a circle of dust filled the dark space at the same time that moldy damp air hit her nose. Chiquita poked her head in, took a sniff, proclaimed it not worth her effort, and made a hasty retreat.

"Thanks a lot," MJ yelled. She stood in the doorway uncertain of what to do next. A chill went through her. MJ took a deep breath and looked into the black hole. No way was she going in there. She grabbed the door, slammed it shut, and ran back upstairs.

The phone was ringing when she entered the kitchen.

"Bueno, MJ here."

"Hi," Alberto said. "I saw your car in the driveway." He paused. "Listen, I have carne asada and a bag of tortillas. Are you hungry?"

"Sure, come on over," she said thinking his timing was perfect.

MJ was ashen when Alberto arrived. He gave her a quick hug and studied her face.

"What's wrong?" he asked.

She told him what just happened.

"Do you think it could be the same people who ransacked the house?" she asked.

"I don't know, is anything missing?"

"I was too scared to look. Will you go down there with me?"

Alberto and MJ made their way to the basement. He flicked on the flashlight and quickly opened the door before MJ changed her mind.

"There's a switch on the wall to your left," she said.

The room lit up with the dim wattage of a church. Alberto found a chair and placed it against the door. His flashlight moved slowly over tables around the edge of the room.

"Does it look the same?"

"It's more cluttered than I had remembered."

Alberto moved the light to the floor. Footprints went from the entrance to each table and continued to a tipped chair near the back of the room. From the chair to the door the footprints we replaced by a wide swath that looked like something was dragged. He walked to the door at the back of the basement and shined a light into the opening.

"Nothing in here," he said. He turned toward the chair and focused on two black globs on the floor. Alberto crouched down to take a closer look. He wet his finger, ran it over the spot, and sniffed.

"It's blood," he said.

MJ gasped.

"Let's get out of here," he said. "We can talk in the house."

Later, over dinner, MJ and Alberto spent a long time discussing possible scenarios of what could have occurred in the basement.

"How many people know there's a room below the kitchen?" Alberto asked.

"I haven't any idea," MJ said. "Oliver built the house when Rick was a baby. That was over thirty years ago."

"I didn't remember the place until I walked in there," he said. "Oliver was all over Rick and me for hiding down there one time when we were kids."

MJ pushed the last piece of carne asada around her plate.

"Well, whoever came knew there was a room down there and was on a specific mission."

"Yeah, but the tables were undisturbed so I don't think anything was taken. And there's only one set of footprints going in and out."

Alberto rubbed his hand on his chin.

"My guess is he fell and cut himself, bled on the floor, and never finished the search. We didn't find a body outside, so the person is still alive," he said with a smirk.

MJ smiled. "That makes me feel better. Sure."

"Realistically, it could have happened months ago. In my opinion, it has nothing to do with last week."

After their supper of carne asada and tortillas, they decided to play a game of Scrabble to lighten up the evening. The couples played years ago when Alberto's wife was alive. An hour later the scores were neck and neck. MJ was getting tired. She studied the board with glazed eyes.

"Hey," she said, "You only put one l in the word vanilla." She grinned sheepishly. "I think we should call it quits. Let's call it a draw."

"You're lucky I am a gentleman," he laughed.

MJ handed him the game box. "If you put the pieces away I'll get some ice cream from the freezer."

"Naw," he said as he stood up. "I should be getting home. But how 'bout I come by tomorrow and board up the door."

"I won't be here, I'm going to San Jose. And Monday I leave for Santa Rosario to visit Mama Estrada. But you're welcome to come by and fix it when I'm not here."

"Okay," he said walking toward the door. "That reminds me, Mama has a big birthday coming up soon. I'm hoping I can get away."

"She'd be terribly disappointed if you didn't come."

He turned and studied MJ trying to read her thoughts. "Well goodnight, and try not to worry."

"I'll be fine," MJ said. Besides, Ginger should be back from Cabo soon."

"Say hello to her for me."

It was several hours before MJ was awakened by Chiquita barking. She lifted her head. The clock read almost midnight. Her head was spinning? Did she really drink that much red wine?

"Anybody here?" Ginger asked, bounding into the room. She walked over and looked down at MJ.

"Why is it that every time I see you in this room you look like hell?"

"Be nice. It's late and I've had a rough day."

"And I haven't? I've been up since dawn, spent eight hours on rough seas with two people barfing over the side, tiptoed around a psychotic first mate, and then just when I thought nothing else could go wrong, I sat for two hours in a traffic jam."

Ginger collapsed into a chair, shook the bottle of wine, and took a swig. She continued her tirade.

"A Coca Cola truck sideswiped a farmer bringing watermelons to Cabo. The melons flew off truck like guided missiles and blew the tops off two cardon cacti. The old platform truck pretty much disintegrated. Pieces were strewn all over the road."

"Was anyone hurt?"

"The old man driving the truck was taken away in an ambulance. He was in shock and it looked like he had a broken arm. All of us who were stranded in cars sat around and ate watermelon while the Federales tried to find people to clean up the mess."

MJ reached for another pillow and put it behind her head.

"Did you bring a watermelon for me?"

"Two," Ginger said. She struggled out of the comfortable chair. "Let me find Hanz and Fritz. Then I'll cut you a big slice."

"When you come back, it's my turn to tell you about my day. And pour yourself a glass of wine, it's a long story."

"Is there any left?" asked Ginger walking toward the kitchen with the empty bottle.

"There's an open bottle of white wine in the refrigerator. And don't ask too many questions or we'll be up all night."

CHAPTER 18

MJ could feel the tension when she entered the kitchen to find Ginger with a fixed smile on her face. She'd made breakfast: table was set, perfectly browned toast with butter and jam nearby. She poured coffee before MJ could say a word and blurted, "Do you really want to do this? You haven't a clue whom you are meeting in San Jose. Just because it's near a church doesn't mean it's safe." Ginger placed the cup on the table with a bang. "How do you know it's not some diabolical plot of Ramon Diaz?"

MJ looked up. Yikes.

"I don't know," MJ said. "But I do know there are too many questions and not enough answers about what happened to Rick." She put two scoops of sugar in her cup and stirred. "I have to start somewhere. He didn't call and there was nothing in his journal. I don't understand anything about what happened to him that night."

MJ took a sip of coffee. "Besides, the decision is made, I'm going to San Jose. Let's move on to something else."

Ginger frowned. She knew MJ's every mood and anxiety. Their college years were like boot camp. MJ was the sergeant and Ginger stood in salute. It took years to realize the problem was MJ's low blood sugar and the best way to calm her down was to put food in her mouth.

"How do you want your eggs, the usual?" Ginger asked.

"That would be great," MJ said. She needed change of scenery and a visit to Mama Estrada's home would be a start. Then she would go to the camp in Santa Juanico and have a week of peace with Chiquita. No phones, television, or visitors. Heaven.

After breakfast, Ginger went for run on the beach with the dogs. Los Santos was changing before her eyes. The wonderful intimacy of the village was disappearing. Fifty new homes had already been constructed north of MJ's property and there was talk of building new homes on the dunes. The only place unchanged was the Catholic Church, The Virgin de Pilar. The church, built in 1733, was virtually intact. Of the twenty Jesuit churches built between 1683 and 1767, eight were still standing and only San Javier was untouched. Every Sunday Mexican families along with widows and a handful of gringos on holidays went to church. Ginger missed the intimacy that attracted her to Los Santos. But the weather was still perfect, the lifestyle remained casual, and the cost of living was cheap.

When Hacienda Azul came into view Ginger's mind returned to the bickering at breakfast. MJ was unbending once she made up her mind. The decision was cast in stone. Ginger reflected on her weekend crew to Mazatlan. She softened the information she gave to MJ about the men on the boat and promised to tell her more as soon as she knew something. It wouldn't be easy. The captain would fire her if he found out.

Ginger was dripping with sweat as she walked in the door and ready for a shower. In her path was MJ. She wore a flowered skirt, lavender short sleeve blouse, espadrilles, and a black hat with a veil.

"What do you think?" MJ asked.

Ginger rolled her eyes and suppressed a laugh. "You look like something out of Laura Ashley. Did you buy the stuff at a the clothing exchange?"

MJ glared.

Then Ginger noticed the handkerchief and the bible. "Aren't you overdoing it a bit? You're not going to a funeral."

"I am a widow and haven't a clue who I'm meeting. What am I supposed to wear, jeans and a tee shirt?"

Ginger wiped the sweat from her forehead on her shirt. "Why are you leaving so soon? You don't have to be there until two o'clock."

"I have to get gas, and I'm not sure how long it will take. If I arrive early I can window shop."

Ginger couldn't suppress herself any longer and burst out laughing.

MJ lifted the veil off her head and placed it on the table. She looked in the mirror, appraised her outfit, and crinkled her nose. "The darn thing itches. And I probably don't need the Bible. I'm going to change into something more comfortable."

In the end, MJ wore a navy linen suit with a coral blouse, and plain black shoes. But she insisted on taking the handkerchief.

"I'll see you tonight," MJ said heading out the door.

Surprisingly there was little traffic on the road until she reached the bottleneck around Cabo San Lucas. Then everything changed. She went into red alert at the bottleneck. Trucks turned from any direction without using signals; two hunched over men pushed a car down the middle of the road; a mother, clutching the hand of her child, stepped in front of MJ's car as she approached a green light. The woman never looked. Street venders hawked fresh orange juice and fruit. At the red light, a mime performed a juggling routine, while his buddy walked from car to car with a tip basket.

Finally the slowdown ended and MJ's thoughts turned to the stranger she was meeting, "A." What information could this person have about Rick on the night he died? Should she be wary?

Ginger watched MJ drive down the road. What a relief. Now she had time to relax. She walked over to the truck and retrieved the magazine on gourmet cooking under the back seat. The heck with a shower, it could wait.

Ten minutes later, Ginger was sprawled on the sofa with the magazine balanced between her legs, sipping wine and flipping the pages. The phone rang just as she found a recipe for mango soufflé. She was tempted not to answer. But it could be MJ.

Reluctantly, she got up and went to the phone.

"MJ, thank God you're there," said a familiar voice.

She paused, then said, "Johnny is that you? This is Ginger. MJ isn't here."

There was silence on the other end of the phone.

"Johnny? Are you there?"

"Oh God, Ginger, he sobbed. "Something awful has happened and I need your help."

"Where are you?" Ginger asked in a calm voice. She heard Johnny gasping between sobs.

"I'm hurt. Really bad I think."

"Tell me where you are. I need to know."

"On the dirt road on the outskirt of La Paz. The place with a view of the bay where we went for picnics. Remember?"

"Yes."

"Will you come? I don't know what to do. Please, Ginger."

"I'll be there before sunset. Stay out of sight but near the road. I'll find you."

Ginger was in overdrive a minute after she hung up the phone. First she called Tina, a friend from La Paz. Ginger didn't mince words.

"I have an emergency and need to borrow your truck. I don't know how many days I'll be gone and can't tell you the reason."

Tina said yes. No questions asked. The girls met several years ago while crewing to Mazatlan and still traded homes annually during Mardi Gras. While Tina stayed in Los Santos and walked along the ocean enjoying the quiet of a small town, Ginger visited La Paz, watched the parade, and partied with friends. It was a tradition.

Ginger arrived at Tina's home in La Paz within an hour. She gave Tina a hug and a smile then turned serious. "I promise nothing will happen to your truck." Ginger placed a shovel, pick and First Aid Kit into Tina's truck along with food, a cooler and plenty of water. "I'll call you later tonight if I can, but for sure tomorrow," Ginger said with a reassuring smile. She waved goodbye, blew Tina a kiss, and waved again.

Truthfully, Ginger had no idea when the police would begin searching for Johnny. Eventually it would lead them to Ginger and her truck, a red Toyota with California plates. Not exactly invisible. Tina had a white truck with Mexican plates and a special custom feature, a raised platform covered with a cushion on the back seat that hid Tina's surfboards when she traveled. The design would be invaluable for Johnny.

Fortunately she knew how to administer CPR, a requirement for crewing a boat. The only emergency she ever encountered that she couldn't handle was the gash on her leg from Kevin's knife. The most common illness on a cruise was seasickness. She could stitch a wound if necessary and no one ever got food related poisoning on her watch. Six years ago when she and MJ drove down the Baja the unexpected happened. She delivered a baby boy near Catavina. They both still laughed about it.

The traffic was light as Ginger made her way around the La Paz ring road. She flipped on the radio and listened for the news. There wasn't any mention of Johnny and there were no police cars. Just before dusk, Ginger arrived at the turnoff for the dirt road. Since there was no traffic in sight she turned right. The overgrown brush on the road made it difficult to see anything. Ginger turned on her dims searching for any movement. Where was Johnny?

CHAPTER 19

The road from Cabo San Lucas to San Jose is peppered with the newest signs of prosperity in lower Baja. MJ frowned with annoyance and dismay. Tall stark mega hotels blighted the once pristine beaches. Gone are the hamburger shacks with beat up trucks, surfboards, and coolers of beer. Everything has been replaced with bougainvillea, palm trees, golf courses, and Hummers. MJ was glad to take a right turn off the corridor and head into old town.

San Jose is the colonial town on the tip of the Baja peninsula. Even with uncontrolled growth elsewhere, the city center was becoming more charming. MJ found a nearby parking place and looked around. An old Jesuit Church anchored the plaza. The stately edifice, columned with twin steeples, sat above an imposing staircase. Thick carved oak doors on wrought iron hinges flanked the entrance. In the steeple high above, four men took turns pulling an iron bell hourly by hand. Black wrought iron benches lined the perimeter of the plaza that was shaded by ficus trees. They sparkled from the sun's reflection. Children played tag as their parents entertained family and friends. It was a typical outing for local Mexicans on a Sunday afternoon.

MJ stood in a small cobblestone alley, watching the activity, and waited. She looked at her watch. The church bells began to chime. It was two o'clock.

"Con permiso," a man said as he brushed by with two small children and continued toward the plaza.

The click of high heels caught MJ's attention. She turned as a woman with black hair wearing a purple dress walk toward her. The tight fitting dress had a beaded appliqué bodice, cut low, revealing a long neck and ample breasts. Multi-stranded black pearls with matching earrings hung casually around her neck. Stunning. The woman extended her hand revealing perfectly manicured red fingernails.

"Mrs. Delgado, how nice to meet you," she said. "Thank you for coming."

"You're welcome," MJ said. "And your name is?"

"My friends call me Angelique." The words rolled off her lips with ease and conviction. "I hope you don't mind, but I made a reservation at Las Palmas. It is nearby and we can talk in comfort. Follow me please."

MJ fixed her eyes on the woman's purple stilettos as she maneuvered the cobblestones.

Las Palmas is an old, elegant restaurant frequented by the relatively few Mexicans who can afford it. MJ had never been there. At the entrance a small oval tile sheathed in black said Las Palmas. A doorman opened a simple black mesquite door flanked by etched glass windows and they entered a cool foyer. The walls were covered with photographs of the movie stars who frequented the restaurant. The maître d' nodded to Angelique. She discreetly folded two hundred pesos into his hand and was led to a blue velvet banquette underneath an alcove.

The waiter handed them a menu and turned to a small table. He popped a cork, opened a bottle of merlot, poured MJ and Angelique a glass of red wine, and left.

MJ appraised Angelique. She tried to align her thoughts with the person who sent the letter signed "A." The woman sitting across the table was remarkably at ease with her surroundings. Angelique perused the menu, seemingly oblivious to MJ.

What an amazing face Angelique possessed. It was a storybook of a life full of joy, anger, fear, sadness and success. Her forehead was deeply furrowed and covered with makeup. The ridges were like small valleys. Her brown eyes were thickened with mascara and eye shadow, and her full lips were heavily painted with red lipstick. She could be any age between thirty-five and fifty.

Angelique looked up, smiling through perfect teeth.

"Are you hungry?" she asked. "The service is slow, but the food is fabulous. Does anything in particular appeal to you?"

MJ folded the menu and placed it on the table. "I think I'll have a Caesar salad and fish. Which fish you suggest?"

"I'll ask the waiter what the fish of the day is," Angelique said. She signaled the waiter and reached into her purse and placed a pack of cigarettes on the table.

"Do you smoke?" Angelique asked.

MJ shook her head no and took a sip of wine. She watched Angelique light a cigarette and take a puff. She said nothing. Should MJ start the conversation? Angelique didn't seem to be in any hurry. MJ had many questions so she began.

"Your letter indicated you have important information about my husband's death," MJ said. "Please tell me what you know."

"Of course," Angelique said, her face serious.

"Your husband stopped in San Jose last Monday evening. He almost ran into me as he was leaving a building on Magnolia Street. He was obviously in a hurry."

"How do you know it was my husband?"

"I recognized his face from the newspaper."

Angelique leaned forward and continued,

"I followed him. He walked to the plaza and got into a truck. He was alone. Shortly afterward, another vehicle pulled out and followed him down the street. Both cars were headed north out of town. The road leads to the airport."

MJ cleared her throat, a habit she found hard to control when she was nervous. "Could it have been a coincidence?"

'No it could not. The truck is one of a fleet owned by the man I work for. I'm sure they were following your husband." Angelique's face was composed and serious. Her words were spoken with assurance.

"Why would they follow Rick?"

"Your husband must be involved in some way with Alfonzo Ramirez. He meets clients between six and eight p.m., when there are fewer people milling around. Mr. Delgado would not be in the building for any other reason."

MJ was perplexed. She wanted to take a deep breath but felt she should remain composed and unaffected. "I don't understand. Why would my husband meet with Alfonzo Ramirez?"

"It could be a number of things," Angelique said. "Alfonzo controls all the illegal activities in lower Baja. Maybe your husband bet on the horses and lost, or borrowed money he couldn't pay back. The worst case scenario would be that he needed protection for a crime he committed."

MJ paused, trying to absorb what Angelique said. "But you are speculating. You do not know anything for sure."

Angelique took a sip of wine.

"I want to give you some information about Alfonzo Ramirez. I've known him for years. Nobody meets with him without an appointment. He is a well protected man." Angelique swirled the remaining wine, focused on the glass for a moment, and placed it on the table. "Half of the people in San Jose, including me, do business with Alfonzo Ramirez. We have no choice. He controls most of the illegal money and activities that go through southern Baja."

The blue velvet upholstery on the banquette blurred into a haze of confusion in MJ's head. She was unwilling to believe Rick was involved in something illegal. But didn't she find twenty-five thousand dollars in cash, along with an insurance policy in their safety deposit box? Not to mention that both Ramon and Johnny commented on Rick's involvement in things she knew nothing about.

The waiter approached carrying a platter of lobster tails and baked potatoes with sour cream and chive. His assistant pushed a cart with rolls, wine glasses, and a bowl of salad. The assistant served the main course while the headwaiter prepared a Caesar salad with professional gusto. Each plate contained the perfect amount of anchovies, cubed bread, garlic, cheese and dressing.

MJ's stomach was in knots, her heart was beating like a locomotive, and her head was starting to ache. She was no longer hungry but picked at a piece of salad. "What is your connection with Mr. Ramirez?"

Angelique snuffed her cigarette into the ashtray. "I provide Alfonzo with escorts for businessmen who fly into the Cabo area or any other gentleman wishing to spend an evening with a companion." Her steely eyes looked directly at MJ. "Your husband did not use my services."

MJ leaned over the table. "Why are you telling me this?"

Angelique twirled her finger around a strand of hair near her eyes then folded both hands on the table. "I have been at this game for a very long time," she said. "Every federale, attorney, and public figure in lower Baja California knows who I am. Although it costs me a great deal, I protect my women from physical abuse, provide their children with food and clothing, and I can sleep at night. Or rather, I could until last week when your husband was killed."

MJ's eyes were downcast. Her mind was in high gear, oblivious to her surroundings. How did this information fit into Rick's disappearance? Very few people entered her wall of independence and she was becoming bonded to a woman she barely knew. Could MJ trust her?

The women sat in silence until their intimate mood was broken by the loud voice of a man.

"Angelique, how nice to see you."

Angelique raised her head. Her face froze and her eyes hardened. MJ wondered who could have such a profound effect on her.

"We have a visitor," Angelique said. "Just smile and let me do the talking." She sat upright, shook the hair from her face with defiance, and smiled. Her hand briefly touched her purse. MJ wondered if she was going to light a cigarette.

The deep and bold voice resonated,

"How wonderful you're here," he said. "What brings you into San Jose on a Sunday afternoon?"

MJ turned as a large hand reached over Angelique's shoulder for an embrace. A heavy Rolex watch and an emerald signet ring flashed by. An enormous man with grey hair bent over and kissed Angelique on the cheek. She barely acknowledged his presence.

"Hello, Don Hernando," she said. A pregnant silence followed.

Don Hernando, born and bred a gentleman, turned toward MJ. "And who is the lovely woman you are with?"

Angelique paused before she answered, "Mrs. Delgado, I would like you to meet Don Hernando Cortez."

MJ studied the tall portly man with a hawk nose, rather broad nostrils, bushy eyebrows, and a well-manicured salt-and- pepper beard. He appraised MJ with intense black eyes that she found disconcerting.

"What brings you to San Jose?" Don Hernando asked

MJ put on her most charming smile. "I am chairman of the New Events Committee for the Biblioteca fund raiser in Los Santos," she said.

"Wonderful, will Angelique be on your committee?" he asked with a smirk.

"Perhaps we can convince her," MJ said. "Angelique's name was on my collectors' list. Our featured event is Antique Jewelry of Baja California and she has generously agreed to loan us two pieces from her collection of black pearls."

"Very interesting," he said. "I'm sure my mother will be most anxious to attend. She has a beautiful pair of Mayan earrings she may be willing to submit for your event." Don Hernando reached into his pocket and handed MJ a business card. "Call me and I will put you in contact with her." Don Hernando's face took on a serious tone. "Excuse me for asking, but are you Ricardo Delgado's widow?"

"Yes I am."

Don Hernando looked down at his feet and said, "I am sorry for your loss."

"Thank you."

Then he looked directly into MJ's eyes and continued, "And you must be terribly upset about the accident Mr. Thompson was in yesterday afternoon."

MJ looked at Don Hernando. A surprised look that turned to confusion came over her face. "What accident?"

"Forgive me, I thought you knew. It was on the news earlier today." Don Hernando gave a quick glance toward Angelique then lowered his voice. "The police have reason to believe Mr. Thompson shot a man fifteen miles south of La Paz, left him for dead, and drove away. The victim managed crawl to the road where he was seen by a passing vehicle and taken to a hospital."

MJ cupped her hand over her open mouth. This was too much shock for one day. "I can't believe Johnny would shoot anyone. Are you sure?"

"The victim told the police they were acquaintances. Mr. Thompson's car was found this morning on the outskirts of La Paz. There is an all point alert for his arrest."

MJ was dumbfounded. Johnny wouldn't kill anyone. Something didn't add up. "When did this happen?"

"The man was found just before dark last night."

Angelique stood up from the table and looked Don Hernando in the eyes. "Thank you for the information, but I have an appointment in an hour. Mrs. Delgado and I have to finalize our plans for the museum show. Please give my regards to Elena."

"Of course," said Don Hernando. He nodded goodbye to the women. His mind was ablaze with questions as he walked toward his table near the courtyard. He doubted the story about a jewelry exhibit and wondered what the real reason for their lunch was. Don Hernando pulled a small pad from the inside of his jacket and made a note. The maître d' ushered Don Hernando through a curtain into the office of the manager and closed the door behind him. Don Hernando picked up the phone and dialed.

"Thanks for the lead. You were right. She's in San Jose having lunch with an associate of mine." He paused and listened. "If she knew about Johnny she's a superb actress. I'll be in touch tomorrow." Don Hernando made his way back to the table. A waiter appeared with a glass of wine.

"As you ordered sir," he said.

Don Hernando nodded, picked up his pen, and began to draw arrows toward the name in the center of the page, Ricardo Delgado. What information did he take to the grave? The location of The Lost Mission of Santa Isabel? He crossed out Rick's name and inserted the name MJ Steele/Delgado. He circled it. The key to everything now was her.

Angelique watched Don Hernando from across the room. She took MJ's hand. "Are you all right?"

"Just shaken," MJ said. "I was on Johnny's radio show Friday. He left two messages on my cell phone Friday and the second one sounded urgent."

Angelique reached for her water and took a sip. "Leave it up to Don Hernando to be the bearer of bad news," she said sarcastically. "Misfortune follows the Cortez family, just like the Kennedys in America. The Gods are against them. Every male Cortez has been cursed since the first Don Miguel lost the Jesuit map of the Santa Isabel Mission. Some people say it was stolen by his servant but who knows?"

Angelique shrugged her shoulders and continued. "Don Hernando's father, Don Leon, died in a plane crash when he was a boy," she said. "He was an amateur pilot and got caught in a squall off the coast not far from Tres Cruces. His wife Elena has multiple sclerosis. She lives in a facility in San Jose."

"How terrible," MJ said. "Do they have children?"

"No. She became ill two years after they married."

Angelique leaned over and whispered, "And his mother, Antigua, is beyond difficult."

"I only met her once," said MJ, "At our wedding. She was a friend of Rick's mother."

"She never recovered from the loss of her favorite son, Don Miguel II," Angelique said. "He attended college in Guadalajara, met a woman from Spain with a family fortune from the cement business, moved to Madrid, and never returned to Mexico. The rumor is he never spoke to his family again. I can't say that I blame him." Angelique lit another cigarette and took a puff. "Don Hernando is the last Cortez of a legacy. He is self serving and very dangerous."

"Why do you say that?" MJ asked.

"When you are in my business you hear a lot of things. Some people say he's the brains and money behind Alfonzo's operation. And he hasn't been very discreet. His last affair was with Maria Lopez Garcia, the wife of the Governor."

"Risky," MJ said.

"Apparently not for a member of the Cortez family. The only honorable thing the man ever did was to rescue his brother from drowning in the family swimming pool. And knowing him as well as I do, I find that hard to believe."

The waiter approached with a tray.

"Would you like some coffee?" he asked. "May I take your plates?"

The women said yes to both questions. He scooped up the uneaten food and went back to the kitchen.

"Excuse me," MJ said. "I need to find the ladies' room. I'll be right back."

Angelique was drinking a cup of coffee when MJ returned.

"Would you like some coffee?"

"I don't think so." MJ answered, unsure of what to say next. She stood nervously at the table with her purse in hand. "I'm sorry, but I really must go. I'm too distracted to be very good company."

Angelique took MJ's hand. "Of course." She hugged MJ tightly. "It was a pleasure to meet you. I hope my information was not too disturbing."

"I very much appreciate what you told me," MJ said. "I will be forever grateful for your kindness."

MJ left San Jose exhausted. She headed for Los Santos knowing that she had one more stop to make: a detour to Wiley's house. An hour later MJ pulled to a stop in front of the old homestead. Wiley's dogs came running from the back and started barking viscously. She rolled down the window and spoke in a soothing voice. They sniffed the truck, recognized the scent, and left. A three-hundred year old fig tree stood directly in her path. She ducked around the branches and knocked on the front door. A minute later, the porch light came on. Yellow paint and cement flaked off the casita, the steps hadn't been hosed in years. As she lifted her hand to knock again the door opened.

Wiley's outline stood in the shadow of the hall leaning against a cane. His breadth reeked of whiskey and he looked like he'd been dragged into an alley and beaten. He was obviously surprised.

"What do you want?" he asked.

"Sorry for not calling, but I was on my way back from Cabo," MJ said. "You were on the way home."

Wiley rubbed his eyes and tried to focus. "I was sleeping. It's Sunday after all."

"Well, I'll just pick up the book you borrowed and be on my way," MJ said forcefully.

Wiley jutted his chin out and shook his head no. "I'm not finished with it."

"Well you'll have to borrow it later. Apparently, I'm not allowed to loan any books until the estate is settled." MJ looked at his knee. "What happened to your leg?"

"I fell."

"Oh, I'm sorry. Let me help you find the book," she said taking a step into the hall.

Wiley slammed his cane on the floor. "Close the door and wait here. I'll find it."

———

The sky was a paintbrush of orange and red when Los Santos came into view at the crest of the hill. MJ drove through town on autopilot, allowing familiarity to guide her across the otra lado, and over the windy road to her home. Hacienda Azul was dark except for the light in the kitchen. Chiquita ran up to the car barking with her tail wagging. MJ realized Ginger's car was gone. She flicked on the flashlight, walked to the house, and unlocked the door. She found the switch and noticed a yellow paper on the counter. It was from Ginger.

Sorry. Something came up and I won't be back tonight. Nothing to worry about. Can't talk about it. Private matter. I'll call you tomorrow. Say hello to Mama for me.

Ginger

MJ stared at the note then read it again. What private matter? Ginger hadn't been that illusive since she slept with a priest from La Paz five years ago. Well, a former priest. At the time, Ginger was more worried about his reputation than hers. MJ crinkled the paper and threw it in the trash.

What could it be? Then the light bulb went off. It had to be Johnny. Damn. Did Ginger have any idea what she was getting herself into? She was savvy but this was a different situation. MJ reached for the phone and dialed Ginger. A canned message said the number was out of phone time. Typical. Unless you deposited five hundred pesos into the Telcel account daily there were never enough minutes. The only phone company in Mexico was privately owned. Highway robbery! What a day. She opened the refrigerator and looked for the coffee. It was going to be a long night.

CHAPTER 20

Even though Ginger was concerned about Johnny, she was totally unprepared for the man who staggered onto the road in front of her. He gave a limp wave, raised a hand to shield his eyes, and collapsed into a heap before she could stop the truck. She jumped out and ran toward him clutching a water bottle and a medical bag. When she reached Johnny she knew he was in bad shape. His face was scarlet, his breath shallow, and his shirtsleeve looked like it had been dipped in blood. She yanked off her sweatshirt, rolled it into a ball and placed the material under his head.

His eyes fluttered and he sighed. A faint smile of relief came across his lips. Ginger unscrewed the canteen and lifted his head. He swallowed the sugared water as best he could.

"Thank you," he whispered.

Ginger smiled reassuringly. Inwardly she was deeply concerned. "Can you walk to the truck?" she asked.

He nodded yes.

It took all of Ginger's stamina to maneuver Johnny first to his knees, and then to a standing position. She placed his arm across her shoulder and neck, and they staggered toward the car. Once she got there, every ounce of strength she had left went into guiding him below the hidden platform under the back seat. His body was hot. She reached for the canteen and he drank the water so fast he gagged. When Ginger had him settled enough to inspect him with a flashlight, she placed a thermometer in his mouth. It read one-hundred and four degrees.

She moved her attention to the concentration of blood on his shirt below the left shoulder. With a pair of scissors she gingerly began to cut the bloodied fabric. She removed the cloth with care. A circular hole appeared six inches above his elbow. She lifted his arm to look underneath. He moaned. A similar hole appeared at the back of his arm. During her EMT training Ginger saw similar photos. They were gunshot wounds.

Johnny was as white as a sheet and panting. She washed the wound, made a tourniquet from the gauze in her kit, and wiped his head again with a wet towel hoping it would be sufficient until they found a place where he could get proper medical attention. But where?

Ginger had no idea when she spoke with Johnny that his situation was acute. Her first aid kit could handle a minor accident, but he needed a doctor and quite possibly, a blood transfusion. How far could they travel without medical help? She placed the wooden cover over him hoping he wouldn't suffocate, got in the driver's seat and started the truck. Somehow the dogs knew this was not the time to misbehave. Hanz sat docilely on the front seat while Fritz found a spot near the back. Ginger turned on the lights and headed for the main road. She was already thinking about how she'd handle any road blocks they'd encounter.

Ginger knew how to sweet-talk her way through most situations. Hanz and Fritz were her back up men. They growled on command. The dogs would scare the living daylights out of anyone, especially young Mexican soldiers who were wary of dogs. She worried the military might get nervous and shoot someone accidentally. Did they even know how to release the safety catch? Ginger headed over the mountain toward Ciudad Insurgentes and turned on the radio hoping for some news about Johnny. There was no reception high in the hills. The clock on the dash said it was 9:15 p.m. She was worried. It would be at least two hours before she found a spot safe enough to check Johnny again.

It didn't take long for Ginger to determine their final destination: the Mission of San Javier. Finding Johnny in such terrible shape didn't leave her any choice. The mission was located in a remote village of one-hundred and fifty people. It was only thirty miles west of Loreto, but she had to cross the Sierra de la Gigante Mountains over a treacherous dirt road to get there. She decided on an even more obscure route to avoid the Federale roadblock outside Loreto. Ginger's plan was to head north for thirty miles past Ciudad Insurgentes, bypass any potential roadblocks, and turn right at the sign for Comoundu, a forgotten mission pueblo nobody visited anymore. If the road still existed, it was the safest way to reach San Javier. Her first problem would be getting through Ciudad Constitution. There was no doubt the Federale would have a special roadblock there. But Ginger had no other choice. She hit the radio button to calm her nerves but there was still no reception. Damn.

Few cars approached from the opposite direction and so far, no one came up behind here. It was pretty typical. Only Mexicans with Baja plates drove at night. Ginger was traveling incognito. Her hair was tucked under a Panama hat, the staple of every farmer and vaquero in

Mexico. Anyone who passed the Mexican truck would think she was a man. Her biggest dilemma was she couldn't check on Johnny until she passed Ciudad Insurgentes where it would be less risky. A twinkle of light appeared on the horizon. A sign indicated a Pemex station was one kilometer ahead. Ginger breathed a sigh of relief. The gage on the dashboard read half full. She doubted she would pass another gas station before San Javier.

Mexican Pemex stations all looked the same and the service was quick and efficient. The only caveat was that you had to bring your own toilet paper. Even worse, in the more remote areas, the toilet seat was gone. The approaching lights of the station were bright enough to land a jet, which Ginger found disconcerting given her cargo under the back seat. She opened the door, stepped in front of the back window, and smiled at the attendant.

"Magna," she said holding a thumb up, the universal sign to fill it up.

The man set the meter and headed to the front of the truck to wash the window. Attendants always washed windows for Americans because often they were tipped. Ginger paid the man and pulled out toward the road. A black Federale car passed her and entered the parking lot. The police car indicated there was a roadblock ahead. Sure enough, five miles down the road a temporary sign read Inspección and a soldier flagged everyone to the right.

Ginger knew her best defense was an offense. She was prepared. The truck crawled behind six vehicles moving toward the final stop. Several feet in front of her, Federales were inspecting two trucks: a small Mexican box truck and a blue Volkswagen bus. Three young Americans stood near the blue bus watching a Federale with a leashed dog circle the vehicle. The animal sniffed the tires and doors. Ginger suspected the police were looking for marijuana. The young men looked nervous. She was glad for the diversion and hoped it would last until she passed.

Ginger pulled up to an officer, opened the window, and smiled. Hanz and Fritz were in full view on the passenger seat. Her hat was hidden and a mass of curly red hair framed her face and shoulders. They asked the usual questions. Where are you going? Where did you come from?

Then the soldier asked, "Why are you traveling this late at night alone?"

The question momentarily threw Ginger off guard. She paused. Then she put her hands over her face, burst into tears, and began to sob. She turned to the officer with tears streaming down her face. "I need to drive as far as I can tonight. My mother had a stroke. She lives in San Diego and I have to get home before she dies." As she continued to cry the dogs began to bay.

The policeman was completely unnerved by her crying. He looked at the long queue, shrugged his shoulders, and said, "Pasale."

Ginger drove away slowly, her grief apparent to the officers who stood nearby. When the lights behind her disappeared she breathed a sigh of relief. Earlier she was scared out of her mind, now she cried tears of relief. The ploy worked because Mexican men were perplexed by a woman in tears.

At Ciudad Insurgentes, where the road to Loreto veered right, Ginger went straight ahead. She was worried about Johnny. Would he reach the San Javier Mission?

Ginger recalled her first visit to the mission. It was a weeklong retreat that focused on people at the crossroads of life. She was reeling from the breakup with Johnny after a tumultuous three-year relationship. MJ was newly married and busy with Rick. What were her options? Return to the States, the safe haven where she could get a job as a pastry chef? The idea would lead to a one-dimensional life. There was no edginess in America. She would miss the beat up vehicles repaired by mechanical wizards; the roads with killer potholes; untouched beaches with miles of beautiful shells and driftwood, sand dollars, and a view to make your heart burst. Most compelling of all, were the generations of Mexican families who still lived next door to each other. No, the States lacked the things she loved most about Mexico.

During the retreat, Ginger ate sparingly, prayed daily, developed calluses from digging in the vegetable fields, and made a lifelong friend of Sister Augusta. The woman was blessed with a hearty laugh, a winning smile, and a lifetime of experiences. She was wise, thoughtful, non-judgmental, a patient listener, and a trustworthy friend. Ginger's last communication with Sister Augusta was a Christmas card last year. The simple message mentioned mission festivities and how she hoped Ginger was happy. Sister Augusta didn't mention her health, but the nun was eighty and had a hip replacement a year ago.

Ginger hoped the road she chose for the last leg of her trip would be passable. She'd soon find out. Ten miles later a small sign said San Javier and she turned down an even darker road. She hadn't seen a vehicle pass her for miles. It was time to stop and check on Johnny. As soon as she slowed down, the dogs sat up and yipped. They were anxious to get out of the cooped up truck. The door wasn't fully opened before they bolted outside. The sky was clear. The only sounds Ginger heard were crickets and the dogs thrashing through the brush. The cool night air made her skin prickle. She lifted the cover and peered inside. Johnny was motionless and his eyes were open. Ginger gasped. Then he blinked, and she cried all over again. Wiping tears on her sleeve she placed her hand on his forehead. He was cooler. The antibiotics and acetaminophen did the job. Ginger kissed her fingers and placed them on his forehead. "Hang on Johnny, we're almost there," she said pulling the cover over him.

Just before dawn, Ginger found her way into town. She drove down the cobblestone street toward the spectacular lava cliffs that surrounded the Mission of San Javier. The architectural gem was considered to be the best example of an untouched mission still in existence in the Californias.

Its history was well-documented. In 1699, Padre Francesco Piccolo, a Jesuit priest, arrived from Loreto to spread religious teachings to the Guaycura Indians. With their help, he built a chapel and living quarters before work on the mission began. They constructed exterior walls seven feet thick to keep the church cool in the summer and warm in winter. The design of the Jesuits mission was Moorish. When it was completed Italian and Spanish paintings were sent to the mission to be hung on the walls. Many of the original pieces of art are still hanging in the church. Construction continued for twenty years. From the beginning, priests and parishioners planted crops and raised livestock with water from the aqueducts and dams they built. They continued their progress by building a hospital and a home for the elderly. To this day, olive trees, planted in the garden, still surround the church. They are the oldest in the Americas.

Ginger continued toward the mission for several hours until she approached the mission just before dawn. The truck hobbled over the cobblestone street on the plaza toward the church steeple, outlined by the full moon. She parked the truck at the small stone wall in front of the main entrance and willed herself to move. She had no choice. The door opened slowly and Ginger put her weary feet on the ground. She clung to the frame and placed her hand on the hood to guide her to the front of the truck. Ginger lowered her head to the hood and rubbed her cheeks across the cool wetness. It took a minute for her to absorb the relief she felt.

San Javier loomed tall and stately before her. Mourning doves cooed in the dawn of the coming day as Ginger walked toward the darkened cloister. When she reached the granite stoop, she climbed two steps and knocked on the door. Not a sound. She knocked more loudly. The only thing she heard was the rustle of the trees and a dog barking somewhere in the distance.

Ginger left the main entrance and walked around the side of the mission toward a nearby wall. She nearly tripped on the cobblestones but caught herself and peered over the wall into the parking lot. An old truck and a Jeep, visible through the shadows of the trees, sat in the lot nearby. There had to be somebody inside. She returned to the mission and started banging on the door with all the force her body could muster.

"Hello? Sister Agusta? It's Ginger. Anybody there?"

After a couple of minutes she heard footsteps and the large door opened with a creak. Ginger looked into a black hall and the outline of a figure in a white dressing gown stood before her. Flickering glass sconces outlined the form as a starry aberration. The woman's face was obscured. She spoke.

"My goodness, child . . . what are you doing here at this hour?"

Ginger recognized the voice immediately and was overwhelmed with relief. She shook uncontrollably.

"I have a friend," she stammered.

Sister Augusta reacted quickly when she saw Johnny. Within minutes, the janitor assisted by two nuns pulled him from the truck and carried him on a stretcher into the building. He disappeared down the hall before Ginger had time to understand what was happening. Sister Augusta led her to a long narrow room and pointed to the bench.

"Sit, please," she said. "I'll be back as soon as I can."

Ginger looked at the clock. She'd been sitting on the bench for over an hour. Her eyes focused on door to the room where Johnny lay. Only nuns on a mission came by. A young nun scurried down the hall and returned almost immediately with towels and a brown bottle. Hardly reassuring. Ginger put her head down and closed her eyes. The last thing she remembered was someone placing a pillow beneath her head. She slept soundly from sheer exhaustion until she heard a squeaking noise and opened her eyes. Everything was a blur. She focused and realized the large brown mass in front of her was a brown chest. A cross was hung on the wall above. To her right, a sister pushed a metal cart toward Johnny's room. A plastic bag swayed from a hook on top. Another sister dressed in black passed by with a tray. Ginger sat up and put her elbows on her knees, her hands on her head, and tried to wake up. The door across the room opened. Ginger looked up. Sister Augusta approached her with a grim look.

"He is awake," she said. "Barring any complications he should be well enough to see you tomorrow. He's lost a lot of blood."

Ginger breathed a sigh of relief. "Thank God," she said quietly.

"However, he is adamant about speaking with you now," Sister Augusta continued. "I think he should rest, but he said it is urgent." Sister Augusta grasped Ginger's hand and squeezed.

"Please don't stay long," she said in a pleading voice.

CHAPTER 21

MJ, up to her elbows in flour, kneaded the masa with a look of determination. She had arrived in Santa Rosario an hour earlier. The drive was uneventful except for MJ's dark thoughts about Ginger. She greeted Mama's family, gave the old woman a big hug, drank some strong coffee, devoured three homemade biscochitos, and began the task of making tortillas for the first time. She thought she'd be excited, but her heart just wasn't in it.

Frustrated, MJ glanced at Mama. The thought of making tortillas was a lot more appealing before she stood over a bowl full of mush. Her head was spinning and she was exasperated. What was she thinking? Ginger was right. Cooking was not her strong suit. The whole thing was Rick's idea. He thought MJ could get to know Mama better. He thought it was important to since he had known Mama from the time he was an eager little guy with curly black hair, all arms and legs, one step away from mischief. The only upside for MJ so far was spending a day without the stress of an unexpected event. Rick had said that Mama lost count of the number of times she stood in the kitchen teaching the art of making tortillas to family, friends, and visitors to the restaurant. Steve McQueen sent a film crew to make a short video for his buddies. Mama remembered being center stage, surrounded by bowls, stacks of flour and a tortilla press, doling out lobster to Hollywood's finest. She was the stuff of legends. She knew politicians, actors, racecar drivers, and Mexican people from all over the Baja. Several books had been written about her extraordinary life.

Her father, Lucas, an Italian engineer, migrated to Baja California when he was twenty, worked in the mines, married a Pima Indian, and was subsequently disowned by his wealthy Italian family. Mama, at the time called Maria, was the eldest of ten children. She was born in 1908 just after the start of the Mexican revolution. Her father, concerned for the safety of his family, hitched up a four-horse wagon and sent them to Calexco, California until the war ended. Maria learned to speak English in grammar school. By the time she returned to Mexico at nineteen, she was fluent in two languages. She married Carlos Estrada, had ten children, and was the postmaster of Santa Rosario for twenty years. During the Second World War her pantry was the radio/telephone office of the Mexican Army. Every American traveling down the Baja stopped in Santa Rosario to visit Mama's restaurant and devour the same lobster tortillas MJ was now attempting to make.

Mama eased out of the chair, reached for her cane, and maneuvered her way to the table. "Let me take a look at how things are coming along." Mama squeezed the mixture between her fingers. "The cornmeal should be soft, but not sticky." She held a lump for MJ to appraise. "Be sure you have enough cornmeal on the table to dry your hands each time."

"Like this?" asked MJ thrusting her hand in the corn meal and watching it trickle through her fingers.

"Exactly," Mama said with a big smile on her face.

"How will I know when the mixture is just the right texture, Mama?"

"It's a matter of trial and error, like most things in our lives."

An hour later thirty tortillas were stacked on the counter   stuffed with Mama's lobster filling. MJ bit into her third tortilla and agreed they were indeed deservedly famous. She cleaned her plate and wiped her lips.

Mama took her hand. "MJ, help me to my chair. And sit next to me." Mama pointed to a ladder back chair with a flowered needlepoint seat. "I want to talk about Ricardo. It's a long story."

MJ walked Mama to the chair, placed a pillow behind her head, and sat down.

"I last saw Ricardo a month ago," Mama began. "I was sitting in my chair, almost asleep, when I heard footsteps. I opened my eyes and Ricardo was standing right there." She pointed to the spot across the room. "He handed me a bouquet of wild roses and kissed me on the forehead. He was on his way to Santa Juanico and wanted to say hello." Mama gazed out the window. "He asked about my birthday party and I told him that everybody from the President of Mexico to Hollywood movie stars were coming." Mama's eyes twinkled with excitement.

"Then we talked about my husband, Carlos," she said. "And how different he was the year before he died." Mama's eyes turned serious as she looked at MJ. "Carlos' personality changed after he left mining and started to prospect for gold with his cousin."

"You mean he went out on his own?" MJ asked.

"Yes. It was very hard on all of us," Mama said. "Every week he was gone six days and on Sunday day he came back tired, hungry and empty handed. The situation was getting desperate. Our money was running out and Carlos was very discouraged."

Mama knotted her hands. "Then he came back from a trip happy. He handed me a mesquite box he bought on the trail and asked me to open it."

"Do you still have the box?" MJ asked.

Mama turned her head toward the wall. "Yes. It's in the chest over there."

"When Ricardo was here two months ago, I asked him to bring the box to me. I wanted to show him the parchment Carlos kept inside." Mama lifted her hand toward the chest. It was shaking. "Carlos kept something else there I want to show you," she said. "Will you get the box for me?"

"Of course," MJ said. She stood and walked toward the hand carved chest. She had always admired it but never about its history. The idea would have to wait for another time.

"You will have to take the photos and clothes out first," Mama said. "The box is underneath."

MJ lifted the cover and carefully removed the contents. Sepia photos were stacked on top of beautiful antique clothing. Each one was covered in plastic with a small piece of paper inside. Marco's christening. Tenth anniversary. Then MJ saw Mama's wedding dress. It was creamy silk with tiny daisies embroidered around the neck and bodice. The garment was elegant.

"Your wedding dress is beautiful, Mama. It should be in a museum."

"It is," Mama answered with a laugh.

MJ peered into the chest. "I don't see a box. Could it be somewhere else?"

"It is hidden under the bottom panel. Find the small brass pin in the back left corner. You might need a pencil to get it to spring."

"Found it." MJ pushed the latch. Nothing happened. "You're right about a pencil," she said walking toward the counter. A minute later the latch snapped.

"Please put everything back in the chest and close it," Mama said. "The box is going on the bookcase until after the birthday party."

MJ put everything back, closed the lid and walked to Mama's side. She felt something sliding around inside the box. She handed it to Mama.

The old woman ran her hand over the mesquite, carefully touching every cut and groove. She sighed and kept her eyes on the box as she spoke. "This box sat in my trunk for thirty two years until Ricardo opened it and I gave him the parchment." She looked intently into MJ's eyes. "I want you to open it, too."

MJ put the heavy mesquite box on her lap. She tried to lift the top but it wouldn't budge.

"The key is taped underneath," Mama laughed. "I forget."

MJ found the key and opened the box. She stared at the contents.

"Mama, it's beautiful."

"Take it out."

MJ lifted the gold necklace. The piece was intricately ornamented with swirls, circles, and rectangles that were surrounded by emeralds and black pearls. MJ had seen a similar necklace, a burial piece for an Aztec queen, at the

Prado in Madrid. She turned the piece over. Each contiguous section was an inch by two inches and held together with clasps not visible from the front. MJ placed the necklace on her lap and studied the expression on Mama's face. She looked like a woman who just transferred a heavy burden to someone else.

"What did Ricardo say when he opened the box?"

Mama spoke firmly. "He was overwhelmed."

MJ ran her fingers over the stunning necklace. "Why didn't you share this with anybody until now?"

"The contents of this box have brought a lifetime of sadness to me. Carlos died six months later. He died for this necklace." Mama lowered her eyes and sighed. "I gave Ricardo the parchment because I knew he would do the right thing. But he is dead. Now, it's up to you."

CHAPTER 22

MJ left Mama Estrada's home at two p.m., dazed and confused. Rick never mentioned his visit with Mama, the necklace, or the parchment Mama gave him. MJ was learning there were lots of things Rick didn't mention: hidden money and a life insurance policy. The list kept growing and growing.

MJ clutched the wheel with fierce determination. She'd get to the bottom of what happened. She'd find out who was involved in his death, and why. With time, the pieces of the puzzle would fit and validate the man she knew and loved. The best place to unravel the mess was Santa Juanico where she and Rick shared so much joy. The camp would provide the solitude she needed and she'd be there in a few hours. MJ concentrated on the road. She knew it well enough. Continue until she passed the mission town of La Purisma, then drive fifteen miles through riverbeds and potholes. The sweet oasis would appear on the bluff. Santa Juanico, where fishing camps, perched like paper boxes, sat on the edge of the Pacific. Or they did, the first time MJ visited the place. Unfortunately, much of the original charm was disappearing, very fast. A small airstrip built four years ago, brought young, wealthy Californians from their urban blight a thousand miles north. Several of the old camps were now unrecognizable as two-story structures with a large expansive deck, barbecue, and potted geraniums in clay pots.

Rick's parents arrived in Santa Juanico thirty-five years earlier. They bought twenty acres on the only flat land in town and began organic farming before it was a big deal. Rick spent childhood summers fishing for crabs along the inlet, catching butterflies, and looking for Indian arrowheads.

Five years ago MJ and Rick came here for their honeymoon. After a walk on the beach every morning, they returned to the camp and spent the rest of the day in bed, with a meal or two in between. MJ fell in love with the place. The very first time she walked through the door she was mesmerized by Oliver's collection of Baja artifacts. It was overwhelming. Anything imaginable related to Baja California covered the bookshelves, windowsills, even the dining room table. Now on the lonely ride to Santa Juanico, MJ looked forward to the familiarity of her happiest moments with Rick.

Three vaqueros were camped on an overlook above the village of Santa Juanico. They were waiting for the señora to arrive. It was a hot and barren site; the men were bored and getting weary. They had been there for almost three days. But that was just a matter of time.

One man focused his binoculars on the house, while the other two sat on a serape playing checkers. The board was fashioned from an old cowhide burned with a branding iron that could be rolled and stored under a saddle when not in use. The black squares were colored with charcoal, the red ones with ox blood. Each man moved his colored bottle caps with skill and determination. They had spent many lonely hours in competition.

The third man was focused on the palapa-roofed casita. The old house sat lazily on a lush organic garden casting hues of verdant green that spread from the entry gate to the cliffs above the Pacific.

The Vaqueros arrived two nights ago, found a cool spot for the horses in the underbrush, and began their wait. They set up camp by stretching an old tarp between cardon cacti ribs they used for poles and stakes and then pounded them into the ground. They laid out their bedrolls on cowhide, which served as a barrier against the cold at night. Each evening one man took the canteens to a mountain stream a mile away and refilled them. The other men prepared a meal of the tortillas and beans they carried from home. They were unhappy eating the same food every day and wanted to be with their families or riding in the mountains looking for longhorn sheep.

Vaqueros, the Mexican cowboys of Baja California, still lived in the seclusion of the mountains. The women churned goat cheese in barrels made from wooden planks, and the men herded cattle from family to family on land parceled out generations ago. Recently the Mexican government mandated compulsory education and tried to relocate the families closer to schools. Parents resisted and sent their children to class without clothing. They were promptly sent home. Eventually everyone ignored the edict.

The men were quietly playing checkers when one felt a rock hit his feet. He looked up and saw the lead man waving. The vaquero stood up, tucked a gun into his belt and walked over. He peered through the binoculars. In the distance a dusty truck pulled up to the gate of the casita. A blond woman wearing jeans and a baseball cap fumbled with the lock. A dog barked loudly as he ran back and forth in front of her. Eventually she unlocked the gate, got in the truck, and headed for the casita.

"Time to pack up," the lead man said. "I'll keep an eye on her while you find the horses. And get your gear. We want to be there around sunset so no one will see us."

———

MJ arrived at the casita just before sunset. Hundreds of sunflowers cast shadows against the shed as she drove toward the old adobe. Brilliant pink and white cosmos danced in the setting sun. It was her welcome home greeting. The heavy hat of the palapa roof sat on the whitewashed adobe building. The shutters and threshold were newly painted in cerulean blue, as were the windows and posts over the palo de arco front porch. Everything was recently hosed down. The official caretakers, Lupita and Oscar, now in their seventies, turned over most of he upkeep to their sons. Chiquita ran to the front door, her tail wagging and barking with delight.

"Silly dog, alive and happy," MJ said. "You are one of the good things in my life." She walked up the front steps and opened the door. The house smelled fresh and clean. The scent of herbs hung in the air. A bucket full of wildflowers, rosemary, and thyme sat on a dining room table of carved mesquite. The turned oval legs were covered with an old lace tablecloth gathered in the corner like a bridal veil. MJ noticed the place setting for one. She was struck with sadness and continued to the kitchen.

Chiquita was pushing the metal dish around the floor and wagging her tail having already devoured the food in the bowl.

MJ noticed a note on the counter and walked over.

Welcome home. I will come by tomorrow morning to see if everything is okay. Dinner and apple pie are in the refrigerator.

Lupita

MJ turned to the kitchen window. The sun was three-fingers above the horizon. "Come on Chiquita, we're going for a walk. Only five minutes left to catch the sunset."

The dog barked with enthusiasm.

MJ ran down the path toward the stairs: eighty-five steps to the bottom. She reached the beach just as the sun was falling over the horizon. Chiquita ran toward the hermit crabs. They found hole in the sand and disappeared before she could reach them. She dug furiously to no avail. The incoming tide would bury the hole in a minute or two. In an hour the beach would be pristine and look untouched. Chiquita changed tactics and ran toward Punto Juanico, a sandy treeless rock that was shaped like a whale. Loose boulders fell into the sea below. MJ and Chiquita always stopped there before heading back.

On the cliff, two mirror image casitas, owned by the Rodriguez family, faced the water's edge. Years ago, the family became owners of a large parcel of land granted to them via a primordial by Benito Juarez, the president of Mexico. Beachfront land wasn't of much value since it wouldn't support crops and couldn't be used for grazing cattle. Morning fog and gusty winds left droplets of salt and sand. But to an American, the view and access to the ocean were priceless. In the States, the same land would cost at least ten times as much. The Rodriguez brothers understood the value of property close to the Pacific. They no longer farmed the land; they constructed environmentally conscious homes. The brothers included strict codes for building near the ocean to assure that leatherback turtles could build their nests on the beach and grey whales could swim close to shore. In Santa Juanico, there were only two large parcels of land. One belonged to the Rodriguez family and the other to Oliver Marshall and Lucinda Delgado, who purchased the land from the Rodriguez family when they arrived.

MJ felt goose bumps from the ocean wind and pulled the sweater tighter around her neck. It was time to head back. She whistled for Chiquita. The dog looked up and started running toward her, but flew right by and continued down the beach. As MJ turned to see what excited the dog she heard a distant thumping sound. She looked up to the top of the ridge. A man on horseback was making his way down with one arm in a sling. He wore a Mexican hat; a shotgun was slung over his saddle. Two men riding behind him stopped and watched the lead man continue down the steep ridge. MJ recognized the way he held the reins and tilted his hat. It had to be Rick. He waved. MJ ran toward her husband with her arms waving and screaming madly as Rick was galloping toward her. "Oh my God, Rick it's really you." Tears streamed down her face.

"Hi babe. It's been a long time. It's sure good to see you." With a big grin on his face, he balanced on one stirrup, and lifted his leg over the saddle and on to the ground. He reached over and kissed her, first on the lips, then all over the tears streaming down her face. "Shush," he said holding her tightly. "Everything's going to be okay, I'm fine."

They held each other tightly until the horse began to whinny and Chiquita barked. Rick pulled his head back and stared at MJ. He gave her the perfect smile she fell in love with. "God, I love you so much. I'm so happy to see you again."

CHAPTER 23

The wind howled and the palapa roof of the casita rustled. It was long past dark. In the living room, MJ and Rick watched the fire turn to glowing embers. The dog was curled up on the rug fast asleep. They couldn't stop laughing. Just being together where they first made love and shared so many memories made them happy.

Chayo and the other vaquero left hours ago. After Rick and MJ gave them a hearty meal, they mounted their horses, tipped their hats, and rode off in the black night. It would be two days before they reached their ranchos.

MJ lay on the sofa with her head on Rick's lap. He looked tired and gaunt. One arm was in a sling, the side of his face was puffy, and stitches covered the area above his eyebrow.

"I'm so happy you're alive," MJ said. She took his hand and kissed it. "How did you know I would come here?"

"It was just a matter of time before you headed to the camp," Rick said. "I left you with too many loose ends. You had to have answers. I knew curiosity, stubbornness, and determination would win. It's your nature."

"Well there was an added reason that you don't know about. I came to Santa Juanico because of Elisea."

"So who is Elisea?

"A curandera in the mountains Ginger insisted I see. Elisea told me to go to the home of your childhood, but to stop and see Mama first. Not exactly in those words, but I put two and two together and figured it out." MJ sat upright with a surprised look. "And you know what? She said Mama would have information I needed." MJ paused. "She was right."

"We know so little about folk healing," Rick said. "We are skeptics, babes in the woods." Rick sat pensively as his thoughts went to Chayo's wife Ruita, and her prediction that Rick was alive.

MJ ran her hand over the scar. "Does it hurt?"

"Not much anymore. At the time I was too scared to know I was hit. All I cared about was jumping over the cliff at the right spot."

MJ looked at her husband with bewilderment. "Why would you jump? The ocean is two hundred feet below."

"I knew I had a place to land if I didn't screw up."

"How?"

Rick took a cigarette from the pack in his pocket, lit it and inhaled deeply. Then he told her what happened the night he went over the cliff.

"Wiley told me he never went there with you." She sat up and stared at him with annoyance. "I have a list a mile long about Wiley."

Rick could see MJ was about to start a tirade. Not tonight. He had other things in mind. "That's a story for another evening," he said with a sheepish grin. He ran his hand across her shoulder and drew her near. "Boy, I really missed you." His hand caressed the nape of her neck and brushed against her hair. He clutched it, twisted, and pulled her close. His lips kissed her forehead, then her eyes. He ran his tongue around her lips and thrust it into her mouth. MJ shuddered. Rick continued down her face to the nape of her neck and on to her breasts, where he paused, sighing.

"Let's go to bed," he said as he took her hand and placed it on the bulge between his legs.

———————

They woke before dawn and started again as if they had never made love before. They were hungry, like children, touching and probing and holding back their fulfillment untilthe last possible moment before an explosion that left them breathless and spent. After a few minutes, MJ rolled over and placed her head in the crook of Rick's arm, looking into his face.

"Something else happened the night you disappeared," she said. "I've been waiting for the right time to tell you."

MJ sat up and pulled the hair away from her eyes.

"Our house was broken into."

Rick had a bewildered look on his face. "What?"

MJ explained what happened after the town meeting. She told him everything: her rescue by Alberto; his call to Ginger; and the arrival of the police early the next morning.

"My God, why didn't you tell me? Were you hurt?"

"Just a lump on the head and a bruised ego for my stupidity," MJ said pointing to the spot. She looked intently into Rick's eyes.

"So many things don't add up. We were both attacked that same night. A coincidence? I doubt it. Why?"

For what seemed like a long time, Rick couldn't speak. His shoulders were slumped. He felt defeated. He never thought they would target his wife.

"There's something I have to tell you. It's a long story. When I'm through, I hope you will forgive me."

Rick lifted his chin and looked MJ straight in the eye. This wasn't going to be easy. "Wiley and I joined forces to open the mine at El Triunfo."

When MJ opened her mouth to speak, Rick put his fingers over her lips. "Please let me finish." He stood up trying to gain some advantage over MJ.

"You have to understand where I'm coming from on this. Wiley has been a part of my life since I was a kid. He was my Dad's best buddy." Rick reached into his pocket and pulled a cigarette out of the pack. MJ frowned.

"When dad fell into the mine, it was Wiley who found him. He lit a cigarette and took a puff. "Somehow he pulled dad out and brought him back to Los Santos. Wiley blamed himself for leaving him alone while he went ahead to check on a watering hole in the area. They had a rule that someone always stayed nearby when a man went down a mine. Wiley was so distraught no one saw him for over a year."

Rick paced back and forth as the story unfolded. "I owe him," he said in a pleading tone. "But beyond that, we worked well together. I provided reference maps and historical information about the mine and Wiley used his geology background to make quick work of the consortium's demands."

MJ snickered and raised an eyebrow in disbelief.

"You have no idea. Wiley provided graphs of the geological strata for the meeting in Cabo and an estimate for the cost of equipment to rebuild and staff the mine. He spent endless hours digging through papers figuring out what the daily production of silver would be in today's dollars. He was invaluable."

"Did you pay him up front?" MJ asked defiantly.

"I had to. Not everybody works for free like I do. In the end the development costs were much more than I estimated." Rick stopped and rubbed his thumb on his chin, trying to decide how to tell MJ what came next. Finally he blurted it out.

"I borrowed money." Rick waited for MJ's reaction. She said nothing but her eyes went wide with amazement. "I cosigned the land behind Hacienda Azul as collateral."

"You've got to be kidding," MJ said incredulous.

"But that's not all of it." Rick shook his head still in disbelief of what happened next. "I borrowed more money privately, from a guy in San Jose. I'm paying him three percent a month in interest. The loan is fifty thousand dollars and I secured it with the title to Hacienda Azul."

MJ was off the bed in a flash, hands on her hips and eyes ablaze.

"You did what," she screamed. "Are you crazy?" She started toward Rick and stopped, looking him straight in the eyes. "Thank God the agreement will never hold up in a court of law. I never signed the loan."

"These guys don't play by the rules. They have other methods to collect their money."

MJ was beyond angry. "What is there about our marriage that keeps you from confiding in me?" MJ sputtered. "Damn it, Rick. I'm your wife!"

Rick reached for another cigarette and lit it.

"I thought you were dead!" she said.

He took a step toward MJ.

"No, please don't come near me. Just where are you emotionally? How do you think I felt when I opened our safety deposit box? I didn't care about money or an insurance policy. I wanted YOU."

Rick put his hands over his eyes to cover the tears. "I'm so sorry," he said. "I love you so much. Please forgive me."

MJ knew Rick was a mess. But so was she. Everything he told her was complicated and painful. "I need some time Rick." She walked to the bedroom door, opened it, and turned to him. "Please leave. I need some time alone."

Rick walked through the door and closed it behind him. He heard the lock turn. He stood in the living room wondering how he could have screwed up so badly. He found the sofa, collapsed, and fell into an exhausted sleep. In his dreams his father loomed over him in disgust. "What were you thinking?" he said, again and again.

The room was quiet, but MJ couldn't sleep. Chiquita, who hid under the dining room table during the heat of the argument, was snoring near the foot of the bed. MJ tried to understand Rick's actions. But she couldn't. Her mind went back to the last time she was caught unaware. Her gut wrenching experience ten years earlier made her wonder how she could be deceived again.

When MJ was a sophomore in college she accepted an invitation to attend a seminar in New York during Thanksgiving break. The weekend before she was to leave, her mother called and insisted she come home.

"What's so important it can't wait until Christmas?"

"I'm sorry, dear," she said. "You'll understand when you get here. See you on Monday."

MJ's plane arrived on time, she found a taxi, and half an hour later pulled up to her parents' gracious nineteenth century white house with a slate roof and black shutters. She paid the cabbie, ran up the stairs, and opened the door. She stopped dead in her tracks. The walls were bare, the paintings were gone, and there were boxes everywhere. The oriental rugs were stacked in a corner, the bookcases were empty, and the piano had completely disappeared. Her father stood in the hall.

"MJ, please come and sit down," he said. "We need to tell you something."

MJ wasn't sure where he expected her to sit since the sofa and chairs were covered with sheets. He continued into the kitchen to the old tubular metal table with three chairs and the red and white oilcloth tablecloth. Her mother was seated with her hands folded. She wore no makeup and looked nervous. Her mother spoke first.

"We don't quite know how to tell you dear, but your father and I are getting a divorce," she said. "All of the financial arrangements have been made. Your father has taken a position in Sydney, Australia. He leaves on Friday and will not return for a year." Her mother's eyes filled with tears, but true to form, she did not cry. "We knew you would want to say goodbye before he left."

MJ had a questioning look on her face as she stared at her father. She shook her head back and forth no.

"I'm sorry, honey," was all he managed to say before he turned and walked out of the room.

"No!" MJ screamed, running after her father. "How can this be possible? Why am I the last one to know?"

MJ would always remember that day. After an hour of ranting and swearing, she stormed up the stairs, grabbed her suitcase and left. She arrived back at San Jose and locked herself in the apartment for three nights. She drank wine, watched Audrey Hepburn movies, and ate home delivered pizza. When the room began to smell from the cardboard boxes, and the TV went on the fritz, MJ decided to go out. Rosie's Place, a block away, was the perfect option. She found a booth in the corner and studied the menu.

"May I join you?" asked a familiar voice. MJ looked up quickly.

John Collins, her English literature professor, stared at her. His infectious smile and stubble beard reminded her of the man gracing the cover of GQ.

"Sure, have a seat," MJ said. "But I'm not the best company."

Thirty minutes later, he was holding her hand and telling her he could feel her pain. And that was how, quite unexpectedly, MJ began her affair with John.

It was perfectly timed. He made her feel alive again. She transferred all her emotional anger to physical passion. John took her places sexually she didn't know existed—until she met Rick. At the end of six months, the affair was over. MJ was feeling sad again and wallowing in Catholic guilt. On a lark, she applied to the University of Madrid and was accepted for her junior year. She focused on Spanish acquisitions from the Americas. MJ vowed never to tell anyone about her affair with John. She never did. But the direction of her life changed forever. MJ tossed around in bed thinking about how different her life was ten years ago. Until half an hour ago, MJ thought her life was terrific. Her best friend Ginger lived nearby; she would be curator of the museum for Rick's father's collection; and she lived in Los Santos, a community that supplied her with tons of activities. And most importantly, she was married to the man she loved, Rick Delgado. The man she loved for better or for worse. Until death.

Chiquita's scratching at the door told MJ it was time to get up. She opened the bedroom door and the dog made a beeline to the kitchen. Rick was asleep on the sofa. He mumbled something she couldn't understand as she walked by. So much had happened to them during the past week. Although it would be painful, she knew they had to sort things out. MJ walked over to the sofa.

"Rick?"

He opened his eyes and rubbed them with his hands. He tried to focus. "Where am I?"

"Santa Juanico. Do you want some coffee, or maybe a Coke?"

"Yeah, sure, a Coke would be nice."

MJ returned with the drink. Rick sat up, yawned, and shook his head. "I guess I was really tired."

MJ edged herself onto the sofa and put her hand on Rick's shoulder. "Let's go for a walk on the beach with the dog and see if we can make some sense of what happened." MJ had a motive. She wanted to stroll on the sand at leisure and tell him everything that happened to her during the past week. She didn't know how much could he assimilate at one time. There was so much to share.

CHAPTER 24

Rick and MJ walked back to the casita hand in hand. The stroll along the Pacific with the waves crashing and a gusty wind helped them calm down and gain some perspective. MJ managed to tell Rick about her meeting with Angelique and touched upon Don Hernando. She mentioned Johnny, but everything she knew about what happened came from Don Hernando.

An hour later, MJ and Rick had settled into the living room and made a list of what had happened to each of them during the past week. They were attempting to plow through the information. MJ paced back and forth.

"According to Angelique, you were followed after you left San Jose. Do you have any idea why?"

"Truthfully, no. I can think of a couple of scenarios. First, maybe Alfonzo was upset that I didn't give him any money again this month. Or second, it could have something to do with my earlier meeting with the consortium. A lot of people aren't too happy about reopening the El Triunfo mine."

MJ couldn't suppress a smile. "Come on honey, no one's going to chase you in a car and shoot you over it."

"There has to be a common thread between the car chase and the break in at the house. They tore our living room apart. They weren't looking for money. It was something else."

Rick shrugged his shoulders. "I don't know."

"We're going around in circles on this one," she said. "Let's move on to something else."

"How does Johnny fit into the picture?" Rick asked.

"He called after the interview and said he was coming to the house with papers. But he never came."

"And the next thing you heard was he shot somebody?" Rick asked. "That's not Johnny. There's definitely more to the story."

"I know. Then there is Ramon Diaz. I haven't a clue how he fits into the picture."

"Who?"

"Whoops," MJ said. "I forgot, I haven't mentioned him yet."

MJ told Rick how she met Ramon Diaz in the La Paz market and what happened that afternoon.

Rick was more annoyed with every sentence until he finally interrupted her. "Look, I'd remember if I had a cousin in Spain."

"But he knew so much about you. Where you went to college, the casita your parents had in Santa Juanica. He even said you surfed together."

"He's crazy. I did all my surfing with Alberto until I met you and found a substitute sport. What did this guy look like?"

"Well, he was a bit taller than you and probably a couple of years older. He wore expensive clothing. His hair was longer on the sides and back, sort of a continental look."

"Oh, I get the picture. The suave European type, a raconteur."

"Stop it. Do you want me to tell you or not."

"Tell me more about why you think he knows me."

"He knew about your father. Apparently Oliver stopped in Seville and visited Ramon's family when he was giving a lecture about the Jesuits a few years ago."

Rick shrugged his shoulders. "Maybe he's psychic."

Her voice became cautious. "Rick, he hinted he knew that you were in trouble. And he said he was supposed to meet you last Tuesday, the day you disappeared."

Rick closed his eyes and rubbed them. He frowned. "Last Tuesday? I don't think so. The only thing I remember about last Tuesday was fighting my way up a cliff."

"I told Ginger about him. I was sure I'd seen him before, maybe in a magazine, or a picture. Somewhere."

Rick stiffened. "You told Ginger about him? Why? Do you have to share everything with her?"

MJ bristled. "Excuse me. I thought you were dead and she is my best friend. Who else am I supposed to talk to? Father Leo?"

"I think we're getting off track," he said.

MJ glared at her husband. "Well if you don't have a cousin in Spain, then who is he?" MJ said putting her hands on her hips.

"I don't know." Rick walked to the mini bar and took a Coke and some ice from the refrigerator. He poured MJ a glass and tool a long swig from the can.

"Was he stalking you?" he finally asked. "Do you think he's dangerous?"

"I didn't at the time. Now I really don't know. Please listen to me," MJ said exasperated. "We need to tell each other everything that's going on in our marriage. No hidden secrets or trying to cover mistakes we may have made." MJ walked to the desk and returned with paper and pencil. "Let's make another list of anything that seemed unusual, and anyone we met during the past six months who might help us get to the bottom of what is going on."

Rick was sullen. MJ was always pushing for results. How did she accumulate so much information so fast? And everything she knew led to more questions. He threw the pen on the table. "I've been to hell and back since last week. I'm exhausted."

He stood up and glared at MJ "Can you stop climbing mountains and clear cutting for a while?" He shook his head in disgust, then turned and headed for the door. "I'm taking a walk." The door slammed with a bang.

MJ completed her list and drank the Coke. They weren't making much headway. Why was everything so damn complicated when it came to dealing with Rick? She put her head back and closed her eyes. Just as she began to dose the door opened and burst of cool air hit her arms. She shuddered. Rick walked over and placed a small briefcase on the table.

"I have something to show you. Mama gave me the last time I saw her." He opened the briefcase and took out a picture frame covered with cardboard. He removed the cardboard and waited for MJ's reaction. MJ peered closer and closer. "Is it what I think it is?"

Rick shook his head and grinned. The unusual map was written on a parchment that was curled at the edges from being rolled for many years. The paper was twelve inches wide by sixteen inches long with the typical greenish markings found on old goatskin.

"Have you identified anything?" MJ asked.

Rick pointed the small coat of arms with a sun symbol. "Only this. The design is a Jesuit Coat of Arms not typically used anymore."

MJ perused the map with awe. It looked like the work of a child. Two simple church facades were connected by a river or maybe a path and surrounded by mounds. Could they be mountains? Who knew for sure? Symbols covered the parchment: animals, clouds, a sun and moon, directional arrows in different colors. The four angels scattered throughout the landscape were in symbolic forms. Small multicolored symbols were the most challenging designs.

Rick took the map out of the frame and placed it on a table. They peered at the complicated document.

"God, there's so much to figure out," MJ said.

"I know," Rick said. "I didn't know what it was until I noticed the churches." Rick pointed to a church. "This facade this is Santa Maria, the last church the Jesuits built. The other must be Santa Isabel from the initials in very small script on the steeple. Look."

A tiny SM sat above the cross on the steeple.

"The little symbols with arrows look like Milagros, the metal trinkets we see on crosses," MJ said. She knew many shops in Los Santos that sold Milagros laid out on a display table. The most common designs were a hat, leaf, parrot, fish, eye, heart, foot or a fig leaf.

"Of course," Rick said. "There is a book on Milagtos somewhere in the house."

"Amazing," MJ said. "The map really exists, it's not just folklore."

"MY dad told me the Jesuits made a map before they left Baja California but he wasn't sure it still existed.

When Mama asked me to open the box, I was blown away by the emerald necklace and didn't notice the map.

"It's an Aztec piece from the fifteenth century, " MJ said. "Mama's birthday is the perfect time to wear the necklace in honor of Carlos." MJ ran her fingers along the edge of the frame. "Did she say anything when she handed you the parchment?"

"Not a word. She waited for me to figure it out."

"I don't understand why she kept the secret for so many years. And why share the information with you?"

Rick ran his fingers through his hair. "Maybe it was the connection between Carlos and my dad. They were really good friends. Her exact words were, 'I asked for God's help and he told me what to do.'" Rick shook his head. "She gave me one huge responsibility. And I'm no further along trying to figure out the map now than when I started. Did Mama mention it to you?"

"Not that I remember. All I saw was that gorgeous Aztec necklace. She probably thought you took the map to your grave."

Rick put his arm around MJ and squeezed. "I'm glad that didn't happen. Let's brew a cup of coffee and get started. We have a lot to figure out."

CHAPTER 25

The living room of the Delgado house was a combination of a tornado zone and a science project gone amuck. The dining room wasn't much different. Papers were scattered over the oak table like confetti. A large folding metal table, dragged in from the garage, held stacks of books in semi-confusion or logical order, depending on the pile. Some books were open, others had yellow post-its with red lettering or were stacked on the rug listing toward the floor. MJ wondered what the capacity of the brain was to absorb information before it crashed and burned. She was at liftoff, or maybe impact.

MJ and Rick had compiled a list of questions with two goals: decipher the Map of Santa Isabel, and find a connection between the map and men who chased Rick over a cliff and broke into their home.

MJ concentrated on the emerald necklace trying to verify it's age and locate the reference to a second necklace she remembered having seen before. She found two books that might have the information she needed. They were a long shot. One book listed Spanish treasures of the new world, the other contained photos from the Prado in Madrid. An hour later she threw the books aside in disgust. "I'm positive an identical necklace is in Prado in Madrid. Unfortunately my book on Aztec jewelry is in Los Santos."

Rick stood up and stretched. "Why don't you call Ginger, tell her where you think the book is, and have her bring it to Loreto when she meets you. I'll go look for the short wave radio in the shed."

"Okay. I'll make sandwiches while you're gone."

Rick found the radio in back corner of the shed near old truck tires. God knows how long it would take to get it running again. Probably hours. They were a godsend for the farmers and vaqueros who lived where landlines and cell phones didn't exist. He could ask Lupita and Oscar to use their radio. But Rick wanted to set his own radio up. MJ would be calling from Loreto tomorrow. Besides, it was an imposition. They needed a short wave radio.

Rick returned with the radio, tinkered a while, and finally got the thing to work. MJ called Ginger's house. No one answered. "This isn't like Ginger," MJ said frowning and tapping her fingers on the kitchen counter. "I haven't heard from her in two days."

"Come on. You haven't been anywhere she can reach you. Quit worrying. She's a big girl."

"You're probably right. But I'm going to call our house anyway." Again, no one answered. "Okay. I'm through thinking about Ginger. Next on my list is to browse through the books Wiley borrowed, starting with the one I picked up at his house the other day." MJ started for the dining room and turned around. "There's something that's bothering me and it needs to be said."

Rick raised an eyebrow.

"I'm not sure you pay enough attention to what Wiley borrows. I made a list of the books, maps, and other items he has taken. Most of it is directly related to The Mission of Santa Isabel."

"So? What are you saying?"

"Don't you think that's a bit odd? Do you two ever talk about the mission? Could he possibly know you have the map?"

"Don't be ridiculous. Wiley has always been interested in missions, mines, geology, and Baja history. He and my dad talked about how they were going to find the lost mission and split the money. It was a joke. Who knew that Mama had it in her hip pocket!"

"But a while back I caught him snooping in your office!" MJ said with defiance.

"So what. Wiley is Wiley. He's been writing a book about the lost mission for years. More than likely, he was looking for something to do with the El Triunfo mine. He was in the thick of it with me." Rick was seething. It took everything he had to stay calm. But he was losing the battle. "Let it go, MJ. We have too many important matters to concentrate on. For starters, I'm still trying to figure out the symbols on the map. Dad's old books on petro glyphs look nothing like the crazy doodles. The strange ciphers on the map head in the direction of the occult."

"Then try a book on Curanderos. Maybe you'll find something there."

"Not a bad idea. They're in the study." Rick did an about face.

MJ found the journal Wiley returned to her. It was a strange little leather bound journal written by a Franciscan named Father Romero when he arrived in Baja California in the 1760s. She opened it. The pages were age worn and quite extraordinary. The ink, faded to sepia, was written in classical Roman cursive script on yellowed paper with brown spots in some areas. It was museum quality and very beautiful. She knew Rick would never have loaned Wiley a book like this. Halfway through the journal MJ found what she was looking for.

"Rick, I think I found something!"

He came through the door holding a book. "I'm in the middle of something, what's up?"

"This diary was written by Padre Javier, the first priest in La Paz after the Jesuits left. Listen to this."

MJ read the paragraph about Father Tomas and the trunk he left with Don Miguel Cortez. She paused and continued on about the servant who disappeared. "Is there another way to corroborate the information?"

Rick was perplexed. "Where are you going with this information, MJ?"

"Well, if the servant stole the map and the necklace from the Cortez family and was never heard from again, maybe Carlos found the map and the necklace at the place where the servant died. MJ put the book on the table and gave Rick a knowing smile. "The Cortez family must know this too. They've probably been seething for centuries."

"A possibility, I suppose. All of the documented information on the Cortez family is in La Paz. It's not exactly handy."

MJ tapped her fingers on the table. "Let's start with the premise that we have the real map. Could anyone else know about it?"

"I don't know how? I haven't exactly been waving it around. I didn't even tell you."

"Did you talk to anyone about it?" MJ asked, choosing her words carefully.

Rick sat down, rubbed his chin, and gazed across the room. "I stopped at the town hall in Loreto a few weeks ago and asked for a plot plan of the land around Santa Maria. I thought the government owned most of the land, but I wanted to be sure."

"And what did you find out?" MJ asked.

Rick shook his shoulders. "Almost nothing. The clerk found the book, put it on the counter, and opened it. He pointed to the word Privado and said the land around Santa Maria is privately owned. The parcel was L-shaped and surrounded by government property," Rick said. "I asked him to look up the name of the owner and told him I'd be back." Rick dug into his pocket for a cigarette but decided against it. MJ would know he was nervous. "When I went back a few days later he gave me a piece of paper and told me the land belonged to the Baja Land Corporation and handed me their telephone number. I've got it in the other room."

He returned with the paper and handed it to MJ. "The number belongs to a law firm in Mexico City. I called several times and left messages. The guy who handles the account, Mr. Flamenco, never returned my calls."

"Could Don Hernando have found out about your visit?"

"I don't know," he said shaking his head with annoyance. How does he fit into the picture anyway?"

"Just wondering."

Rick's hands began to sweat. He rubbed them against his pants. He couldn't stand it any longer, pulled out a cigarette and lit it.

MJ waited for him to continue.

"Well there's something else. The day Mama gave me the map she told me Carlos filed a quitclaim deed on the land where he found the gold, but she didn't know what happened to it." He looked around for an ashtray, found one, and flicked his cigarette. "When I was leaving the clerk's office I asked him to look up quitclaim deeds in the name of Carlos Estrada. He called me back and told me to come by. He had found the information. But I never picked it up."

"There has to be a connection," MJ said. "And I'm going to Loreto to get the deed and find out what it is."

"That poor clerk," Rick said grinning at MJ. "I came in here ten minutes ago with something I wanted to show you. He opened the book he'd been carrying and flipped through the pages. "Look at this. Curanderos carry amulets that have a special significance: coins, beads, silver from old jewelry. Items similar to the Milagros you mentioned earlier."

MJ and Rick studied the page of hand woven bags with amulets of various sizes and colors hanging from the bottom. Rick continued to turn the pages before they found the section on the special meanings of color.

"Stop," MJ said. "Do you think there is a connection between the small colored arrows on the map and the colors they list here?"

"I don't know. Read what it says."

"Okay." MJ ran her finger down the page to the area of interest. "Gold signifies the need for money. Silver represents harmony, copper relates to the poor, green and red release a person from envy and other bad things, and a horseshoe signifies wealth."

"I'll go get the map," Rick said as he darted out of the room.

MJ turned to another page and continued reading. She looked up when he returned. "It says a lodestone is a symbol of good luck and fortune. What's a lodestone?"

"A stone with magnetic qualities," Rick said. "Mexican people collect them. Crusaders brought them back to Spain from the Holy Land. I have one in the other room. Let me get it."

MJ sat with the open book, intrigued by the photos and their meanings. A few minutes later Rick returned with a box. He placed it on the book she was reading. She frowned.

"Here take a look," he said handing her a grey rock. "The Spanish conquistadores brought them to the new world. Curanderos call them Piedra Iman."

MJ looked into the box of rocks. Her eyes widened. "Oh my God," she said jumping up from the sofa. "I forgot something." She dashed out of the room. MJ returned with a cardboard box she placed next to Rick's. "Just before I left Santa Rosario, Mama handed me this box.

She told me your father and Carlos collected them and she wanted me to have them. I didn't think it was very important."

Rick took out each rock and placed it on the table. A couple of times he paused and studied them remembering the first time his father identified one to him when he was a boy. Rick placed several rocks on the table before he lifted one up to the light and held it there.

MJ turned her attention to Piedra Iman designs and paid scant attention to what her husband was doing.

Rick stood up, walked over to the desk, and returned with a magnifying glass. He held one rock up to the light and studied it. "Honey, take a look at this," he said handing her the stone and magnifying glass.

MJ stopped reading when he nudged her. She took the magnifying glass and peered at the symbols on the smooth cool rock. Then she looked at the drawings in the book. The stone was painted with the same symbols. The book, the Piedra Iman and the map of the Mission of Santa Isabel had identical symbols. The circle was complete.

"This may be the connection we were looking for," Rick said.

MJ and Rick spent their next hours trying to decipher the combination of arrows, colors, symbols and their possible meanings. At ten o'clock MJ yawned and turned to her husband.

"I'm quitting for tonight. My head is going around in circles and my brain is mush."

Rick looked up bleary-eyed from the Milagros that he pried off an antique cross and stacked in a pile. His father would be mortified. He was comparing the similarities in design between the map and early twentieth century Milagros. "What?"

"I said, I'm having a glass of milk and going to bed."

"So soon?" he said looking at his watch. "I'm just getting started."

"Damn. I never did call Ginger again."

"Call her tomorrow before you go to Loreto. By then we'll have a better idea of what we need."

"We are still missing something important that will help solve the map," MJ said. "Maybe tomorrow when our brains aren't dead we can figure it out."

CHAPTER 26

The call came through at two a.m. in Baja California Sur and rang and rang before anyone answered. Don Hernando couldn't believe it was possible someone would call him in the middle of the night. The ringing didn't go away. His hand fumbled toward the night table until it brushed something. A glass of brandy hit the floor and shattered. Don Hernando's fingers finally found the phone.

"Bueno."

He heard static on the other end.

"May I speak with Don Hernando Cortez Sanchez?" a woman asked.

Sanchez was Don Hernando's mother's maiden name and the formal way to address someone. It was rarely used except for legal documents.

"This is Don Hernando Cortez speaking."

"One moment please," she said.

Don Hernando continued listening to the noise. Only curiosity kept him from hanging up.

"Is this Don Hernando Cortez Sanchez?" said a male voice.

"Yes. Who is this?"

"Allow me to introduce myself. I am Monsignor Jaime Ruiz, calling from the University of Saint Ignatius Loyola in Seville, Spain."

"Yes, go on."

"I have important information involving documents in our archives that concern the Cortez family. First, I have to ask a few questions. It is a simple formality."

"What questions? I have no idea what you are talking about." Don Hernando could barely hear the man. The clock on the table said two a.m., and too much brandy was sending a throbbing pain across his head.

"This will not take very long, Don Hernando. We just want to verify who you are," the Monsignor said.

Don Hernando opened the bedside drawer and reached for a silver flask. "Just a second please," he said unscrewing the top and taking a swig of vintage tequila. "Continue. What were you saying?"

There was a pause on the other end of the phone.

"I would like to confirm some family history," the Monsignor said.

"Listen Father, it is two in the morning. I'll give you the number of my attorney and you can call him tomorrow and tell him what you need. He will take care of it." He gave the Monsignor his attorney's name and number and slammed the phone.

"What the hell was the man thinking?" Don Hernando turned off the light and went back to sleep.

———

Antigua Cortez was reading when the phone rang. She looked at the time. Two a.m. Who would be calling at this hour? Antigua had a mother's instinct about a phone that rang in the middle of the night. It was bad news. However, with a son like Don Hernando, it could be a business associate with no regard for other people.

Antigua stepped out of bed, pushed her toes around the freezing floor, and found her slippers. She padded to her desk. The phone rang for a long time before it finally stopped. She sat down, picked up the receiver, and listened.

Antigua was appalled that her son was so rude to a Monsignor. His lack of respect was dreadful. When Don Hernando slammed the phone down, Antigua also hung up. She pondered what to do. The priest's message was intriguing. She suspected her son was drunk. He should have understood why the Monsignor called.

Antigua decided to ring the family attorney in the morning. She would say that Don Hernando was too busy to handle the matter and suggest the attorney contact her after speaking with the Monsignor. Antigua knew the call required immediate attention. She sensed the urgency in his voice. She would get to the bottom of the matter.

Monsignor Jaime Ruiz hung up astounded by the rudeness of Don Hernando. The priest was only trying to be courteous and prevent any long-term repercussions from the error in judgment made by a priest in his office. The priest, Father Sanchez, was unaware he could not forward historical information to a third party without notifying the family first. The legal department had instituted parameters dictating prior consent a few years earlier. It was an honest mistake. Only a handful of Spanish dynasties in the Americas fell into the category of continuous ownership of the same property by family name. And fewer still were granted ownership from a land grant by the king. The Monsignor could only recall one other case, and the family resided in Peru. But the damage was done. All the University could do was try to mitigate any future problems.

The Monsignor would not call Don Hernando's attorney tomorrow, or the next day for that matter. He would send a letter by regular mail to the Cortez family stating an outside party requested Jesuit documents about the Cortez family. The Monsignor had no idea how long it would take for the mail to arrive in Baja California.

It was two in the morning, but Wiley couldn't sleep. He was thinking about the package he'd received twelve hours earlier. The phone call to Seville two weeks earlier paid off in spades. The Jesuit library did indeed have a copy of the reference guide that Padre Tomas Ortega carried back to Spain. The library book of records verified its existence from Wiley's letter. Wiley sent an official letter on embossed stationary stating he was the Dean of the Department of Geology and Professor Emeritus of the University of Oregon. He requested the information for his continuing research on Jesuit contributions to Baja California. Wiley listed everything he needed and said he would be in touch.

The call took several transfers before he was connected to Father Jose Sanchez at the University in Seville. The priest received the letter and was delighted they had a copy on file of the reference guide he requested. Did Professor Wiley need anything else? Really? Father Sanchez would check the archives for a map of the Mission of Santa Maria and Santa Isabel.

Wiley was ecstatic. And what a surprise the package contained when it arrived. The library had a copy of the reference guide Padre Tomas carried back to Spain. But just as intriguing, Oliver Marshall translated the material in 1966 when he was a visiting professor to the University of Seville.

"Well, I'll be damned," Wiley said. He was positive Oliver never documented the information. Wiley read the guide, but was hard pressed to see any connection between what was listed in the guide and the Mission of Santa Isabel. Far more importantly, among the materials sent to him, was a copy of the map of The Mission of Santa Isabel. Wiley studied the small designs. How hard could they be to figure out? He would visit the library in La Paz tomorrow. The curator would know the meaning of the designs.

CHAPTER 27

Rick pushed papers and books around all evening until he was bleary-eyed. It was midnight. He could no longer remember what book he was reading. He sat down on the sofa, puffed a pillow under his head, put his feet on the table, and hoped his brain would reroute from confusion to sanity. There was nothing in the map, symbols, or clues that made any sense. MJ was right. Something was missing. But what? He was still empty handed. He closed his eyes. The ghost of his father surrounded him. Oliver was reading a journal and cataloguing an out-of-print book. Then he was sitting at his desk preparing for a lecture. His father was relentless. Everything Rick knew he learned from his dad.

Rick wondered if his father's journal would add any new information. Oliver kept a list of every book or item in the collection that he loaned out with a notation that included the name of the borrower, the date borrowed, the date returned. Rick had continued his dad's tradition. MJ brought the journal from Los Santos, but where did she put it? Rick walked into the dining room and sat on the chair his mother bought an eternity ago. He let out a soft moan. It was hard as a rock and his body ached. He glanced around the room. A red book should be easy to spot, even in his weary state. He bent his head under the table and voila, the book sat near the top of a stack at his feet. He pulled it out and flipped to the last entry, the two books Wiley requested. The first book, The Diary of Father Javier, was picked up by MJ last week. The second book was a The Jesuit book of Records of 1768, a ledger listing everything carried back to Spain. MJ had made a pencil notation "can't find." Rick knew from his father's decimal system the book was in Santa Juanica. Rick wandered from room to room until he found the ledger, opened it, and leafed through several pages before he recognized his father's handwriting. His heart quickened. Handwriting was almost like seeing his father again. Oliver Marshall had made a small check note in pencil on Page 23 next to a book that Padre Tomas carried to Spain named Seventeenth Century Witchcraft of the Guaycura Indians; it read "Possibly regarding Santa Isabel?"

Who was Padre Tomas and why was he so important? Did his father ever find the book? Rick realized he wouldn't get much sleep tonight.

———

MJ and Rick awoke early to the roar of the waves. A woodpecker tapped under the palapa roof outside their window. Rick's watch said he had five hours of sleep. He leaned over and planted a kiss on MJ's cheek. "I'm heading for the shower. When I come back I'm taking you to a place you'll love."

MJ rubbed her eyes, and threw a pillow over her head. "I don't have time."

"Don't you think of anything else? I've something in mind that's really important. A visit to the bodega behind the barn."

"What?" MJ said, sitting bold upright and suddenly alert.

"Yesterday, when I went hunting for the short wave I ran into Lupita. I asked her where my father could have stored boxes other than the house. She mentioned the bodega. After mom died, dad locked the door and told her that no one was ever to go inside again. No one has." Rick rustled MJ's hair. "So if you're planning on going to Loreto today, you better get a move on."

"Maybe, but first I'm going to call Alberto and see if he can meet me at the town clerk's office. Ginger is traveling incognito and it can mean only one thing. She must have hooked up with Johnny. Not good."

"Like I said before, Ginger can take care of herself. Stop worrying," Rick said heading for the bathroom. "By the way, you were right as usual. There's a missing link between the map and the symbols. My dad referenced a book that Padre Tomas took back to Spain named Seventeenth Century Witchcraft of the Guaycura Indians. We're going to search for it in the bodega." Rick removed the towel and sauntered into the bathroom. "Of course, you could always go to Loreto early tomorrow," he said closing the door.

An hour later MJ and Rick were headed toward the bodega, the Mexican catch all name for a storage area. MJ wore hiking boots, her heaviest jeans, a windbreaker, and leather gloves. Her hair was covered with a red babushka. She looked like a Che Guevara commando. Rick skipped the gloves and hat, but wore a long sleeve shirt, jeans and boots. He carried an axe and a flashlight. The bodega was tucked behind a wall and hidden by chamisa. Rick and his boyhood friend, Pancho, were convinced the place was spooked. When they were kids, they hid in the bushes smoking cigarettes and telling jokes every evening.

"Lupita told me the lock was rusty," Rick said at the entrance. He smashed the lock with a blow from the axe, kicked the door open, and stepped inside. The room was dark and musty and smelled of mold, gasoline, mothballs, and cinnamon. The big old flashlight cast a yellow light as Rick moved it slowly around the room.

"MJ, I need your help," he said in a calm and reassuring voice. He heard the rustle of every creepy crawly thing that was suddenly under invasion. The bodega was surprisingly empty. A rusted old shovel and pitchfork lay in the far corner next to a sawhorse. Old frames were stacked on a low table.

MJ tapped Rick's shoulder. "I'm right behind you. She took a deep breath, grabbed his arm, and then let out a squeal. Something ran over her foot.

Rick shined the flashlight on her boots. "A mouse."

"Can we hurry?" MJ said, in a voice an octave higher than normal.

"Shouldn't take long. Looks like the only possibility is the old bureau." Rick shined the light on a tall columned Empire chest.

"I'm surprised it isn't in the house. It's a nice piece of furniture."

Rick handed MJ the flashlight. "Here, take this while I look inside."

The stately old bureau had Sandwich glass pulls and a curly maple facade. The frame looked to be cherry. Rick tugged, but the top drawer wouldn't budge. As he tried to shimmy it from side to side it suddenly let go. "Damn." He closed his eyes, wincing from the weight of the drawer. He pushed the drawer onto the runners of the frame, pushed it back in, and poked his hand inside. "I think there's some truth to ghost stories. I have an eerie feeling something is in here."

MJ looked at Rick with fear and turned to the door. He grabbed her arm broke out laughing. "Just kidding." Rick braced his hands against the side of the bureau and pulled the drawer a bit more. The scent of his mother's rose-petal perfume wafted up his nose. His flashlight shined on a black decoupage box, covered with snippets of birthday cards, photos, and postcards. Rick gave the drawer another tug. He reached in and opened the familiar heart-shaped box. His mother's diamond ring was inside. He continued to a tin box that said Harrods Shortbread. It contained stacks of handkerchiefs. Rick sighed. "My father left the bureau intact because he wanted my mother's memory to remain intact. Everything reminds me of her."

MJ placed her hand on Rick's shoulder. "Are you okay?"

"Yeah," he said. "I might as well get it over with now. There are only two more drawers." Rick opened the middle drawer easily. It was heavy and full of cookie tins. Each one was labeled. He opened a tin that said Our First Year of Marriage that was full of photos. The picture on top was of his mother standing in front of the Eiffel Tower holding an umbrella. Rick picked up each box, shook it, and read the label out loud: Trip to California; Rick's first birthday; Rick surfing; Trip to Europe in 1980."

"I didn't know you went to Europe when you were ten," MJ interrupted.

"I didn't. Mom and Dad left me home with Grandma Delgado the year before she died. I probably added to her demise."

"I believe that. You certainly are adding to mine."

Rick continued reading. "Summers in Los Santos."

"Stop," MJ said. "Let's take that box back to the house."

"Why?"

"Because Ramon Diaz said he spent a couple of summers with you. Maybe a photo inside will rattle your memory."

"I already told you, I never met the guy."

"Humor me," MJ insisted. "And maybe we should take the box on your first year of surfing too."

Rick pulled the boxes out and handed placed them on the bureau. Then he turned to the bottom drawer. It opened easily. Mice had chewed on shreds of newspaper to make bedding inside the drawer; the pieces fell over the top of the drawer and onto the floor. "Put your hand inside and find out what's in there," he said with a grin. "You're wearing gloves."

"Forget it, wise guy. I haven't had a rabies shot."

Rick started from the outside edges and moved his hands toward the middle. "I've got something," he said lifting out a small green metal box. "If I'm not mistaken, my father gave me this toolbox for Christmas years ago. Let's see what's inside."

Rick pushed the hinge and tried to lift the cover. "It's locked. There was a tiny key attached with a string to the handle when he gave it to me. He shook the box and heard metal tapping against the edge. "I recognize the sound of rare coins. We can retire, move to Bali, and live in luxury the rest of our lives."

"Let's close the bodega and go back to the house first," MJ said.

Back inside, Rick pondered the best way to open the toolbox and not destroy it. "I'm going over to see Oscar, he'll know what to do. Be right back," he said heading out the door.

MJ tackled two boxes of photos. She soon realized old pictures of Rick were a looking glass of his childhood and documented images of his mother's love. Rick was in every photo: charging over a difficult wave, sitting on a beach, or reading a book with his dad. Alberto was in most of the photos too, but not Ramon. She covered the first box and moved on.

The second box contained photos of special events: people dancing, singing, milling around. They were all unsmiling. MJ flipped through several photographs when one caught her eye. She gazed intently at it. Rick was on one side, Alberto on the other, and Ramon in the middle, a head taller than both boys. His smile and intense eyes were the giveaway. MJ turned it over. The back said summer of 1978. Rick and Alberto were eight. Ramon was a couple years older. She looked through the rest of the photos but the only picture of Ramon Diaz she found was sitting on her lap. She was staring at the photo when Rick burst through the door flashing a small leather book and envelope. I think I found what I was looking for."

"Can it wait a minute? Come here and look at the photo I found in the box labeled "Summers in Los Santos." I'm pretty sure the young man standing between you and Alfredo is Ramon Diaz."

Rick walked over, reached down, and took a quick look. He handed the photo back to MJ. "Him? That's Rusty Torres, from Seville. His dad was a professor at the Jesuit University and a good friend of my father's."

"I'm sure the man I met in La Paz named Ramon Diaz is the same person. He was from Seville. Why would he say he was your cousin?" MJ asked slightly ruffled.

Rick shrugged his shoulders. "Well the part about being from Seville is accurate. And I guess I could loosely call him a cousin. It was a term my father used because we were all thick as fleas the two summers he spent in Los Santos. The third summer he didn't come back."

"Did your father tell you why?" she asked, taking a sip of her drink.

"It was something about Rusty spending more time with his dad. His mother passed away that winter. It happened pretty fast. I remember my father debated flying over for the funeral, but he decided against it."

"You never saw him again or wrote to each other?"

"No, not really." Rick caught the look of disbelief in his wife's eyes. "Listen babe, guys are different from girls when it comes to stuff like that. Sort of like out of sight out of mind."

"I've known several men like that," she answered sarcastically.

Rick placed his glass on the table. "Besides, we were from two different worlds, geographically and socially."

"What do you mean?"

"Rusty came from old Spanish money. His mother was a countess, or maybe a duchess. She had a title. I knew he went to boarding school, but he never talked about it. He was a pretty regular kid."

"That would explain the way he was dressed and his manners."

Rick raised his eyebrows, but decided to let it pass. "As the years went by we lost touch. My father went to Spain a couple of times for lectures, but he never mentioned Rusty or his father again."

MJ took a step back and gave Rick a steely-eyed look. "Don't you think there's something strange about the timing on all this? The fact that Ramon Diaz showed up at the same time you drove over a cliff and almost died and I came home and found thugs searching our house? Maybe it's not a coincidence that he was looking for you last week."

"Maybe not," Rick shook his head and sighed. "If you're asking if I'm worried about you, you're damn right I am. But what I think or say doesn't mean very much. You're going to do exactly what you want. Would my concern for your safety keep you from getting in the car and going to Loreto? Not in a heartbeat. And we both know it." Rick put his hands on MJ's shoulders. "Thank God no one knows where you are, not even Ginger. Alberto is meeting you in Loreto in less than three hours." Rick kissed her on the forehead. "Now's not the time to get distracted by Rusty, or whatever name he goes by. If your instincts are right, it's me he's after, not you."

Rick waved the small book he'd been holding since he came in the door. "Now give me a minute. I want you to take a look at the witchcraft book that was in the toolbox. It may be the missing link."

CHAPTER 28

There was no holding Rick back once he found the book. He cleared the dining room table, placed the map on his left, a spiral notebook in the center, Padre Tomas' book on his right, and began cross referencing the symbols, colored codes, and compass against the information he found in the old text. Rick quickly realized the Padre was a very clever man. The title of the small volume, Seventeenth Century Witchcraft of the Guaycura Indians, was deliberately misleading. Padre Tomas' quasi-historical book combined early curandero witchcraft with information on how to locate the map. Only someone with access to both documents could decipher the clues he gave. Rick took a break and headed into the kitchen and opened the refrigerator door.

MJ walked in pulling a suitcase. She stopped. "Would you like to tell me about the envelope you found in the tool chest along with the book?"

"Not now," he said frowning. "It's a long story. Do you want a Coke?"

"No thanks. I already grabbed some water, a banana, and a couple of cookies." MJ leaned her suitcase against the kitchen counter. "Maybe we should take a minute to go over our game plan before I leave."

"Sure." Rick took a gulp of the Coke.

"The first thing I'm going to do is meet Alberto at the town clerk's office. With his help, I'll pick up the quitclaim deed for Carlos' property that you never retrieved. When I get back to the hotel, I'll call the Baja Land Corporation in Mexico City. Maybe I can finesse the information on who owns the property from a junior lawyer," she said with a mischievous grin.

"Good luck on that one," Rick said.

"Mama's party is tomorrow at two o'clock. There's no sense in telling her about you with so much going on. She'll find out soon enough." MJ's face turned serious. "But I'll definitely keep an eye on Don Hernando. If Mama wears the necklace, you can bet money he'll know what it is."

"Do you have the map I made of where we're going to meet later?"

MJ unzipped a pocket of her suitcase and put her hand inside. She nodded. "Um Hum. I should be there about six o'clock. It doesn't get dark before seven-thirty."

"I'll be leaving here by noon. If anything changes, call me."

"Anything I've forgotten?" MJ asked.

"I think that about does it," he said.

MJ pecked Rick on the cheek, took her suitcase, and headed out the door. A minute later she was backing the truck out the driveway. "I'll call you from Loreto tonight. She threw a kiss, waved, and drove through the gate. The remainder of her afternoon was mapped out. MJ was lucky Alberto answered the phone earlier. He agreed to meet her and handle any translation problems she might have. He was going to Mama's party, too. MJ's Spanish was good, but she didn't want to risk trying to understand the records clerk on such an important matter.

MJ arrived in Loreto half an hour early, parked the truck, and headed to the visitors center. She found a flyer with a photo of the mission on the cover and the history of Loreto inside. The weather was balmy. She wrapped the sweater around her waist and read the booklet as she walked toward the mission: Nuestra Señora de Loreto, the headquarters for the Jesuit mission chain, is just over three-hundred years old. Padre Juan Maria Salvatierra completed construction of the church in 1704 with local stone, clay mortar, and hand-hewn timbers cut in the Sierra de La Gianta Mountains and dragged by oxen. The decorative bricks in the walls were ship's ballast, and came from Italy. The original brass bell, thought to be stolen but recently found in the bay by fishermen, was restored to its original condition and hoisted to the belfry. The bell is rung daily to announce mass in the chapel.

MJ evaluated the handsome well-maintained building that had aged gracefully. She entered the chapel. Tourists with muffled voices were taking photos of anything that didn't move. She continued to the courtyard. The first ten feet of the wall was original. The upper portion was reconstructed from brick and stone found nearby. The belfry was elegant, rebuilt with more consistency than the wall. The centerpiece was the old brass bell, aglow in sunlight, reflecting against the tower walls.

MJ glanced at her watch. The municipal building would be opening soon. She opened the brochure and continued reading:

The Municipal Building is constructed from the same granite that was used to build the Jesuit mission in 1697. The original walls and presidio were demolished, but the remainder of the compound, including the Museum of the National Institute of Anthropology and History, is original. The Municipal Building was initially a storehouse for corn, tomatoes, and squash. The vegetables were harvested twice a year by Guaycura Indians and dried under palm fronds. The buried vegetables were placed in the ground to make compost, and then covered with adobe to keep the animals out.

MJ approached the Municipal building and was about to turn the handle of the front door when she came eye to eye with a small sign:

Hours are 9 a.m. to 1 p.m. and 3:30 p.m. to 7 p.m. Monday through Friday.

Damn. She forgot that in the more traditional areas of Baja California, county municipal buildings, as well as businesses, were closed during the heat of the day. Nothing was open at two. Mexicans ate seña, their main meal of the day, at that time. Then they took a nap. The custom was no longer practiced in Cabo San Lucas and San Jose, cities that now overflowed with tourists, and the custom was quickly fading in Los Santos too. In the more traditional cities, like La Paz and Loreto, it was still the norm. MJ looked at her watch. Alberto was due any moment. MJ stood at the locked door pondering her next move when she heard a siren. She wheeled around. A black Federale car sped by. MJ caught a glimpse of the woman in the back seat with red hair. No one had a mass of hair that color. No one except Ginger.

MJ approached two pedestrians staring at the black car that just zoomed by. "Excuse me, please, do you know where the Federale are going?"

"Probably to the local jail a block away," a man said.

MJ watched the flashing red light disappear around the corner. She ran after the vehicle and turned left. Several black Federale cars were parked in front of a large brick building down the street. A crowd was gathering outside as she approached. A man in a baseball cap was in a heated discussion with a policeman who was shaking his head no.

MJ pushed her way toward the front. "Excuse me, excuse me, let me through, my friend is inside."

The man turned. "Do you know who went in?"

MJ instinctively knew the man was a reporter. She addressed the policeman. "Officer, I'm a personal friend of that woman. I'd like to speak with her."

"I'm sorry lady, it's impossible," he said. "Come back later."

"Will you tell me what the charges are so I can call her attorney?"

He shook his head no and saw the stricken look on MJ's face. "Just a minute. Wait here." The officer pointed to a spot in front of the door and went inside.

The chatter of the crowd grew louder as more people gathered. An American woman who was taken to jail and put behind bars wasn't an everyday occurrence in Loreto. MJ heard a tap on the door. The policeman signaled MJ with his finger. He barely opened the door enough for her to squeeze through. "Wait here," he said locking the door. "I'll be right back."

The small room was overflowing with people busy at work. Two women were typing, the fax machine was humming, and a man in a sport jacket and tie was shouting into the phone. Two policemen guarded the door to the adjacent room. Nobody seemed to notice that MJ was there. Metal file drawers were edge to edge against one wall, the one on the end was leaning precariously from the weight folders. MJ counted the people twice and came up with the same number, fourteen.

MJ busied herself by studying the old photographs of Loreto on a nearby wall. She observed that there were no women among the important people. She looked to the other walls. There were no women anywhere. She moved her eyes to the cobwebs above the windows, the peeling multicolored paints on the walls, a cast iron stove sitting in a corner. She was becoming more obsessive-compulsive by the minute. She closed her eyes and tried to relax. When she opened them, a well-dressed man sporting a handlebar mustache approached her.

"May I help you madam?" he said, addressing her in perfect English.

"Yes, please. My name is Martha Jane Steele Delgado and I believe my friend Ginger Hughes is in the next room. May I speak with her?" MJ extended her hand.

"Mucho gusto. I am Estevo Lorenzan, the legal representative for the city of Loreto." The man assumed a sympathetic professional persona. "I am very sorry, Mrs. Delgado, but it is not possible to see Miss Hughes until after her arraignment."

"Oh," MJ said, somewhat flustered. "Can you tell me why she's being held?"

"Not until the charges are drafted. All I can tell you now is a warrant was issued for her arrest yesterday in La Paz. She is being photographed and fingerprinted now."

MJ tried to keep her voice calm. "What happens next? I mean after her arraignment?"

"It is possible she could have a hearing today after the arraignment, but it depends on how quickly everything proceeds."

A stern looking young man approached. He nudged between the attorney and MJ and cleared his throat. "I am sorry to bother you, Mr. Lorenzan, but we are ready for you in the next room."

MJ had a split second for another question. "If I return within the hour with an attorney, can we have the hearing late this afternoon?"

"Perhaps," he said. "Now if you will excuse me Miss Delgado."

MJ made her way down the front steps and through the crowd with her head down.

"Can you tell me who is behind bars? Are you a friend? Do you know the charges?"

MJ felt the beginning of a massive migraine headache. She had to find Alberto. The rules of the Mexican legal system were different from those in United States. A person was considered guilty until proven innocent. MJ hoped Alberto was still waiting in front of the Municipal Building. She breathed a sigh of relief when she spotted him across the street talking with a young American couple. The woman's sneakers were a dead giveaway. Mexican women always wore shoes. Only their children wore sneakers.

"What's going on?" Alberto asked.

"I have a serious problem," she began.

An hour later, Alberto came down the front steps of the jail running a hand through his hair. He looked around.

"Alberto, over here." MJ was sitting in front of a café across the street stirring a cup of cold coffee. A late afternoon Sea of Cortez wind was gusting against her legs. Her sweater was buttoned. Her face was pale.

"My God, you look beat," Alberto said. He took off his jacket and placed it on her shoulders. "Let's go inside."

They made their way past the crowd to a couple of red stools at the counter.

"Sorry it took so long," he said. "I had a lucky break. The judge they called on short notice is originally from La Paz. He's a decent sort and knows me. The hearing is scheduled for four." Alberto looked at his watch. "That's an hour from now."

"Thank God," MJ said. "Did you speak with her?"

"Briefly. She's pretty shook up."

A waitress brought glasses of water and handed them a menu. "Be right back to take your order."

Alberto took a sip of water. "She was a mile south of Loreto when a cop passed, did a U-turn, with lights flashing. He asked for license and registration."

Alberto drank down the water. "The cop held her until a Federale arrived. They put her in the car and drove her to jail where they handed her a warrant for her arrest."

"For what?"

"Possession of a stolen vehicle. She was driving Tina's truck."

MJ's eyes widened and froze. She had a terrible sense of foreboding.

"What's the matter?"

"Nothing. I'm just so worried. What happens next?"

"Unless there's something they haven't told me, she will post bond at the hearing."

The waitress approached with a notebook and pencil.

"You must be starving. Let's order," he said.

CHAPTER 29

"Father Leo, how wonderful to see you after all these years," Ramon said approaching the priest's desk.

"Let's sit over here," Father Leo said motioning him to a chair. "Carla is bringing coffee and bisquitchitos. They were your favorite when you were a boy."

Ramon smiled. "I haven't eaten Mexican cookies since I left Los Santos. It's amazing you remembered."

"I remember your nickname too. Rusty. Or don't you go by that name anymore."

"No one has called me Rusty since Oliver gave me the nickname in Los Santos."

"Then Ramon it is. Your letter arrived several months ago. I thought you'd be here sooner."

"I know. My father's estate took longer than I anticipated. I donated my mother's summer home to the Jesuit University in Seville. The paperwork was completed two weeks ago."

A young woman entered the room carrying a silver tea set and a plate of sugared cookies.

"Thank you Carla," said the priest.

"It was the right thing to do after my father died," Ramon said. "My sons are in boarding school and have no interest in the place." Ramon took a bisquitchito. "And my sister was killed a year ago in car accident on the Costa del Sur."

"I am very sorry for your loss. I had no idea."

Neither man spoke. Finally Father Leo said, "I remember that your father was a professor at the University of Seville. Oliver spoke very highly of him. They met when Oliver was on sabbatical in Spain."

"Yes, he was Chairman of the Theology Department. Actually Oliver met my mother first." Ramon spread his fingers across his knees. "When she was a research assistant in the Department of Rare Books." Ramon studied Father Leo during the pregnant silence that followed.

"Well, tell me the urgent matter you wish to discuss."

Ramon took a leather pouch from his briefcase and unzipped it. He handed a yellowed document to the priest. "Father, your signature is on the bottom of the page. Would you please explain the reason the document was issued and why I found it among my father's papers after he died?"

Father Leo's eyes went to the bottom of the page. His face flushed when he saw his signature and the Vatican seal. He looked down and folded his hands in prayer. Then he reread the paper and handed it back to Ramon.

"The document is an appeal to the Vatican for the annulment of the marriage in Portugal between your mother, Consuelo Diaz, and your father, Oliver Marshall. I forwarded the paper along with the original marriage certificate to the department in Rome that requested the information."

"Thank you, Father."

The priest was ashen, but composed. The heavy weight was now lifted from him. "I am very sorry Ramon. I hope you will forgive everyone involved who wanted to protect you and your family."

"You are the only person alive who could confirm what I already knew in my heart." Ramon returned the paper to his briefcase. He rubbed the signet ring on his hand, momentarily lost in thought. Then he said, "My decision to return to Mexico was twofold. I wanted you to confirm the document and I wanted to see Ricardo. However he was killed shortly after I arrived in Baja and we never met again."

Father Leo shook his head in disbelief. "His death was a shock to everybody. It was strange indeed."

"I met his wife briefly last week. She had no idea who I was."

Father Leo seemed to be deep in thought. Then his mood brightened. "I have an idea. Mama Estrada will be one-hundred years old tomorrow and Santa Rosario is celebrating the event. Please come as my guest."

"Mama Estrada is one-hundred? Amazing. We only met once when Oliver took me hiking to an abandoned gold mine above Santa Rosario. We stopped by her house for directions."

"It's a perfect opportunity for you to see her again. I'm sure you'll know other people as well."

"Will Alberto be there?"

"Of course. So will Ricardo's widow, along with most of Baja California."

MJ was way too tired for dinner but she knew Alberto was waiting for her. She made her way through the empty dining room past the expectant waiters and sat down with a groan. "Sorry I'm late. I fell asleep."

"No problem," he said.

"So bring me up to date on what's going on with Ginger."

"Good news. I called Tina. When she arrives tomorrow she can sign a release for the stolen vehicle. Then Ginger will be free on bond."

"Great. Is there bad news?"

"Yeah. The police are testing the truck for fingerprints and won't release it for a week."

"Why?"

"They won't say, but it's unusual." Alberto pulled a sheet of paper from his breast pocket. "The other bad news is the size of the bond, $100,000. It's very high. I have a list of bondsmen, but it will be tough to raise the money on short notice."

MJ stared out the window. A boat pulled up to the pier across the street and banged against the dock. A boy ran over and tied a rope around the mooring and waited for his tip.

"MJ, did you hear what I said?"

"Yes." I'm sorry. I'm tired and not really hungry."

"Listen. Why don't you go back to your room and order room service. I'll make some calls to bail bondsmen." He folded the list and stood up. "Get some rest, you look exhausted."

MJ headed through the lobby toward the guest rooms. When she reached the hall and walked past the glass-framed door leading to the courtyard, she stopped. Perhaps a walk along the Malecon would relax her. She opened the exit door and stepped onto the path toward the swimming pool. Two couples were playing water tag with a fluorescent ball. The pungent scent of evening jasmine wafted under her nose. Tall palm trees surrounded the property shrouded by red bougainvillea. She found a small opening onto the Malecon and looked around.

In the distance she saw the small whitecaps crashing against the breakwater. She headed in their direction. MJ needed to clear her head. The traffic thinned out and there was little activity on the dock. She heard the pinging of ropes against the mast of sailboats and the waves swishing as they hit the water's edge. She understood why Ginger loved the ocean. MJ wandered along the water for a while then turned toward the plaza. She walked for half an hour, deep in thought. She neared a building that looked familiar. It was the rectory. On the second floor, a light shined. She climbed the steps and rang the bell. The sound of footsteps came down the stairs.

Father Leo opened the door. He recognized MJ immediately. "MJ, how nice to see you. Come in."

———

The jailhouse in Loreto was an adobe structure originally built by the Jesuits to store winter vegetables. It was rarely occupied after the large prison was built ten miles south of town ten years earlier. The old jail was connected to the town office building by a long hall. The jail had a separate outside entrance that was only used when a night guard was on duty.

Father Leo knocked on the door, turned the handle, and stepped inside. Ezio, the night guard, was napping in a wooden swivel chair. His feet were on the desk, his head rested on layers of chin above his ample stomach. His head rolled around the makeshift pillow with every snore.

Father Leo coughed without creating so much as a stir. "Ezio," he shouted. Not a move. Father Leo reached for a newspaper near the edge of the desk and smacked it on the arm of the chair.

Ezio opened his eyes and stared until the priest came into focus. "Sorry Father, I must have dozed off."

The priest laughed. "I have a favor to ask you," Father Leo said. He walked toward the door and motioned Ezio to follow.

Ezio lifted his bulk off the chair and made his way to the door. "Yes, Father?"

Father Leo opened the door a crack and nodded. "I have a young woman outside who would like to have a few words with Ginger Hughes."

Ezio opened his mouth in disbelief.

"Five minutes would ease the mind of both women. You have my promise that no one will ever know."

"If anyone finds out I'll lose my job."

"I'll be standing guard behind the bushes. There is no one around. We came through the wooden gate in the alley. We never saw a soul."

Ginger tossed from side to side on the squeaky cot. She couldn't sleep. The room was chilly and damp; the floors were cold, uneven, and loosely-plastered adobe; the walls were impenetrable stone blocks. The guard left her a scratchy wool blanket and a pillow. She immediately tossed both of them into the corner. Any bug within a mile had already made a nest in her hair, and the blanket and pillow would only add to her problem. The faint glow of a light at the end of the hall cast a shadow on the wall into her cell. The barred window was a black hole.

Ginger wiped away the tears drying on her cheeks. She wondered how long it would be before she could leave, if Johnny was alive, what her parents would think if they knew, or if there really was a Mexican justice system for expatriates. The iron door at the end of the hall clanged and she heard footsteps coming down the hall. When they reached her cell a light flashed through the bars. She sat up but the bright light glared in her eyes. Ezio turned the key in the lock and opened the door.

"You have a visitor," he said.

MJ entered the drab cold cell and adjusted her eyes to the figure on the cot. "My God, Ginger, are you all right?"

Ginger began to sob. MJ walked across the cell, sat down, pulled Ginger to her, and held her tight. She stroked her hair and patted her on the back. "It's okay. Everything's going to be okay," MJ said with tears rolling down her cheeks.

"How did you get in here?"

"You can thank Father Leo," MJ said, as she appraised her best friend. Ginger's eyes were puffed, her cheeks were streaked with dirt. Her beautiful hair hung in clumps. She was shaking. MJ took off her sweater and put it around Ginger's shoulders. Then she took her hand. "Now tell me everything that happened."

Ginger's story was riveting. What an ordeal. She explained everything that happened after Johnny's call.

When she was finished, MJ said, "We have very little time. I'm in here without anyone's knowledge, but I have something very important to tell you. "Rick is alive." She pulled Ginger close and whispered. "It's a long story, but somebody tried to kill him."

Ginger was astonished. "Who?"

"We're still not sure. We suspect whoever was involved in the car chase also planned the robbery at the house. Until we figure it out, he's staying out of sight. He's not coming to Mama's party."

The women heard the key clanging at the end of the hall. It was time for MJ to leave. They stood and hugged each other. MJ took Ginger's hand. "I'll see you tomorrow. Alberto has everything under control. Don't worry."

MJ took a cab to the hotel and reentered the grounds the same way she left. The swimming pool was dark. She found the sliding door that led to her bedroom, unlocked it, and entered the room. The bedside lamp was lit. The maid turned down the blanket and left a chocolate on her pillow. A red message light flashed on the phone. It was probably from Alberto.

MJ opened her purse and took out the envelope Ginger gave her from Johnny. Ginger had hidden the letter under the bra of her ample breasts. It said, For MJ. She recognized his handwriting. Ginger was fortunate that the police didn't strip-search her. They needed a woman police officer on site to proceed. MJ tore the envelope open with a pencil, unfolded four pieces of paper, and flattened them. The first page showed a parcel of land that said "Privado." It was surrounded by government property. On the bottom left corner the words "Sta Maria" were written above a cross. The second page designated the name of the owner of the property, The Baja Land Corporation. A Mexico City law firm, Espinoza, Espinoza and Rodriguez, was the law firm to contact. A list of their satellite offices throughout Mexico was also included. The third page contained the names of all of the owners since the first quitclaim deed was issued to Carlos Estrada in 1957.

MJ read the names with interest. In 1962, the land was transferred to Maria Estrada. The Baja Land Corporation purchased the property in 1975. The forth page listed anyone who requested information about the deed. Maria Estrada made an inquiry in 1962. Espinoza, Espinoza and Rodriguez requested information from 1965 annually until the land was transferred to The Baja Land Corporation in 1975. There were no further inquiries until Ricardo Delgado requested information this year.

MJ was perplexed. This meant that after Carlos died, Mama inherited the land from her husband. The same land where he found the map and necklace. Mama sold it to the Baja Land Corporation twelve years later. Bingo. This was the information she needed. Whoever bought the property from Mama knew there was a possible tie between the land and the lost Mission of Santa Isabel. MJ had a gut feeling that if she could find out who owned The Baja Land Corporation she would know who tried to kill Rick. But how could she find out?

MJ kicked off her shoes. She lay on the bed, put her head on the pillow, and closed her eyes. After a few minutes of tossing possibilities around, she came up with two people who could help her: Angelique, who knew everyone and everything in lower Baja, and Alberto, who as an attorney could call the office of Espinoza, Espinoza and Rodriguez on MJ's behalf.

She walked to the mini bar, found some ice, and poured a glass of ginger ale. Angelique was the better choice. MJ wouldn't have to explain why she wanted the information. Besides, Alberto was busy trying to get Ginger out of jail. She looked at the clock. Was it too late to call Angelique?

CHAPTER 30

On the morning of the much-anticipated one-hundredth birthday of Mama Estrada, everything unfolded as preplanned thanks to her daughters. For more than a year the girls had spent countless hours preparing for the occasion.

Sophia was in charge of Mama, who was seated in her carved mesquite chair awaiting further instructions. Earlier Mama insisted the style of her hair remain basically the same. She would have a bun tied with a ribbon at the back of her head. Sophia convinced Mama to change the color of the ribbon to pink velvet, braided into a bun, and tied at the base with a bow. Mama fussed every inch of the way, especially about her manicure and pedicure. "A complete waste of money. And who is going to even see my feet?" Sophia rubbed aromatic lavender cream into Mama's fingers. "With this smell on my hands, I won't be able to make tortillas for a week," Mama complained.

Andrea organized the entertainment: a mariachi group from La Paz. They would perform with Marco Gomez, who would make a surprise appearance. The famous lyric tenor flew into Loreto earlier in the day. Marco was born in Santa Rosario and knew Mama. She was a good friend of his grandmother for many years.

Corinda was responsible for food preparation. Every cook in town worked on the menu for Mama's birthday.

The meal included: tortillas, empanadas, chile rellenos, tacos, tamales, mole, quesadillas, barbequed beef, and a roasted pig. Mama's best friend, Lupita, insisted on making the tres leches cakes with fresh strawberry sauce.

The catering truck arrived at seven in the morning, and by nine a.m., the tents, tables, and chairs were in place for two hundred and fifty guests. The effect was stunning. Each table was covered with rose eyelet fabric, pink napkins, and multicolored roses. The metal chairs were covered in a rose damask sleeves. Each table had an invitation, tied with a rose ribbon that held a photo of Mama taken by Lisa Lioness from Los Santos. The original painting was a gift from Lisa and hung in the dining room of the restaurant. The head table was set for twenty people and covered with a pink hand carved maypole in the center. Streamers cascaded to each end of the table, huge bouquets of pink roses anchored at the front.

The fiesta officially began at noon, but several people arrived earlier by shuttle from the airport in Loreto. MJ was among them. She found Mama in the living room and gave her a big hug, hastily greeted the family, and asked if she could use the short wave radio in the garage. Sophia handed her the key and told her where to find the light switch. "If you have any problems come back and get me," Sophia said as she headed toward the tent with a platter of cookies.

MJ had no trouble turning the lock or finding the lights. But locating the right radio frequency was another matter. She toyed with the dials for several minutes before everything connected and the phone began to ring in Santa Juanico. She hoped that Rick was nearby since he expected her call last night. But he wasn't. The phone rang twenty times before MJ hung up and decided to go next door, have a cup of coffee, and return in half an hour.

The dining room was lively with guests. Everyone was dressed in party attire, laughing and nibbling on sweets. MJ found the coffee and bit into a polvorone, a round cookie made with powdered sugar, ground almonds, cinnamon, and lard. She looked around for a familiar face. Almost immediately she noticed the tall lanky frame of Father Leo in a brown cassock. He was laughing with a broad shouldered man who was wearing a navy sport jacket and gray slacks and had his back to MJ. Father Leo waved and the man turned around. MJ was surprised to see the face of Ramon Diaz. He gave her a slight nod of acknowledgment and both men headed in her direction. Father Leo gave her a hug, stood back, and smiled. "You look lovely. Such a wonderful occasion, and a beautiful day."

"Thank you," she said. MJ wore a vintage capped-sleeve cerulean blue cocktail dress that she found in a box in her mother's closet destined for Goodwill after her father moved to Australia. She had never worn the dress until today.

"Let me introduce you to an old friend from Spain I have not seen for twenty years, Ramon Diaz," said the priest.

"Mucho gusto," said Ramon with a smile and a twinkle of knowledge in his eyes.

"Oh my," said Father Leo, "There's Señora Orozco. She called me yesterday and I haven't had an opportunity to get back to her. I've got to catch her while I can." The priest dashed off before MJ or Ramon had time to react.

MJ bit her lower lip. "I owe you an apology."

"No, I'm the one who should apologize. You had no idea who I was. It would have been better if Alberto had arranged an introduction."

MJ was befuddled. A quizzical look came over her face. "Alberto? I don't understand."

"Alberto knew the reason I came to Baja was to see Ricardo. He made arrangements for us to meet at his office in La Paz on Tuesday. Unfortunately Ricardo died the day before."

"I'm confused. Why didn't you contact Ricardo?"

"It's a long story that cannot be told over coffee and a cookie at Mama's one-hundredth birthday. I'd like to explain everything to you. Can we meet sometime soon?"

MJ glanced at the clock over the door. She didn't have much time to call Rick. "Perhaps in a few days," she said, opening her purse and taking out a small pen and notepad. "Here's my phone number in Los Santos." MJ handed him the paper. "Please leave a number where I can call you."

"It is very nice to see you again," Ramon said.

"Thank you. Now if you'll excuse me I've got a meeting and I'm late." MJ turned away and looked for the nearest exit to make a call to Rick.

Five minutes later she dialed the number. He answered on the first ring. "Thank God you're there," she began. MJ explained Ginger's predicament, brought Rick up to date on Johnny's information regarding the Baja Land Corporation, and told him that she'd just run into Ramon at Mama's birthday party.

"Be careful. You have no idea who's dangerous in that crowd. Just because Ramon sweet talked you doesn't mean he should get a free pass."

MJ opened the door and peeked outside. No one was in sight.

"ey, how are you getting out of there unnoticed?" Rick asked.

"I'll work something out with Ginger when she gets here. And I'll be at the meeting place before dark as planned."

By the time MJ finished the call and returned to the party, the mariachis were in full swing. Her head was swimming from the final details of their rendezvous. She made her way into the tent behind the crowd. MJ scanned the room looking for Alberto and Ginger. She knew they'd be late. The phone message from Alberto last night said he had found a bail bondsman, but the paperwork for Ginger's release would take all morning. "Go on to Mama's party and we'll meet you as soon as I can get Ginger through the bureaucratic process," Alberto had said. "And don't worry, everything's fine. I met with Ginger earlier and told her that she'd be released tomorrow morning."

MJ stopped dead in her tracks. Wait a minute. Why didn't Ginger tell her about Alberto's visit and her probable release last night when they were together? That was strange. MJ looked around for a familiar face to ask about the seating. She stopped again. She was perplexed. Why was Alberto everywhere she was? Alberto found her on the floor the evening she was mugged. MJ learned Alberto set up a meeting between Ramon Diaz and Rick.

She thought back to the night Alberto called and came by with an impromptu dinner. The same evening she mentioned she was going to San Jose the next day and leaving Monday to visit Mama in Santa Rosario. Did she also tell Alberto that she was meeting Ginger in Loreto? She couldn't remember.

No, this was too ridiculous. Alberto and Rick had been friends their whole lives. They met for lunch once a week in either La Paz or Los Santos. But how much did she really know about him? They traveled in different social circles mainly because Alberto had spent most of his time with his family since his wife died. The only thing MJ knew for certain was that he practiced law in La Paz. Rick did not retain Alberto for legal work. He used another firm, Parra & Prieto, the one his father retained decades ago to administer the trust for the Baja collection. Besides, Rick didn't believe in mixing business with friendship.

MJ had no idea who Alberto worked for in La Paz. She reached into the bottom of her purse, felt for Johnny's envelope, and looked for the nearest bathroom. One page of the letter mentioned the satellite offices of the Mexico City law firm. And they had an office located in La Paz.

Five minutes later MJ was sitting in Mama's bedroom prepared to make a phone call to the La Paz office of Lopez and Carey. She heard laughter outside the window. She walked across the room and closed the curtains. Then she locked the door and dialed.

"Bueno, Lopez and Carey," a man said.

"Ah yes, I'm calling from Tijuana on behalf of Villarino and Plaia," MJ said," muffling her voice with her hand over the mouthpiece. "We are sending a FEDEX package to your firm and would like to verify the address."

"Certainly. It is 2411 Fifth of Febrero, La Paz, BCS, Mexico 23000."

"And could you tell me the name of the attorney who handles The Baja Land Corporation account so we can send the package to his attention?"

"Just a moment, I will look it up."

MJ could hear another line ringing in the background and a drawer open and close. "Yes, his name is Alberto Cordero."

"Thank you." MJ hung up the phone. Her hand was shaking. She sat in disbelief trying to regain her composure. It just couldn't be. Alberto was Rick's oldest friend. His integrity was unquestioned.

"Someone you trust will betray you," Elisea said the day she and Ginger visited the curandera. She was right.

"Why Alberto, why? I trusted you, we all did."

CHAPTER 31

Two hundred miles from the scene of the birthday party, Wiley grunted and slapped his burro on the rump. "Get on up there now," he said navigating the animal over the side of a barren cliff. He looked at his watch. It was noon.

"Damn unfair that I'm sweltering in the heat while Don Hernando is enjoying Mama's party with a glass of wine and the best meal anyone has had in decades," he said to the burro.

Wiley frowned and swiped at a fly. But it couldn't be helped. The blueblood Don Hernando was joining him later. He'd have plenty of trouble making his way over the mountain in an overland truck. Worse yet, Wiley knew he'd never be able to navigate a burro. The real problem was Don Hernando would slow down his efforts to find the lost mission. Wiley would have to babysit him all the way to Santa Isabel.

Wiley wasn't happy about the way things turned out. He spent the last twenty years leafing through papers, books, journals, maps, and records, sorting the information, and laying the foundation for his search. The timing was damn unfortunate. Wiley was at the end of his quest when Don Hernando called him last week. A call out of the blue? From Don Hernando Cortez? Wiley knew immediately the man was up to something. Privileged people always acted the same way.

"Wiley. I have heard so much about you over many years. I think it's about time we met. I have a business proposal for you. I would like you to have lunch with me tomorrow at The Palm in Cabo San Jose. Are you available at two o'clock?"

What did Don Hernando really know about him? Probably a lot, he had spies everywhere. Wiley found the only suit he owned in the back of the closet, hung it on the line, and sprayed it with Febreeze to get rid of the smell of mothballs. Frieda ironed his white shirt. He squeezed his feet into a pair of cordovan loafers, covered the gap in the front of his pants with a belt, and headed down the mountain in the old Jeep, creating a layer of dust over his outfit before he even reached the main road.

When he walked to the door of The Palm Restaurant, Don Hernando greeted him with the confidence of a man who held all the winning cards. As soon as they finished ordering lunch, he immediately presented the facts. "A while back you requested and received information from the University of Seville," Don Hernando said. "The papers that were sent to you are private and belong to the Cortez family." Don Hernando's hands were folded on the tablecloth, a gold signet ring with a carat diamond sparkled on his chubby finger. "A young priest, unaware of the legal repercussions, mailed information that required our approval," he continued with assurance.

"Since that unfortunate incident, my family has done a thorough investigation of your background and credentials. We know that you have considerable knowledge of the history of Baja California and that you are finishing research on a book about the California missions, most notably, the lost Mission of Santa Isabel."

Don Hernando put his elbow on the table and rested his chin on his thumb and fingers. "We also know that you requested a map of Santa Isabel from the library in Seville and they sent you a copy. The library sent us the original," Don Hernando lied.

Wiley felt the palms of his hands begin to sweat as he tried to maintain his composure. He opened his mouth to speak, but Don Hernando brushed away his efforts with a swipe of a hand.

"The Cortez family knew of the existence of the map which had been stolen from my family centuries ago. We did not know there was another original in Spain. Until now." Don Hernando took a sip of his wine and peered into Wiley's eyes. "My family and I would like to thank you for all you have done." He smiled. "More importantly, we would like you to continue your search under our supervision. You will be generously rewarded when the treasure is found. And, of course, we will assume any costs you may incur and provide you with all of the equipment needed to carry the search to completion." Don Hernando went on to say again how grateful he was for Wiley's efforts on behalf of the Cortez family.

Wiley nodded in agreement. He realized that it was prudent to accept Don Hernando's offer of equipment and complete the job as soon as possible. There might even be a way to beat the Cortez family at their own game. Wiley regained his composure as he developed a plan. With a calm and confident voice he said, "From the research I've done, I know the general location of the mission. With enough supplies, food, water, and animals to last a week, I could begin the search immediately. However, the mission is located in a remote place surrounded by mountains. Our chances for success will be a lot better if fewer people are involved."

"Consider it done," Don Hernando said. "However I have one other request that is very important to my mother and me. I would like to join you in the search. The Cortez family has waited for several generations for this moment to arrive."

Wiley felt the muscles in his chest tighten. He reached for his wine and clutched the glass. "Of course." Did Wiley have any choice? Not really. But at least he didn't have to worry about Rick Delgado anymore.

CHAPTER 32

By the time MJ gained enough composure to rejoin the party, people were making their way to assigned tables under the tent. MJ had no idea where she was sitting. She asked a couple where to find the listing. The man motioned toward the bandstand. "The names and tables are posted on a billboard near the head table," he said.

MJ continued through the crowd to the billboard and found her name. She and Ginger were seated at a table on the far side of the room next to an exit. She searched for Alberto's name. He was seated in front of the head table. The distance between them was about as far away as she could hope for. She was delighted. He'd have a difficult time keeping tabs on them. MJ walked across the room to her table and gauged where Alberto would least be able to see Ginger and her. She placed her shawl on her seat and a napkin on the other. Plan one complete.

Somebody began to tap on a plate and others joined in. The noise decreased to a hush when Marco Gomez walked to the podium and blew into the microphone. "Ladies and gentlemen, will you please be seated."

MJ continued to stand, hoping to spot Ginger and Alberto. Three couples walked over to her table and sat down. MJ followed suit. They introduced themselves as Californians who met Mama ten years earlier on their first trip through Santa Rosario with the Vagabundos, a group of motorhome enthusiasts who toured Mexico.

After the crowd thinned out, the time had come for members of the head table to be seated. First Mama's three daughters and their husbands walked to the head table followed by Father Leo. Then Don Hernando entered with an elegantly dressed matron on his arm, no doubt Antigua Cortez. The stately woman had elegant carriage and wore a mauve dress with long white gloves. A diamond necklace and matching earrings lit up the room even from where MJ was seated.

The crowd hushed as they awaited the guest of honor, Mama. The drums rolled, the music played, and Marco Gomez began to sing Jurame. Mama Estrada, looking poised and reflective, entered the room on the arm of Ramon Diaz. Her dress, designed by her daughter Corinda, was made of rose taffeta with a lace bodice and long sleeves. She wore dark rose satin shoes with a matching ribbon in her hair and carried a bouquet of tea roses.

Mama, who never wore any jewelry except for her wedding band, looked elegant. Pearl earrings, a stunning pearl, and emerald necklace surrounded her face. Mama had a look of assurance knowing that she made the right choice and the jewelry would be noticed. MJ recognized the Aztec piece she had seen a week earlier. MJ looked at Don Hernando trying to gauge his expression. At first he seemed unaware. Then his eyes widened with surprise, their gaze never leaving Mama's necklace. He whispered into his mother's ear. The elegant old woman stretched her head to get a better look.

Ramon ushered Mama to the table and seated himself. Father Leo stood and gave the blessing. The mariachis began to play, everyone relaxed, and waiters wearing rose bandanas and plaid cummerbunds swooped into the room carrying trays of sizzling fajitas above their heads. Waitresses in floral embroidered blouses hovered nearby ready to ladle the fajitas, tortillas, chilies, and slices of pork onto the plates of hungry guests. A waiter circled and offered a selection of red or white wine.

MJ glanced at the empty chair next to her and wondered if she should make a plate of food for Ginger. She was about to ask the man next to her the time when she spotted Ginger and Alfredo. They were across the room reading the billboard. Ginger was always easy to find with flowing red hair. Today she was a knockout in a lime green dress that clung to her shapely body like a glove. So much for escaping unnoticed later. Alberto had a frown as he glanced across the room and realized how far away Ginger would be seated. He whispered something to her and walked to his seat facing the exit wall. Ginger made her way across the room as a contingent of eyes followed her every move. She had a huge smile and a relieved look on her face when she saw MJ. The girls exchanged hugs.

"Wow, you look fabulous. Let me introduce you to everybody," MJ said.

Ginger, always effusive, felt the need to apologize. "Sorry I'm late, but my suitcase never arrived. Luckily I found a consignment shop on the way." She reached over and took a taco. "I'm starving," she said biting into it while she navigated a tortilla chip through guacamole. "I haven't eaten anything since yesterday." Ginger continued stuffing more food into her mouth oblivious to the startled looks of the other guests.

The music quieted and Marco Gomez walked to the podium. "Ladies and gentlemen, may I have your attention please." Everyone stopped talking and looked up. "There are several people here who would like to say a few words about the wonderful woman we are honoring today, Mama Estrada. First, let's welcome her daughter Corinda." Mama's youngest child stepped up to the microphone.

MJ took a pad and pen from her purse, and began to write. She passed the paper to Ginger.

MJ: Where were you? Bond bail problems?

Ginger: Yeah. Going to LS tomorrow with A. Part of bond agreement. Posted by Don Hernando!

MJ: Careful. DH wants Johnny. We need to talk.

As each friend and relative paid tribute to Mama, MJ and Ginger passed notes back and forth until they developed a firm plan for their next move. They looked at each other and nodded in agreement. It was almost time to go. MJ took Ginger's hand and shook her head no when Ramon Diaz was introduced as the next speaker.

Ramon paused at the podium for a moment and surveyed the room. "It's a great honor to be here among all of Mama's friends and an even greater honor to speak about the beautiful woman who is seated here before us." The audience clapped in agreement. "I met Mama the summer I was twelve and visited Oliver Marshall and his son, Ricardo, in Los Santos. One weekend, Oliver decided to take me to visit the cave paintings in his old Jeep." Ramon stopped and placed his hand on Mama's shoulder. "And as everyone in this room knows, no adventure would be complete without a visit to Mama Estrada's home and a meal of her famous lobster tortillas." The audience stood and clapped.

MJ nodded to Ginger and they stood to make their escape. Only one guest at the table looked in their direction. Ginger mimicked powdering her nose. "Be right back," she whispered.

Once they were outside, MJ turned and gave Ginger a hug. "Listen to me carefully. Alberto has been spying on me since the night I was mugged and he found me on the floor. I've told him everything he knows: my trips to La Paz and Cabo San Jose, my visit to Mama. I even asked him to meet me in Loreto. But he has no idea that Rick is alive." MJ glanced around. "He works for Don Hernando. And they are up to something."

"How do you know?"

"Long story. For starters, using Don Hernando for the bail bond. They want to keep you under wraps. And they want Johnny because he knows too much."

"Are you sure?"

"Just trust me on this. And find a reason why you can't go back to Los Santos with Alberto tomorrow." MJ motioned toward the guest entrance. "You go back inside and create a diversion. I'm going to meet Rick."

CHAPTER 33

MJ was an hour late for their rendezvous. When she didn't appear on schedule, Rick went back down the dirt road looking for her. MJ was ten miles below their original meeting place. He signaled for her to follow him until he reached the edge of a cliff and pointed to an area behind outcroppings where she should park. Rick knew how exhausted she was as he watched her maneuver the truck. He waited for her to open the door. She stepped out and didn't move. He walked over and waited. She took a deep breath, reached into the back seat for her backpack and boots, and handed them to him.

Rick squeezed her shoulder. "I have sleeping bags and all our equipment on the horses. We have plenty of food. I even stashed some chocolate and a couple of cookies. Do you want a piece? You look beat."

"I'm so tired," MJ said. Everything unraveled after we spoke on the phone." She rubbed her eyes. "You're in for quite a shock when I tell you everything that's happened since we spoke earlier."

Rick checked the area where they parked the trucks to be sure they were completely hidden. Then he motioned to the bushes across the road. "The animals and supplies are over there."

MJ walked over and stood next to her horse hoping she had enough energy to get on. Rick, sensing her dilemma, guided her onto the saddle and adjusted the stirrups. Each horse pulled a burro carrying enough gear and food to last a week. Rick made all the arrangements for the transfer when he arrived earlier in the day. He knew the local vaqueros. They were happy to help him. His loyalty with these contacts ran deep.

"Okay, let's go. We have two hours before sunset."

High on a mesa in the Sierra de Camalli Mountains a yellow light glowed through a tent. Inside, MJ and Rick sat on a blanket on the floor. MJ held a flashlight and listened intently as Rick explained how he deciphered the map. Her purple fleece was zipped to her neck but some fabric stuck out of the nylon windbreaker under her chin. The fleece covered her wrists and provided an air lock over her gloves. Wind blew off the Sierras through the cardon forest, dropped to the mesa, and swooped around their feet. She could hear the gentle flapping of the tent and coyotes howling in the distance, their frenzy heightened by a full moon.

"The key to solving the puzzle is the Mayan compass on the Piedra Iman," Rick said. He reached for a stone and held it near the map.

"Look here," he pointed. "The compass has the cardinal directions, N,S,E,W. Each one has a small symbol next to it of a different design and color. Most compasses only have four points, but Padre Tomas added the ordinal directions, NE, SE, SW, and NW. They each have their own design and color, leaving a total of eight directions."

Rick pointed to north on the map. Next to the N was a green hand. He then located the same direction and color on the Piedra Iman. "Each direction has its own design and a total of six colors are used. They are the three primary colors of blue, yellow, and red, as well as green, gold, and silver."

"They're difficult to see in this light," MJ said.

"I know. I brought a magnifying glass we can use tomorrow when this information is critical."

"The Mayan people used the four basic colors of blue, green, red, and yellow to signify important events. However, sometimes they changed the normal color of a symbol to convey a different meaning. For example, the color blue signifies the sky and the symbol is a cloud. If the cloud is not blue, let's say it's gold, it could mean wealth or money beneath the cloud."

"Here," he said, pointing to the gold cloud over the mission Santa Isabel.

"It's gold," MJ said.

"Exactly. Padre Tomas was sending a different message. The color green relates to the environment and this is where things get tricky." Rick shined the flashlight evenly over the map. "The Maya revered many animals and plants. If the symbol is yellow instead of green, it signifies a harvest celebration during the month they plant corn. Look here at the yellow foot next to the SW ordinal." Rick pointed to the foot.

"The cieba, a cottonwood tree, is the symbol of power in nature and is usually green. But sometimes it can be red and would signify fire. The Maya burned cottonwood trees in censers during the rainy season. The spiritual ceremonies involved sacrificial animals."

Rick placed the Piedra Iman and the map on the blanket, and motioned for MJ to come closer. He put his arm around her shoulder. "I didn't mean to fill your head with symbols tonight," he said. "I just wanted to give you an overview of what I've learned."

MJ put her head on his lap. "I'm sorry that I'm so distracted," she said. "I left Ginger without telling her very much. She has no idea what's going on." MJ closed her eyes. "Alberto is bringing her back to Los Santos tomorrow morning. I warned her to be careful."

Rick leaned back using his arms to hold up his weight. "You had a rough day. We both did." He leaned over and kissed her on the forehead. "Tomorrow will be longer but if my map is accurate we'll be at the mountain near Santa Isabel by early afternoon." Rick looked down at MJ. Her eyes fluttered. She was breathing evenly, her mouth slightly open. She was exhausted and sound asleep. Not a surprise considering the day.

He reflected on what MJ told him earlier about Alberto. At first he was mystified, then he felt betrayed. It just didn't make sense. How long had Alberto been setting him up? And why? Don Hernando and Alberto had nothing in common except the fact they were both Mexican. Maybe that was enough. But what could Alberto possibly have to gain?

CHAPTER 34

While MJ was sound asleep in the mountains, Ginger was holed up in her motel room. Guests on both sides of her were still celebrating Mama's birthday party. A television blared. Guns went off, cannons were fired, and a stampede of horses shook the walls. Finally the gravelly voice of John Wayne echoed in her room. A cowboy movie, in Spanish? She walked to the bathroom, rolled some tissue, and stuffed it into her ears. Not great, but better. Ginger ignored the phone even though it rang several times. She knew it was Alberto. He banged on the door and hour ago yelling her name and MJ's. A Do Not Disturb sign was on the door. She pretended she was asleep.

Alberto slammed the receiver and pounded his fist on the table. "I've been calling them for hours. Why don't they answer? I haven't seen MJ since Mama's party. I don't like it and I certainly don't trust Ginger." He turned toward Don Hernando. "You sat facing them, did you notice when MJ and Ginger left?"

Don Hernando shook his head no. He looked totally nonplussed as he leafed through a Spanish newspaper. "To tell you the truth, I was trying to figure out why Ramon Diaz, who hadn't been in Mexico in twenty years, was sitting at the head table and giving a speech about Mama." He picked a piece of lint off his pants and brushed them down with his hands.

"MJ's car isn't in the parking lot," Alberto said. "Where could she be?"

"Why are you so concerned?" Her car is gone? So what? Maybe she went to visit somebody in town. Ginger is the one we should worry about. She can lead us to Johnny tomorrow. The question is what to do with her after that." Don Hernando brushed his pants with his hands one last time and stood up. "I'm going back to my room. Mother is expecting me to stop by and say goodnight, and we have to be up early. I'll see you in the lobby at six."

An hour later Alberto was still wide-awake in his bed, too angry to sleep. Don Hernando was down the hall and most likely sound asleep. The guy was as cold as ice. His mother, Antigua, was across the hall in a suite. Hardly a suite, her room was equipped with a small refrigerator, a wet bar, and a pull out sofa. Alberto couldn't understand how Don Hernando could be so casual about MJ, or Ginger for that matter. If one woman was trouble, the two of them were an explosion waiting to happen.

Alberto closed his eyes and tried to relax. Childhood memories flashed before him like short vignettes in a movie. He was ten, sitting in the back yard under a coconut palm tree. Their dog Chica was licking her new puppies under the fender of an abandoned car near the fence. At his feet was a matchbox dump truck, a holiday gift from Rick who found ten cars and trucks under the tree on Christmas morning.

"Take any one you want," Rick said. "You are my best friend."

Alberto was lucky to have Rick for a friend. Every summer they went camping for a week with the Boy Scouts. Although nothing was ever said, Alberto knew that Oliver paid for his trip to camp. Alberto's dad was a gardener, his mom cleaned houses for rich people, and he had four brothers. No way could his parents afford to send him to camp. Besides, none of his other brothers went. No matter what Alberto did, Rick did it better. Whether it was surfing, getting into a good college, flirting with girls, playing baseball, getting a summer job, everything was easier for Rick. Life just wasn't fair. That was until Don Hernando approached his law firm six months ago. Alberto knew the Cortez family had retained Lopez & Carey to handle their family land holdings in Baja California. One day six months ago Don Hernando made a special request from the firm. He wanted Alberto Cordero to handle all the legal work for his family properties. The partners were surprised but not about to question anything Don Hernando wanted.

Alberto had to hand it to Don Hernando. He was subtle, smooth, polite, and charming. Come in to my parlor said the spider to the fly. Alberto was lured into a web of moral compromise before he understood what was going on. From the very beginning Don Hernando had special requirements. The first was a private weekly meeting weekly between the two of them. Don Hernando always arrived with a list of questions and seemed very interested in what Alberto had to say. One day, after their usual meeting, Don Hernando made a suggestion.

"From now on let's meet at La Perla Hotel. They have a private dining room where we can discuss matters over lunch in a more casual setting."

Initially everything was strictly professional. Then Don Hernando started to veer off the subject, asking innocuous questions. "Aren't you friends with Rick Delgado? I knew his father Oliver Marshall. He did a lot for Baja California. He was quite a man."

And so it went. You and Rick are neighbors? Didn't you buy your land from him? Do you see him often? A few months later the owners of the firm, Miguel Lopez and Luis Carey approached Alberto. They offered him the position of junior partner, which included a thirty percent increase in salary and a corner office. There was a condition: his main responsibility would be to handle the Cortez family properties. He no longer would have to file briefs for other clients. In essence, Don Hernando made the firm an offer they couldn't refuse. If Alberto didn't like it, his only other option was to quit. He had no choice in the matter. One evening Alberto received an unexpected call from Don Hernando.

"Meet me at La Perla in an hour. It's urgent."

When Alberto arrived, a grim-faced Don Hernando greeted him. " Please sit down. Would you like a glass of port?" Alberto shook his head no. He had never seen Don Hernando ruffled and couldn't fathom what could unnerve him. "I need your help regarding a complication with Rick Delgado. He may have discovered information about landholdings that belong to the Cortez family. Information I don't want him to pursue. What I'm about to share with you is very confidential."

Did Don Hernando ask him to do something illegal? Not really. Or was it? Alberto knew only one thing for sure. He was caught in a web of deceit and there was no way out.

———————

Ginger pulled back the curtain of her bedroom window and looked outside. A full moon peeked through the clouds, casting light across the cars in the parking lot and the road beyond. The family in the bedroom next door crashed an hour ago. Alberto had not knocked on her door or called her for several hours. She lifted the window with the edge of the curtains, gradually allowing the moonlight to filter into her room. It was very quiet outside. She got on her knees and pushed the window up as far as it would go. Cool damp air washed over her face and neck. She stuck her head out and looked around. Nothing. Not a peep except the drone of the air conditioner from the hotel kitchen around the corner.

Ginger reached for the tied sheets and secured them with the leg of the bureau. She threw the other end over the side of the window and said a prayer that they would hold as she shimmied down the edge of the building. It was slow going. Her legs scraped against the thorny bougainvillea and it hurt like hell. But she dared not scream. She touched the ground and groaned with relief. She was fortunate that the curtains were closed in the room directly below her. Every other room on the side of the building was dark. The backpack she wore had a change of clothing, a flashlight, a sweater, and the windbreaker that she had carried from San Javier. She left her beautiful new dress and shoes under the bed along with any other non-essential items.

Ginger headed for the parking lot. She didn't have a car, but she had learned how to hotwire one in college. Long story. She scanned the lot. A Ford truck from the late '90s, the easiest type to hotwire was nearby. The solenoid was mounted on the inner fender well, instead of the starter. A peek through the window at the dashboard told her it was not armed. Perfect. Plan one complete.

CHAPTER 35

The sun glowed on the horizon, docile, pensive, and ready to begin another day.

At six o'clock, Don Hernando and Alberto drank a quick cup of coffee, got in a Hummer, and drove out of a Santa Rosario. They used Wiley's makeshift map to check their route and headed north toward the mountains. The road quickly became steep, windy, and their speed dropped to twenty miles an hour. Neither man spoke. By late morning the sun radiating off the dashboard was oppressive. Alberto pulled the visor down and flipped up the air. He gripped the steering wheel of the Hummer, plowing through everything in his path. The fenders, hood, and roof were covered with twigs and leaves; the engine roared in anger.

The drop over the edge of the cliff was two hundred feet to the bottom. The right fender scraped against the shale and loose stones cracked against the hood. Fragments of stone hit the windows and doors. The big truck could barely maneuver the road. Alberto swore under his breath and clutched the wheel ready to gun the engine if a tire slipped. Don Hernando didn't utter a sound and barely moved. If Alberto didn't see the shadow of the man's body, he wouldn't know he had a passenger on board. The guy had nerves of steel. Don Hernando had the map on his lap. If he had any guidelines or advice on what to do, he kept it to himself. They rounded another corner but this time the road ahead of him disappeared. All Alberto saw was horizon over the hood. He eased his way toward the precipice.

Ten feet from the end, the road took a sharp right and edged down at a sharp grade for another twenty feet. Then it disappeared again. Alberto wondered if he was driving the first vehicle to come down the trail. How long it had been since any man or animal had trespassed over this path? "Are you sure we're on the right road?"

"Yes," Don Hernando said.

Alberto looked ahead and saw trouble. The passenger side of the road was covered with outcroppings. "Do you see the bushes in front of us hanging from the ledge above? I think the hood will clear, but I'm not sure about the roof." Alberto nodded in the direction of the problem, not daring to take his hands off the road.

"I'll put the window down on my side and pull the branches into the truck," Don Hernando said. "As they pass through the cab they'll snap free when they go past the back windows." Don Hernando looked behind him. "Go slow. I'm getting into the back. I'll guide them out."

Alberto held the wheel tightly and gritted his teeth. He eased the Hummer into the thicket. The front right tire ground against the shale, spun, jerked, and pushed forward. Long branches covered most of the windshield, snapping against the hood, cracking and falling off the front. Some of them bent a full ninety degrees before they finally slammed into the open window and flew toward Alberto's face and arms. Every muscle in his body was taut, desperately holding on to the wheel. His head moved around the branches trying to find an open spot to see where he was going.

The Hummer filled with more and more branches that clung to each other, forming a massive leafy cluster inside. Alberto stopped and put the truck into low gear. Then he pushed down the pedal and inched the truck forward. He was afraid that too much gas would send the vehicle out of control after the branches snapped free. "There are no more branches coming in," Alberto said. "Stay down back there. Eventually they'll pass out of the back window. The truck weighs three tons and should be able to handle it."

"I hope so," Don Hernando said. "I can't begin to push them out. They're everywhere." Don Hernando crawled over to the area behind Alberto and faced the back window. He was unaware of what was happening until he heard a crack and the frame around the rear window bent outward and the roof buckled. The window shattered within seconds and the limbs, suddenly free, whooshed out of the new opening in a flash. Don Hernando screamed, "Stop, stop!"

The force of the branches flying out caused the truck to skid pushing the left rear wheel of the truck toward the edge of the cliff. The loose rock underneath began to crumble. Alberto knew what was happening. So did Don Hernando who dived to the right side of the Hummer trying to move his weight from the danger zone. Alberto drove the truck directly into the cliff gouging the shale and smashing the right front fender and bumper. Then he straightened the vehicle. He felt the stability of four wheels back on the road, drove for ten feet, and stopped.

The sun was directly in front of the Hummer. It shined on Alberto's face and threw white streaks of light across the windshield. He looked out the window. The valley below was serene, empty, and desolate. Nothing moved. There was no sound except the thumping of his heart and the heavy breathing of Don Hernando.

He almost died. If the truck had gone over the cliff no one would find them smashed against bottom of the mountain for months, maybe years. Don Hernando in his life was a curse.

———

Mama woke up early, still excited from the gala affair. The clock told her it was not yet seven and there wasn't a reason why she should get out of bed. The girls did everything. Mama only had to walk through the kitchen and dining room daily, check the silverware and china for cleanliness, the supply of flour, sugar, and lard for the tortillas, and ask about the price of whatever fish was running in the bay. She was truly amazed how expensive fish had become. And lobster, the price was sky-high. Thank goodness she was the first person to recognize its value as a restaurant item. Fishermen, out of respect, always came to Mama first with their lobster catch. She bought every one. Any leftover lobster was cooked, picked clean, and frozen for later use.

Mama was more keyed up this morning than she was yesterday. My goodness she was up late last night. She, Father Leo, and Ramon talked and laughed till the wee hours of the morning. They were having breakfast together at eight. Then Father Leo had to leave for a wedding rehearsal in Loreto. Ramon thought he might take a hike up the trail that he and Oliver took so many years ago.

Mama was happy that Ramon seemed to have made peace with his father's past. She knew that Oliver was Ramon's father. That he met and married a woman in Seville, returned to Mexico, fell in love with Lupita Delgado, and never returned to Spain. Ramon's family was well connected to the papacy. Once Father Leo signed the necessary papers, the marriage was annulled. Mama could still see Ramon when he was a boy, and Oliver, so stoic and composed, beaming about his friend's son from Seville. She should have seen the signs then but she never suspected until Carlos told her. As Mama lay in bed trying to put her thoughts together, she heard a knock at the door. Corinda poked her head inside. "Are you awake?"

"Of course. What is so urgent that you appear at my door before eight in the morning?"

"Someone is here to see you," Corinda said. "You remember Ginger, MJ's friend? She said it was urgent. Ramon and Father Leo are with her."

Mama sat up slowly, located her cane and put her feet on the floor. "Give me five minutes and have some good strong coffee. Do we have any leftover cake?"

Corinda smiled. "And if we do?"

"Put some on the table for our guests. We might as well finish it off before the rest of our family does."

"Okay Mama. I'll tell them you'll be out soon."

Ginger, Ramon, and Father Leo were talking when Corinda made her way back to the waiting room of the restaurant. Ginger was shaking her head no. A braid hung down her back and wisps of hair were flying around her forehead. When she saw Corinda, she stopped her conversation and looked up.

"Mama will be right out," Corinda said. "Take a seat at a dining room table while I make coffee. Would anyone like bacon and eggs?"

"No, thank you," was said all around. Corinda headed for the kitchen.

"Ginger, you need to calm down," Father Leo said, motioning her to a table. "When you tell Mama what you know she will need time to process what you are saying. You do not want to frighten her. What you want is her wisdom and her help."

They sat in a booth and Father Leo gave Ginger a moment to gather her thoughts. "Mama may ask you questions," he continued. "Tell her everything you know. When you are finished, I will share with her anything I can say that is not privileged information."

Corinda arrived with the coffee and cake and placed the tray on the table. "The choice of what we are eating was Mama's idea," she said. The she turned and left.

Ramon poured a cup of coffee and handed it to Ginger. "Try to think positive," he said. "Mama is a grand old dame and she has more knowledge and information than the rest of us. What she doesn't know she can find out. Mama knows everyone in Mexico. She's the person who can make things happen."

CHAPTER 36

Rick knew about dynamite. He was introduced to the explosive as a teenager working alongside Wiley and his father. They blasted their way into to abandoned mines all over southern Baja: Old sites that were covered with debris, fallen shafts, rotted framework, and in some cases, earlier blasting attempts. ANFO, a more powerful plastic explosive, had been used since the fifties but it was only available to the military. Dynamite, on the other hand, could be purchased with a special permit from the government. Rick was fortunate that his father stockpiled the material years earlier, before Mexico decided to regulate its access more carefully. His home in Santa Juanica had dynamite hidden away in metal boxes in the garage. Rick didn't mention the fact to MJ who would insist he get rid of the stuff.

Several years ago, Rick and Wiley used explosives to unearth one of the few a gold locations in Baja. Gold was discovered near San Andraś Ranch in 1893 and a mining camp was established. By 1904, seventy-five thousand dollars worth of gold had been extracted. The men knew from books in Oliver's collection, and from local legend, that there were rich placers in the area. They blasted around other sites, but their efforts went unrewarded.

Rick surveyed the mountain then set as many charges as possible in the natural handholds of the scattered rocks. The charges were no further than five feet apart over unequal distances. Since he didn't know the exact location of the mission, it was prudent to lay the charges carefully and with less force. By using smaller sticks of dynamite set further apart, he could detonate the area and the mountain wouldn't collapse. He studied the hill looking for any signs of fallen rocks. Anything buried underneath could be destroyed by a heavy charge. He saw nothing suspicious, at least not to his untrained eye. His father would recognize anything unusual from an indentation, or a group of equal size rocks of a different color, or strata located too low on the hillside to have formed naturally. Wiley had an even better eye. He could recognize anything out of the ordinary with one scan of his binoculars.

From the endless hours Rick spent solving the map in Santa Juanica, he knew that Padre Tomas was a clever man. Everything he did had a purpose. One clue led to another, and then another. Rick unrolled the map and focused on the small designs. Previously, he matched the designs with Milagros, interpreted them, checked the color for specific meaning, compared them to the Piedra Iman, and referenced everything against the notations in Padre Tomas' small leather journal. Several times the directions went full circle. If Rick was missing one piece of the puzzle, everything would fall apart and the map would lead nowhere. The interpretation of Milagros depended on their color and what was nearby. A green fence next to a white cloud meant one thing, a green fence next to a blue cloud, another. Rick was secure that he deciphered the information correctly and that this was the right mountain. But he had no idea how deep the mission was hidden under the landslide. Anything that was buried inside had to be found with as little damage as possible.

MJ watched her husband and the methodical way he placed chargers into the rocks. Taut and anxious, MJ was totally uncomfortable with situations she couldn't understand or anticipate. She needed facts whenever possible. Laying dynamite on the side of a mountain was completely out of her learning curve.

"Hon, how many feet did I say the charge should be from the large boulder over here?" Rick asked.

MJ looked at his notes in the red folder. The distances were guesswork and based on Rick's interpretation of the designs. "Fifty feet. Then you head N/NW for twenty feet and place as many charges as you think you need there. After that, you come back and we start praying."

"Have a little faith, will you?" Rick placed the last two sticks of dynamite and pulled the lead lines over to the main detonator several feet away. "You head back to our meeting place now. I'm almost finished." He checked the wiring on the blast caps. The delay mechanisms were set to detonate from right to the left. He walked toward the end of the lead line and timer. It was located on a primer charge a thousand feet from where MJ was waiting. He set the timer for ten minutes and headed toward his wife. He allowed plenty of time and would be there in less than five minutes.

Rick felt a sudden gust of wind that started at his ankles, continued up his body, across his chest, and blew the hat off his head. He looked around. There wasn't a cloud in the sky but it was beastly hot. The hat twirled up in the air and landed against a chamisa bush twenty feet away. Damn. His dad gave him that hat on his twenty-first birthday. He still remembered the day.

"Now you won't have to borrow mine anymore," Oliver said as he handed Rick the soft straw sombrero woven in Guadalajara. There was a photo of them grinning like Cheshire cats hanging on the wall in his study. Rick wanted the hat. He had plenty of time and headed toward the bush. He snatched the sombrero and secured it firmly on his head. As he turned around to head back he heard MJ shouting. She was pointing to the mesa in the distance where a large funnel, poised few hundred feet above them, began to ease down the side of the hill like a slow motion film.

The budding tornado grew more ominous as it neared the valley. A second gust of wind knocked him off his feet. Rick knew that when the funnel reached the bottom of the mesa it would be a devastating tornado. Rick got up, kept his head down, and ran directly into the path of the funnel. He was at MJ's side in less than a minute. "We've got to get the animals. Come on."

By the time they reached the horses they were hurling themselves against the tree in their effort to get loose. Rick reached into the side pocket of his saddle and grabbed a knife.

"I'll cut them loose. Take your backpack and the map and papers. Throw my bag over here." Rick pointed to the cliff behind her that he could barely see. "Wait for me under that ledge over there. I'm right behind you." He could see how worried MJ was from the look in her eyes.

"You have a whistle in your pack. Use it to call me when you get there." MJ hesitated.

"Go now, dammit."

CHAPTER 37

Wiley was smoking a pipe under a cholla bush with a gun on his lap and a thermos of water at his side. He wore a long sleeve shirt, a broad brim hat heavily stained at the rim, high boots, and chaps. They were damn hot but necessary. Wiley took special care before he parked his backside on the dirt under a tree. Any hole in the ground was suspect. It could be a rabbit, a mole, or a snake. Rattlesnakes loved the coolness and protection of their den under a cactus, the edge of a boulder, or the area around a gnarled dead tree.

Wiley wasn't taking any chances. He raised his head and looked around. The burros were chewing on the dead grass under a mesquite tree. The gear, which he took off the animals earlier, was in a shaded place, but they still had their saddles on. The animals got ornery when you came too close to their underside. He sniggered. Most people would too, he guessed.

Wiley's face was rough, wavy, and deeply crevassed from a lifetime of hanging around mines with a compass, shovel, and pick, looking at rock strata and trying to determine its composition and age. His crotchety temperament had etched a permanent frown line at the bridge of his nose so he always looked slightly annoyed. He took a deep breath of fresh, hot, dry mountain air and contemplated his choices over next twenty-four hours. He had a problem: Don Hernando. And he didn't like any of the options. He laid his head against the base of the tree. In the distance he listened to the wheeze of an engine shifting gears, then silence. After a few seconds the engine shifted again.

He sat up, reached over to his backpack, took out binoculars, and focused them on the mesa. A horizontal line of heat and dust ran back and forth along the horizon like a ribbon. He moved his location to the lower level. A Hummer was slowly coming down a steep incline. He was amazed the large vehicle had maneuvered the pass. Don Hernando was a damn good driver. He had hoped the truck would go over the cliff. Indeed, he expected it would happen and take care of his problem.

A glance at his watch said it was quarter past twelve. Before another twenty minutes passed he had to make a decision. He stood up, dusted off his pants, found the small flask in a pouch under his shirt, and took a swig of tequila. The liquor would clear his head. He lumbered toward the burro, lifted the Savage rifle from its holster, and checked the ammunition. It was loaded. The rifle had an accuracy range of almost a half a mile. He was a good shooter, but he had to hit his target the first time. The whole idea unnerved him.

Wiley had not killed anybody before, having convinced himself that Oliver's death was an accident. He had told the story so many times to so many people that he believed it himself. The accident happened more than eight years ago on a rock hounding expedition to an old mine. That particular day, he and Oliver were meeting on the outskirts of Santa Rosario. Oliver made a quick stop at Mama's house to pick up a map of their destination. Mama had told him about a mine located on property that

Carlos visited. She thought he should investigate and find out if the mine still existed. None of her boys cared a wit about mining and had never been to the site.

Wiley and Oliver arrived on a beautiful sunny day. The lime cast mountain reflected spring growth, birds swept in and out of cacti searching for food, and even a stray rabbit peeked out of its den. Unfortunately, the mine had been abandoned long ago and was strewn with litter and decaying wood. The men walked over to the entrance to get a closer look. The structure was precarious and dangerous. The frame around the shaft had gaps of missing wood and the walls didn't have rungs for the men to hold going down. They discussed their options. Both men were knowledgeable about the potential problems of old mine shafts, but they decided they could handle it. Oliver volunteered to go first. He walked to the nearest place to tie a secure rope, a cirio cactus, and lowered himself into the shaft. He wore a backpack and headlamp and carried a pick and hammer on his belt. They had agreed that Wiley would take the second shift if there was anything worth going back for.

Oliver stayed in the mine for a long time. After a while, Wiley called down to be sure everything was all right. Oliver said that everything was going great. He chuckled that Carlos had held out on him. Thirty minutes later Oliver gave Wiley a shout that he was coming up. Oliver emerged from the shaft pretty grubby. His shirt was torn, his face black with soot, and he had a gash on his arm. When he took off his backpack it hit the ground with a plop. Wiley knew there had to be something heavy inside.

"What's in the backpack?" Wiley asked.

Oliver opened the bag and dumped out several large quartz rocks. He picked one up and handed it to Wiley. "I couldn't believe it. And they are all pretty big in size." He pointed to a yellow oval stone. "Each rock has at least one nugget inside."

The rock Wiley was holding had a piece of gold the size of his thumb. His jaw dropped. "Wowee. We finally struck pay dirt."

"Not really. By rights, this gold isn't ours. Everything on this property belongs to the Estrada family."

"Now wait a minute. It's my turn to go down and see what else is there."

Oliver put his hand on Wiley's shoulder. "No. I think we should come back another day."

Wiley looked grim. This was a switch for Oliver. He never felt this way about the other mines they found. If there was silver or any other metal, the men immediately went to the town clerk's office, checked the ownership, and if the land was unclaimed or had back taxes, the men paid the taxes and made a claim on the property. Over the years they had yet to find anything that paid off. But why should they even worry about filing a claim this time? They could dig some nuggets out of the mine, take them to a town near La Paz, and sell them. No one would be the wiser. Wiley was tired of schlepping around the countryside with Oliver in the damn heat risking broken bones and asthma. Shouldn't they be rewarded?

"Did you leave a marker where you found the quartz?" Wiley asked.

"I didn't expect to find anything. Never put pins in my rucksack."

Wiley reached into his pocket, pulled some out, and handed them to Oliver. "You'd better go back and mark the spot. It'll make things easier when we come back."

Oliver frowned. "I suppose you're right." He stuck the pins in his pocket and descended into the shaft. Wiley waited under a honey mesquite tree, snapped off a pod, and chewed it. He was getting hungry and mesquite pods were resource rich in sugar and protein. He listened to the ping, ping of the hammer hitting the rock. The pounding stopped and Oliver shouted, "I'm coming up."

By then Wiley had made up his mind. He took the knife from his belt holder and walked over to the cholla. Without any hesitation he cut the rope.

When people of Los Santos heard the news about Oliver's death, they were shocked and saddened. According to the story, Oliver was down in the mine when his rope gave way. Wiley, who was on the expedition with him, was sick with grief and went into mourning for a full year. Everybody understood. The men were best friends.

When Wiley finally had enough courage to return to the mine the following year, he found the pins that Oliver had placed but nothing else. He searched the walls for several months looking for the gold. Every time, he'd emerge from the mine with his back about break, covered in dust and sweat. But he never found another piece of quartz. His luck had run out.

That was until now. Wiley wasn't going to allow anyone to take what was rightfully his this time. He walked back to the tree and found his binoculars. In the distance the Hummer was coming toward the final slope. He placed his eye in the sight and moved the rifle toward the truck. The truck had turned another corner and the driver was on the far side of the vehicle. He waited for the truck to appear again and aimed the rifle. The man's shoulder was visible just above the frame of the window. He'd aim as low as possible for the body. The picture was getting hazy. Why? He moved his eye above the scope and saw a huge funnel cloud coming down the mesa directly at him. He'd only have one shot and he'd better hurry. The truck had slowed down and was barely moving, a lucky break. He pulled the trigger and fired. The driver jerked and threw his hands toward his face, letting go of the wheel. The hummer continued to roll down the slope until the area in front of him became a cloud of dust. Wiley could see nothing.

The tornado moved toward Wiley with fury. He lowered his head and pushed his way toward his animals. They were secured at the base of the mesa where he had stopped earlier. Once the tornado landed on the bottom it would dissipate and not be much of a problem as long as he wasn't directly in its path. The animals were digging their hooves into the dirt and whinnying. They had to get under cover fast.

The explosion that came from the other side of the mountain took him by surprise. He recognized the sound of dynamite immediately. Only one person had access to dynamite and the ability to use it. But as far as he knew, Rick Delgado was dead. If not, Santa Isabel was closer than he thought.

CHAPTER 38

MJ and Rick made it through the storm unscathed except for a flying branch that clipped the side of Rick's chin that left a small gash and a large bruise. An hour later they had rounded up and harnessed the animals, found their gear, and checked for missing items. They couldn't find a backpack stuffed with food and two blankets. Rick thought they should head for the mountain to see how successful the explosion was. Any missing baggage could wait until later. The dust was so thick that their eyes seared. They fumbled toward the entrance with Rick holding a compass, a map, and two flashlights. He carried chocolate bars, chips, canned salsa, water, and two jackets in his backpack.

The mountain was clearer as they approached and boulders were visible at the base of the ledge. More importantly, the blast penetrated the middle of the mountain and created a large black hole. They jumped across the large rocks as quickly as possible toward the opening. Rick was confident the burros could get across the stones without any trouble. Just before the entrance he realized a boulder had settled between the rocks and provided a secure wedge for the double exit. Rick stopped and surveyed the opening. "I'm going in the right side, it's larger. Stay here until I give you the word." He tossed his backpack to MJ and maneuvered the last few feet to the entrance. He checked the opening for support, poked his head inside, and disappeared.

After what seemed to be a long time to MJ, Rick reappeared. He had a big grin on his face. "Come on," he said and disappeared inside.

MJ stepped into the blackness of the cavern with a flashlight pointed at her feet. During the time she had waited outside she practiced deep breathing exercises to calm her nerves and curb her dreaded claustrophobia. The glow of a light ahead her assured Rick was close by. "Mind your feet," he said.

MJ knew from the excitement in Rick's voice that he had found something hidden in the cave. She adjusted her eyes to the darkness and moved forward. Rick's flashlight was poised on a wagon. A closer look told her it had a wooden frame and metal wheels and was covered with a ragged tarp full of holes.

"I suspect many creatures thought the wagon was their home during the past two-hundred and fifty years." Rick pointed to the area behind him. "There are three more wagons over there. I've only peeked under this one."

"Find anything?"

"Yeah, take a look. As Rick tugged at the tarp it crumbled. Two frightened mice went scurrying for cover. Mold and dust rose from the bed of the wagon. MJ began to sneeze and cough.

"The darn thing is fragile," Rick said, reaching into his pocket and handing her a handkerchief. "Put this over your nose and mouth." He shined the flashlight over the wagon.

MJ surveyed the altar vestments spread across the wagon. Many items were partially shredded. All were decayed, moldy, or stained. Animals, insects, and water dripping from the ceiling for two centuries had taken its toll on liturgical clothing. The vestments were made of satin and silk and folded and stacked by seasonal colors. MJ recalled her course on the history of Catholicism. She remembered that white was worn on Christmas, violet on Advent, and the other times of the year, the clergy wore red, gold, green, black, or rose, depending on the occasion. Many of the vestments she surveyed were intact but in fragile condition. The intricate gold and silver threads still had a luster and the various jewels around the collar and sleeves were dusty and dull with age but still beautiful. The wagon contained items worn by a priest for any mass or celebration in the Catholic Church. Vestments, altar clothes, liturgical headpieces called copes, maniples, stoles and albs. Everything was stacked by color.

"Why do you think they stored altar garments?" Rick asked.

"They were planning on coming back or else they would have taken them to Spain," MJ said.

"Let's see what else is here," Rick said.

They walked to the next wagon. Rick shined his light and pulled aside the tarp. This time they found religious items that related to the church: icons, rosary beads, and items used during mass. The icons were locally painted and meticulously detailed in vivid colors that portrayed the Madonna and Child, or Jesus on the cross. Lavish gold paint was displayed on clothing, halos, and the frames. Nearby rosary beads were lined up in a row. All of the beads were hand carved, some made of wood, others of marble or semiprecious stones.

"This is truly amazing," MJ said. She moved her eyes past the beads to the far end of the wagon and saw sacred items used during mass. Chalices, ciboriums, flagons, patens, and incense burners were still standing where they were placed two hundred years earlier. The items were made of either gold or silver, encrusted with jewels, and etched with a classic Roman motif.

"The Jesuits must have stripped bare every mission before they returned to Spain," Rick said.

MJ thought about the effort and planning that went into the display. She hypothesized what might have happened to create the scene before her. Two hundred years earlier each Padre in the Jesuit missions received a letter stating they would be leaving for Spain, but all religious items or anything else of value would remain in Baja California until they returned. The Padres were requested to take everything to a central place, most likely the Mission of Loreto, by wagon. In Loreto, the items were sorted, individually wrapped, reloaded on wagons, and taken by burro over a virgin trail north to the mountains. When the wagons arrived everything was unwrapped, sorted by content, and placed aside. Four special wagons were pulled into the cave and every item was placed exactly as they stood today. A priest blessed everything, a landslide ensued, and nothing was moved for two hundred years. MJ was overwhelmed with the enormity and skill that was involved.

"We are half way through," Rick said. "So far we've seen nothing that relates to the Manila Galleon." They continued to the third wagon where they found more religious items. Statues were lying across two-thirds of the bed. They were carved of wood, marble, or stone and ranged in size from a few inches to several feet. Spanish armor covered the last third of the bed: swords, helmets, guns, breast-plaits, leg wraps—anything a soldier might wear for a parade, a holy day, or to intimidate the local Indians. MJ shook her head in amazement. "You're right. They didn't leave much behind."

They approached the fourth and final wagon. This wagon was different, smaller than the others and more elaborate. MJ was drawn to the metal wheels that had filigree designs on each spoke. More amazingly, each side of the wagon was painted with a different Baja California scene. The first panel presented a picture of the Bay of La Paz. Ships sat around the crescent shaped harbor, children played at the water's edge, the streets were laid out in squares, and men rode on horses near the shore. The second panel showed the village of Loreto with the Sea of Cortez in the background. Bright, colored houses and the Mission were the focal point. The third panel had a painting of the Sierra de Laguna Mountains with deer, birds, coyote, and red fox roaming through the forest. The forth panel had an illustrated map of Baja California with small crosses scattered from north to south that showed the location of the Jesuits missions.

"Wow," MJ said. "It's beautiful."

"Yeah. They must have burned a lot of candles trying to paint the panels in the dark."

MJ turned to Rick with a frown. "I suspect the wagon was painted by European craftsmen from drawings provided by local Mexican priests. The wagon could have been a gift from The Pious Fund."

"The what?"

"The Jesuits in Baja created an endowment from benefactors in Spain to sustain a Jesuit California. It was called The Pious Fund and was independent from the controls of other Jesuit missions throughout the Americas. Historians believe it was the smoking gun that finally convinced King Carlos to bring the Jesuits back to Spain."

"It's time to see what's underneath this display," Rick said. "Look at this leather." The wagon was covered with several pieces of leather sewn together and tucked around the perimeter. Rick pulled at a corner, lifted the flap, and continued around to the next corner. "You hold the flashlight and I'll roll it back. It's going to be heavy." Rick only had to roll the leather a few inches when MJ gasped.

"It's incredible."

The Jesuits, meticulous to the end, had once again displayed everything by category. The first row displayed a line of twenty-two karat gold buckles used for dress shoes that men wore in the 1700s. The following rows uncovered other items worn on clothing: silver and gold buttons inlaid with jade, turquoise, and coral. Dresses, shirts, pants, and jackets were decorated with the buttons. MJ marveled at the intricate detailing. She couldn't think of a museum in the world that owned a collection as complete.

"Let's stay a minute more," MJ said. "The items are incredible in their detailing."

"Let's finish uncovering the wagon first. You can come back later and review everything."

"You're right. Best finish unrolling the leather first."

"Yeah. But it will go faster if you put down your flashlight and grab an end."

MJ gripped the leather and they continued to roll. "Do you think everything came off Manila Galleon ships that was headed for Spain?"

"Most of it" he said. "The ships were destined for Acapulco after they left the Philippines. Their route was to cross the Pacific and skirt the shore of lower California until they arrived at their destination. Ships that came near the shore of Cabo San Lucas were an easy prey for pirates hiding in the Sea of Cortez where the majority of the lootings occurred."

"Wow," MJ exclaimed they unrolled the leather. Hand carved combs, fans, buttons, and chess sets made of ivory sat before their eyes. Elephant tusks carried from Africa and carved in Asia dominated the array.

"Look at the detailing on the queen," MJ said. "And see how fine the teeth are carved on the combs?"

"Which fan would look good in my hair," Rick asked with a sheepish grin.

"Only have a couple of feet to the end, keep rolling."

As they unrolled the remaining leather, Rick and MJ were dazzled by what lay underneath. Rick whistled.

MJ just stood there with her mouth open. "Overwhelming." She gazed over the assortment. "One thing's for certain. None of this jewelry came from Asia. Everything here is Mexican and very old. The pieces are probably Mayan or Aztec. They're more valuable than I can begin to comprehend and definitely belong in a museum." MJ gazed from left to right then back again. "How did the Jesuits ever get their hands on this?"

"I have no idea," Rick said. "But we should be thankful everything has been hidden for two hundred years. Otherwise this stuff would be scattered all over the world."

"What do we do next?"

"Stand guard while I go over there," Rick said pointing to the back of the cave. "There's a small opening where I took a quick look before I called you. It may be a tunnel. Don't go far." Rick disappeared into the darkness, flashlight in hand and whistling a tune.

MJ, overwhelmed by the display, was trying to catalogue everything according to age. She was reluctant to touch anything, afraid that any item she dropped would disappear in the dark and never be found again. A pair of earrings with a matching bracelet caught her eye. Wasn't the design similar to the necklace Mama had worn at her birthday party? MJ shined the flashlight on the bracelet for a better look. Perhaps it was the same design, but she wanted to see it in natural light. MJ carefully picked up the bracelet walked toward the opening. Brilliant sunshine momentarily blinded her as she walked outside. She squinted trying to adjust her eyes to the light, placed the bracelet on her wrist, and gently turned it.

"What you got there, gal?" said a voice. "Find it inside the cave, did you?"

MJ recognized Wiley's voice and looked up at his crooked smile and beat up dusty hat. His feet were spread apart and he carried a silver pistol pointed in her direction.

"Throw the bracelet over to me. Now!"

MJ did as she was told.

"Where's your husband?"

"What?"

"Don't play stupid with me, MJ. I heard the dynamite blast a while back." He motioned toward his feet. "Come on over here where I can keep an eye on you. And turn around when you get here. I won't have any problem shooting you in the back if you try anything funny."

They stood in the hot sun. Wiley breathed with a rasp, shuffled from foot to foot, and once, just for fun, poked the gun into MJ's back. She stood very still.

A few minutes later, Rick came out of the cave looking for MJ. "What's going on?" he said trying to focus on two people standing in front of him through the glare of the sun. Then he saw the problem. Wiley's gun was pointed at MJ.

"Well well, what have we here," Wiley said. "The dead man was only playing hooky." He motioned them toward the cave. "Don't try anything funny 'cause I won't think twice about shooting both of you." Wiley prodded them on as they slowly made their way toward the back of the cave. Wiley glanced at the contents of each wagon and chuckled. His wait was finally over. At the final wagon Wiley stopped prompting MJ and Rick to stop too. "Keep going," he barked. "I think our time together has finally come to an end."

MJ and Rick didn't say a word as they entered the tunnel. The opening got smaller and smaller as MJ and Rick moved further in. They were stooped over with MJ walking behind Rick. Their heads scraped the top of the tunnel and their shoulders bounced against the walls.

"Throw your flashlights behind you," Wiley said. "Now." Rick and MJ did as they were told.

"Take my hand," Rick whispered. "And breathe deeply. Everything will be okay."

"Hush," Wiley said. Wiley pointed the flashlights into the tunnel and watched them disappear into the darkness. He aimed the pistol on the ground and fired. The thunder echoed down the tunnel. He put the gun in his pocket, reached in his backpack, and pulled a flashlight from a small pocket. He fit a small powerful headlamp onto his head and tilted the light into the tunnel. Rick and MJ were gone. The rest of Wiley's backpack was full of dynamite. He reached for a packet and measured the distance from the final wagon to the tunnel opening, about seventy-five feet. He placed the dynamite against the tunnel wall and scratched his head thinking as if he'd forgotten something. The most valuable items were in the wagon closest to the tunnel. They needed to be relocated.

Within minutes Wiley had his burro in the cave hitched to the wagon ready for action. The treasure was moved to the entrance. The dynamite was double-checked to be sure it was in the right location at the wall. Wiley set the timer for three minutes, and lit the stick. The explosion would be strong enough to close the tunnel, create a barrier between MJ and Rick, and small enough not to damage the wagons. Wiley hustled toward the exit where he came to an abrupt stop. A very frightened burro stood near the opening and blocked his path.

CHAPTER 39

Rick yelled the second he heard the dynamite go off.

"Get on the ground, now!" He knew the blast would create an air pocket that would blow through the tunnel creating thirty mile an hour winds.

MJ threw her arms forward and dove toward the ground at the same moment Rick grabbed her. She fell on top of Rick's body scraping her knees against the ground hard. When the dirt and fumes hit her nose she began to cough. MJ rolled over and put her face into the crook of her arm and breathed deeply.

"You all right?" Rick asked.

She touched her knees and felt sticky blood on her fingers. "Nothing's broken. You?"

"I'm okay. Stay down until the dust settles."

MJ slowly opened her eyes. Everything was black, her worst nightmare. She'd be claustrophobic soon if she didn't do something. She hated tight dark spaces. The problem was compounded if she couldn't breathe. But she knew what to do. Maintain a clear head, don't panic, and evaluate the options. There might be way out.

Rick took MJ's hand. "Don't worry. I got this far earlier. This is the narrowest part. Keep moving ahead we'll be able stand again. Let's go."

"Okay." The blackness helped MJ focus. She had a small Velcro pouch hidden at her waist. With unsteady fingers, she undid the plastic snaps and withdrew a powerful tiny LED flashlight. Earlier she was fearful Wiley would see the glow and shoot at them again. MJ pushed a button. A circle of light appeared.

"Holy cow, where'd you get that?"

"Dad sent it from Hong Kong. I was saving it for your birthday but decided to bring it along."

"The light bounces off the walls. Hey there's light at the end of the tunnel."

"Aren't you funny."

"Not really. Cause when I get out, I'm going to beat Wiley to a bloody pulp. If I don't kill him first."

They struggled along in silence. Rick's heavy breathing told MJ that he was trying to control his anger. After a few minutes they could stand again and move their arms freely. The tunnel was getting wider, and wetter. MJ's shoes squished on the soft surface.

"Do you hear anything? Flowing water?"

"Not yet. You'll be the first to know. Hand me the flashlight." Rick shined the light on the walls. Tiny stalagmites appeared on the ceiling. "Looks like there's an open area ahead. Put your hands on the wall for more balance, it's getting slippery."

Rick stepped into a cave and flashed the light around. The opening appeared to be about ten feet wide, fifteen feet long and sixteen feet high. A trickle of water flowed from the far left corner, continued down the wall, and emptied into the tunnel.

"Where's the water coming from?" MJ asked.

"The lake above us. Our route through the tunnel runs parallel to an arroyo on the other side of the mountain. I remember the details from the map at the town clerk's office. Santa Isabel is flanked by the Pintura Mountains and there's a lake near the top."

MJ appraised the area. "Turn off the flashlight. I think I saw something and I want to check."

They stood in the black space listening to the sound of water dripping as their eyes adjusted to the darkness.

"Look on your left," MJ said. "There's light at the top of the wall."

"Where's it coming from?"

"It's a reflection from the other side. Turn around. It's coming from an opening above a ledge. See? Turn on the light. I'll keep my eyes on the opening."

With the flick of the flashlight, the wall lit up and MJ zeroed in on the wall. It was rough, ridged, and vertical except for a five-degree slope to the top. She walked over to the opposite wall and peered back. The ledge wasn't visible unless you knew what you were looking for. She'd give a lot for the binoculars in her backpack right now.

"Turn the flashlight off again so I can gauge the size of the opening."

"And what are you going to do then? Wave a magic wand and appear on the ledge? Get serious. I can get us out of here."

"And I can't?" MJ said with annoyance.

Rick moved the flashlight up the side of the wall.

"Hold this. I'm going to climb the wall."

MJ looked at his heavy hiking boots knowing they would be a challenge. Rick moved his hands over the surface of the wall looking for handholds. He found what he wanted and placed his fingers securely in the holds. He used his boots to brace himself against the wall and his arms to lift his body. Almost immediately, his feet began to slip against the wet surface, but he clung onto the wall with his fingers until they began to bleed. He had to let go. Rick shook his head in disgust.

"Why don't I—" was all MJ managed to say before they heard a sharp crack that penetrated the cave. She turned pointing the flashlight in the direction of the sound, and focused on the wall. Water gushed through the enlarged crack, continued down the side, and flowed across the floor into the tunnel.

"Flash the light through the tunnel," Rick said.

MJ focused the light on the opening.

"We were walking at an upward incline until we got here," he said. "The water will fill the lower end of the tunnel, flow back, and when it reaches here, it will go to the top the cave."

———————

Wiley waited for the dust to settle from the blast. He pulled the flask from his pocket and took a swig of tequila. Damn nice of the Marshalls, father and son, to lead him to his fortune. Too bad they got their comeuppance in the process. He took another swig. What a surprise to find the burro blocking the exit. It was a pretty close call. Thank God he was a quick thinker. Couldn't have gotten this far if he wasn't smarter than most people. Yeah. When he saw the problem he fell to the ground, crawled through the burros' legs, and pulled the animal from the opening just as the blast went off.

Flush with hubris from his accomplishment, Wiley whistled as he approached the cave, eager to load the bounty from the lost mission. He led the burro inside, jockeyed him to the painted wagon, and lifted his blinders. Wiley opened his pack and reached inside. "Have a carrot," he said popping the treat into the animal's mouth. The next item of business was to find out what he would take. He headed for the wagon with the scenes painted on the outside thinking the best items would be there. Wiley threw back the leather tarp. Wow. He was going to be rich. He began to stuff the gold buckles and jewelry into the pouches. Nearby, the burro was rasping from the thick film dust in the air. Wiley stuffed more carrots into his mouth and tied a bandana over his nose. It would be a shame if the burro collapsed and died before they got out of there. He loaded as much as he could fit into each bag. The wagon was almost empty before Wiley threw the tarp back over the remaining items, blindfolded the animal, and headed for the opening. It was time to get this show on the road. What a pity to leave things behind, but there was no sense in being greedy. Outside, Wiley looked back at the opening. He wanted to cover the cave but there was no time. God forbid some guy in a private plane with nothing to do found the Hummer. Wiley wasn't sure the truck went over the cliff, but he knew that Don Hernando was dead. Served him right, the selfish old bastard.

Wiley pulled himself onto the burro headed down the hillside. He was exhausted. This was way too much activity for a seventy-year-old man. He put a hand above his eyes to cover the sun's glare. The day had ebbed and the sun would set shortly. Not wanting to push his luck, he decided to skirt the road. He dug his heels into the burro and smacked its hindquarters.

"Get moving," he said. "We're gonna stop in an hour."

The sky was crystal clear, disconnected from the havoc of the earlier storm. Birds swooped and dived for rodents. A cirio cactus, weary from its ordeal, lay drooping against a bush. Jagged orange flowers clung to its tips.

A disheveled Don Hernando dragged himself toward a plateau thick with dust. Blood dripped from a gash on his head. His chest and leg ached with pain. It was a miracle that he was alive. Alberto was dead. Shot through the chest. Don Hernando left him in a heap with blood all over the steering wheel, climbed over the back seat, and made his way down the road. Pure revenge motivated him this far. He should have heeded his mother's advice about Wiley. "Better the devil you know, than the devil you don't know," she had said.

Don Hernando followed the road to the bottom of the hill and stopped. The landscape was blurry. His hand shook violently, but he needed to use the binoculars to lift his broken arm. He winced with pain and focused in the direction where he heard a dynamite blast. A white figure moved through the haze. Don Hernando dropped his arm in pain. When he closed his eyes a light flashed across his forehead. He shook his head, opened his eyes, and, with gritted teeth, lifted his arm again. Across the arroyo he could see Wiley riding a burro down the side of a cliff. Another burro, tethered behind him, struggled with bent knees to maintain his footing. Wiley dismounted and checked the huge packs hanging low on the animal. He opened one pack and threw something over the side of the cliff. He unhitched the other pack and dragged it to the burro he was riding. What was Wiley carrying? Of course. He had the treasure from the Mission of Santa Isabel.

Don Hernando's blood began to boil. He was a driven man, desperate to beat Wiley at his own game. Wiley and the burros were headed in his direction. All he had to do was wait. He'd devise a way to get the treasure back. But how? He looked around. The stand of Madrono trees appeared to be a good choice for a hiding place. He looked again. A large boulder, masked by two small challah bushes, sat off to his right. It was a better choice. He'd wait behind the boulder. The old bastard was his only hope to survive. Wiley had the gun, food, water and camping supplies that Don Hernando had paid for and sorely needed.

Don Hernando was lightheaded and exhausted. His tongue ran over his parched lips. He'd give a lot for some liquid from a nopali, or even an aloe. He had searched along the trail but didn't pass anything edible. He dragged himself behind the rock and collapsed.

CHAPTER 40

Mama walked down the hall to the suite at the end of the corridor with determination, her eyes were alert and focused. She wore a simple pink cotton flowered dress and no jewelry. She placed her cane against the door and knocked.

"Who is it?" Antigua asked.

"Mama. Open the door. I need to speak with you."

It took a while before Antigua opened the door. She seemed bewildered by Mama's unannounced visit. Mama brushed by and looked around the room. "I've asked Corinda to bring strong coffee and biscuits for us. We will be a while. Would you like anything else?"

Antigua shook her head no.

"May I sit down?" Mama asked.

"Of course," Antigua answered, motioning her to a chair in the corner.

Mama walked across the room, found a comfortable place, and waited for her old friend. It was obvious Antigua was surprised by her visit. Mama planned it that way so Antigua wouldn't have an excuse for not seeing her.

Antigua was dressed in a blue chenille bathrobe she had folded over her legs, ever careful of propriety. A lace nightgown curled around the collar of her neck, a long braid hung down her back. Painted toes peeked through her satin slippers. Antigua wore no makeup but years of

293

attention to her face revealed skin barely wrinkled by age. The deep circles under her eyes indicated she might be worried or hadn't slept well.

"Do you know why I am here?" Mama asked.

Antigua crossed her hands on her lap. Mama noted one hand shook.

"Not really," she replied.

Mama looked directly into Antigua's eyes. "We have known each other for seventy-five years. During that time we've attended the same state functions, religious events, as well as the marriages and birthdays of our children. But we have never discussed personal matters that affect both of us." Mama paused. "Until now."

Antigua rubbed her fingers together but said nothing. Mama continued. "Twenty-seven years ago you purchased land which I inherited from my husband. You used the guise of The Baja Land Corporation to hide the purchase."

"Our family reacquired what was rightfully ours," Antigua said.

"And why was it rightfully yours, Antigua?"

"I don't have to discuss our personal land holdings with you."

"You are correct, you don't. But if you care about your son, you need to answer some questions."

"Are you threatening me?"

Mama shot Antigua an annoyed look. "Of course not, but Don Hernando's life may be in danger. He left early this morning with Alberto. Do you know where they were going?"

"I don't know what you're talking about," Antigua said. She pursed her lips, unwilling to say anything else.

"They were headed for the mountains above Santa Maria. Do you know why?"

Antigua ignored Mama's question.

"Tell me something," Mama said. "Is finding the lost mission more important than your son's safety?"

Antigua looked up. A smile of recognition came over her face. "So we were right. Don Hernando and I were always suspicious you knew where the treasure was hidden, but we couldn't prove it."

"And what made you change your mind?"

"The Aztec necklace you wore last night. The Cortez family has the original drawing. It was given to us by a Jesuit priest shortly before he left for Spain in 1768."

Mama waited for Antigua to continue.

"We also had a map of Santa Isabel. But a family servant stole the necklace and the map, and he was never heard from again." Antigua stopped when she realized the scope of what Mama might know. She stood up and walked over to Mama.

"Since you have the necklace, do you have the map?"

Mama was nonplussed. She smiled and waited.

"Do you?"

"No."

"I don't believe you. You have the map or you wouldn't be here. You need to find out where Don Hernando is so you can stop him."

A knock at the door caught both women by surprise.

"That must be Corinda," Mama said.

Antigua tied the belt of her nightgown and ran her hands through her hair as she walked to the door.

"Good morning," Corinda said. She walked across the room and placed the tray on the table and glanced at her mother who nodded with assurance that she was fine. "Would you like anything else?"

"No, thank you," Antigua answered.

After Corinda left, both women sat in silence. Mama took a bite of a cookie, placed it on a napkin, and waited. Finally Antigua spoke.

"Let me ask the question another way. Do you know where the map is?"

"Yes. I gave it to someone for safekeeping."

"Are you telling me you had the map all these years and you never looked for the treasure?

"That's correct."

"Why not?"

"There was nothing to be gained. The treasure has brought grief and pain to anyone who touched it."

Antigua shook her head in disbelief.

Mama took a sip of coffee. "But I have hope that things are different today. The government is not as corrupt. They are operating on a more level playing field." Mama placed her cup on the small table. "The Cortez family can no longer pay off every politician they want, or hide things under the rug."

"I wouldn't be so sure," Antigua said smugly.

"Listen to me." Mama leaned forward, her anger apparent in her eyes and steely, measured voice. "The treasure doesn't belong to you, or to me, for that matter. It belongs to the people of Baja California. It's their treasure, their history."

Mama reached for her cane and lifted herself out of the chair. "Enough blood has been shed already. No good will come from Don Hernando's search. If you care about your son, you will tell me where he is."

Fifteen minutes later Mama, leaning heavily on her cane, returned to the restaurant. Corinda grasped her arm and ushered her to the booth where Ginger, Father Leo, and Ramon waited. Mama was grim. Cordina, with the flat of her hand, motioned them to stay calm. "Let me get you a cup of tea and a piece of birthday cake, Mama," she said. "Would anyone else like something to eat or drink?"

"No, thank you," they said.

"I'll be right back."

The group remained silent and waited for Mama to speak. She composed herself and turned to Father Leo. "I want you to call Rubio Gomes and tell him to come to Santa Rosario as soon as possible. Cordina will give you his telephone number. Tell him that Marco will be waiting at the landing strip here in Santa Rosario with two people and they are to leave immediately. I will provide a map with the location of their destination."

Father Leo left the room in search of Cordina.

Mama looked at Ginger and Ramon. "I know where Don Hernando and Alberto went this morning. Rick and MJ are nearby and their lives may be in danger. They are all searching for the Mission of Santa Isabel." Mama pointed to the entrance of the restaurant. "In the sideboard you'll find the map that shows a road leading to the Pintura Mountains. Get it. We need a plan."

CHAPTER 41

MJ watched water flow into the tunnel in stunned silence. She gazed into Rick's worried eyes. "We don't have much time," she said. "The water will fill the cave within an hour. We have no idea how long it will take before the side of the mountain caves in." She hustled over to the wall that Rick attempted to climb earlier. "I think I can get us out of here. Trust me."

MJ ran her fingers over the surface of a two-by-two foot square, and tried various handgrips. In training school, she was the best rock climber in her group. That was years ago. Now MJ wasn't sure she could climb the sixteen feet she needed to reach the ledge, or what she would do if she got there. "Rick, will you come here?"

Rick walked over to where MJ was located. "Stand here, like this." Her elbows and knees were bent, her feet were spread apart hip length, and her face was six inches from the wall. MJ gripped her legs around his waist, and quickly followed by putting her feet on his shoulders. "Stay very still. Don't move from the wall."

MJ ran her hands over the surface trying various handholds. She placed her feet against the wall and maintained this position for ten seconds. Then she put her feet on Ricks' shoulders and took a deep breath. "All right, I'm ready. But stay where you are in case I fall."

Rick watched his wife's precision climbing with amazement. She swore and stopped to take a deep breath.

Near the top her feet slipped and she hung by her hands. When she caught herself she pulled her body onto the ledge and banged her head in the process.

MJ looked outside. The opening was a circle of blue sky. A light breeze ruffled her hair as she crawled to the edge and poked her head out. There was a narrow ledge with a path three feet below her that gradually sloped to the right until it vanished. To her left, the path along ledge narrowed and disappeared when it reached a corner. She rolled on her stomach, exited feet first, and touched the ground. Below her, in the distance, a trail wandered over the valley, crossed an arroyo, and was gobbled up by the next mountain range. Nothing looked familiar.

She chose the wider ledge, walked two hundred feet and came to a shear drop. A small stream gurgled from the top of the mountain and spread wider just above her. Most of the water disappeared into the rock. If memory served her right, the water coming down the wall of the cave was in the same place. She made a beeline back to the opening and crawled in far enough to see Rick standing in water up to his knees holding a flashlight. MJ yelled, "Hey."

"Christ MJ, what's going on up there? Is there a way out?" Rick's panic echoed through the cavern.

"Yeah, I think so. The first trail I tried didn't work. It ran down the side of the mountain and had a shear drop at the end. I'm going the other way now. Back in a minute."

She hit the ground and scurried to the left, navigated the two-foot wide ledge with care, and rounded the corner. It immediately widened into a long straight trail up the side of the mountain. MJ peered down the hill. In the distance were two brown burros faded into the horizon.

One had Wiley astride. He was miles away and the least of her worries right now. She had to move fast. The cave was unstable and could collapse at any time.

The rocky wide slope up the mountain was a welcome sight. With her head down and eyes focused on the uneven terrain, MJ continued, oblivious to any danger. The trail narrowed so quickly she stopped a split second before it disappeared. Christ. She almost went over the end. Another larger problem loomed before her. She'd reached another dead end.

The sudden movement under her feet caught her by surprise. MJ looked back to see jagged rocks careening down the cliff followed by a loud crack that threw her against the wall. She grasped her hands against the wall and leaned in to steady her balance. She watched with astonishment as a section of the trail below her slowly separated from the cliff and fell down the mountain. A ten-foot gap stood between her and the route to the cave. There was no way back.

The mountain was eerily quiet. How much time did she have before another quake shook the hillside? The dynamite blasts combined with the hidden tunnel and the stream flowing from the top of the mountain had created a perfect storm. The internal void of the cave would cause the mountain to adapt to the change.

MJ had to get around the cliff's edge and find out if the trail continued on the other side. The idea was perilous. If she slipped she would fall to her death. But did she have any other choice? She eased toward the precipice, bent her right leg, and placed her knee against the cliff. She leaned over the edge, and ran her fingers along the surface of the other side until she found secure holds. Then she shimmed her body closer to the edge and extended her leg around the corner looking for a flat platform for her foot. When she felt secure that she had found one, MJ took a deep breath, counted to three, and swung her body around the corner into the unknown.

The single engine five-passenger Robinson R44 helicopter flew above the Pintura Mountains at a speed of 140 mph. Rubio Gomes had two passengers, Ramon Diaz and Ginger Hughes. Gomes was an old pro who navigated the Sierras on search and rescue missions for twenty years looking for hikers and climbers, usually Americans. They often underestimated the difficulty of the terrain and the freezing weather of the Baja California Mountains. Gomes now worked for a private company whose main job was to medevac injured personnel from oilrigs located on the Gulf of Mexico.

As soon as Gomes got Mama's call, he dispatched another pilot to cover him and headed for Santa Rosario. Hell, he'd never have become a pilot if it weren't for Mama. In the sixties she built the first small private landing strip in Baja California for The Flying Samaritans. The story went that Mama rescued a family flying back to the States that ran out of gas and landed in a field nearby. Mama, who spoke English, welcomed them into her home, prepared dinner, and dispatched someone to get airplane gas. The closest place was forty miles away. That chance meeting cemented an annual trip by a group of pilots and doctors who came down every December with gifts of food, medical supplies, dry milk, clothing, and other supplies.

As a kid, Gomes hung around the new landing strip, mesmerized by aircraft. Mama encouraged him to hitch a ride with anyone heading to El Mármol, Magdalena Bay, or even La Paz. Gomes was the envy of every kid in town. In high school he worked as a junior mechanic fixing engines. When Mama offered to send him to aviation school in Utah, he jumped at the chance. From the moment Gomes saw his first helicopter his mind was made up. It was the only aircraft he wanted to fly.

Ramon was seated behind Gomes trying to align a map Mama had given him with the Guia Roja, the Mexican bible of maps. He hoped he'd have some recollection of the trip with Oliver twenty years earlier but in truth, he was grasping at straws.

Ginger, in the copilot's seat, was Gomes' extra pair of eyes. She didn't lack a curiosity about her surroundings, peppering Gomes with constant questions that he found so distracting he asked her not to talk until she saw something that related to their search. He dug under the seat and handed her a list of things she should do when they landed.

Earlier, Ginger assured Mama and Gomes they didn't need a medic, the standard requirement for an S&R mission. She had EMT training and used her knowledge regularly on sailing trips. And no, she wasn't concerned about the possibility of being lowered in a harness from a hovering helicopter. Gomes wasn't so sure.

"We're getting close to the area Mama highlighted on the map," Ramon said with less than positive assurance. Directly in front of them a dirt road ran in a straight line to a mesa, continued half way up the incline, curved around the side, and couldn't be seen.

"I'm going to swing around the hill," Gomes said. He maneuvered the helicopter toward the mesa aware that a downdraft could affect its stability. "Did you say this is the first road that goes over a mesa since we left Santa Rosario?"

"Yes," Ramon said. "On the Guia Roja it continues to the next mountain range."

Gomes followed the road over the thick shrubbery that impeded his visibility. The west side of the mesa caught clouds that dropped rain and produced the verdant hillside.

"Hey, look over there," Ginger shouted, pointing to the right. "There's something white in the trees."

Gomes handed Ginger a pair of binoculars and circled around. He slowly lowered the helicopter toward the hillside aware that by hovering in a confined area the helicopter could fall into its own downwash and crash.

"There's a white truck lying on its side," Ginger said. "Don Hernando and Alberto were driving a white truck. Can you get any closer?" Gomes dropped the plane very slowly and hovered over the truck.

"Oh my God," she said. "A man is slouched over the steering wheel. I can't see his face."

"Can I take a look?" Ramon asked. He scanned the binoculars around the bushes, and back over the body. "He's not moving. It looks like he's dead. There's no one in the passenger seat or the area around the truck."

"I'll radio the office and they'll dispatch a helicopter with a medic," Gomes said. "Our instructions are to continue the search until everyone is accounted for."

Gomes lifted the helicopter from the hillside and veered to the left. "We're heading for the next mesa."

Ginger continued to stare back until she could no longer see the truck. Her stomach was in knots. "Why is there so much dust in this direction? The first mesa is still clear when I look back. The one ahead is hazy."

"Good question," Gomes said looking thru the rear view mirror. "It looks like a storm came over the area where we are headed and dissipated in the valley below us. It has the markings of a small tornado."

"A tornado?" Ramon and Ginger said at the same time.

"Yeah. We see them from time to time up on the flats between the mountains. Be happy it passed by, or we'd be on our way back."

Don Hernando lay in the dirt sound asleep. In his dream a burro whinnied but he ignored it. When he heard the whinny a second time he opened his eyes and tried to sit up. His legs were numb. He braced against the rock and peeked around the edge. Two burros were tied to the Madrono. Large heavy packs sat against the tree. A campfire glowed and crackled as Wiley stirred onions in the frying pan. He hummed a tune and stopped every minute or so to take a swig from a brown bottle.

Nothing much happened during the three hours Don Hernando waited. He wondered when Wiley would finally slow down. Throughout the afternoon and into the evening the old man drank constantly. After he finished the first bottle he started working his way through a second one. The fire was dying, the pan sat in the embers. Whatever food left was too burned to eat. Wiley's head had fallen twice but he righted himself, blinked his eyes, and tipped the bottle to his mouth. Don Hernando was planning his next move. It would be when everything changed. Wiley let out a holler, collapsed on his back, and began to snore. The embers cast enough light for Don Hernando to make his way over to where Wiley had passed out. He glanced at the burros. They didn't even twitch their ears. Wiley lay on the ground with his arms straight out and his chest heaving with every breath. The knife he had used to prepare dinner sat near the base of the fire. Don Hernando walked over and touched the handle. It was hot. He kicked the knife away and ground it in the dirt with his foot. Then he approached Wiley, knife in hand. Wiley's mouth was open. Drool dripped across his lips and down his cheek. He was relaxed, content. The trace of a smile extended across his lips.

Don Hernando knew his target. He plunged the knife into Wiley's heart. The old man barely grunted. He stabbed him again and again. Spent and drenched in blood, he lay down next to the body, took two long gulps from the bottle of tequila, and fell asleep.

CHAPTER 42

MJ swung her body into the unknown. A hot gust of wind greeted her at the turn, but she balanced on one toe and reached for the next hold. Two moves later she stopped and looked up. No end in sight. Nothing but a sheer cliff as far as the eye could see. She was bouldering—no rope or gear—she had only one choice: go up. Thank God she'd stuffed Rick's socks into her shoes. The tight fit kept her feet from slipping. Hot sun scorched her back. She concentrated on what she learned in training. Keeping her hands dry was the biggest challenge. Earlier, she filled her pocket with some loose dry dirt. Would it help? Maybe, but eventually her hands would get raw and start to bleed.

After fifteen minutes, MJ wondered if it would ever end. She was discouraged, her back ached, and she was frantic with worry about Rick. How far had she climbed? Fifty feet? She scanned the cliff again. There was a slight dip in the wall above her to the right. She moved toward the area and realized she was near the top. Two feet from what she thought was the end of the climb, everything fell apart. MJ moved her hands across the surface above her and couldn't find any handholds. No way. This couldn't be possible. She'd reached a flat. She made a wider arc. Still nothing.

"No!" she cried out. She was too close. MJ rubbed her eyes on her arm and cried wet salty tears that made her wince. There had to be something she could grasp. She'd come too far to give up. She squinted and looked to her right and left, praying for something, anything to grasp. There seemed to be a slight ripple on the edge to her left. She looked again, and went for it. The fingers of her right hand grasped the ledge. She reached way up with her left hand and caught a handhold. With both hands secure she gradually moved her feet up the rock until her body was in a disproportionate position. Her right hand screamed with pain. She had to pull her body up as much as possible with her left arm and reach with her right hand for an unseen hold. MJ threw her right arm over the top, found a hold and with every ounce of strength she had, pulled herself over the top.

Tears of relief gushed down her face. She had survived. But her happiness quickly turned to fear over Rick. She felt helpless. She was safe, but his life was in peril. Lost in self-pity, she put her head into the crook of her elbow and sobbed.

At first, the noise from above didn't penetrate her mind. But it grew louder and finally MJ rolled over and looked up with surprise. A helicopter hovered above her. The wind was fierce and the loose gravel it threw stung her face and arms. She shielded her eyes with her elbow and didn't move knowing the downdraft could push her over the cliff. Who was it? Where did it come from? The helicopter remained stationary and a door opened. Someone strapped to a harness was lowered from the plane. Red hair peeked through a leather cap and a hand waved furiously. MJ started to laugh. Ginger unstrapped from the harness and didn't move until the helicopter lifted. Then she ran over to MJ.

"Where's Rick?" Ginger asked as she helped her best friend up. MJ ran toward the helicopter. "Tell him to come back. Rick's trapped below. We've got to leave right away."

————

Gomes circled the edge of the mountain while MJ scanned the surface. "Over there," MJ said pointing to the rock. "Rick's in there."

Gomes moved the helicopter toward the mountain slowly and with precision. He didn't want to get into a vortex ring state and cause the helicopter to be caught in a downwash. He took his time. When he felt assured, he signaled Ramon to strap the girls in the harness. Ramon opened the door and lowered them toward the ledge. As they descended, MJ beamed her flashlight through the opening of the cave. All she could see was the black hole. Ginger clutched a safety rope and a medical kit and tried to remain calm. As soon as they touched the ground, MJ unstrapped herself, ran to the opening, and dove in headfirst. Ginger, right behind her, reached over the opening and placed the rope and kit inside. She signaled to Ramon to lift the harness.

MJ shined her flashlight on the water and couldn't believe the mess. Loose rocks were falling through water from the opening above, which had doubled in size. Rick was panicked. He was at the edge in the dark trying to find a secure rock to grasp but the swirling water pushed him around. MJ shouted but he didn't hear her. As she watched him and planned her next move, the rocks above Rick's head came loose. A large boulder fell on his head, glanced off his shoulder, and he went under. MJ jumped into the murky water so fast she didn't have time to take off her shoes. With her eyes closed, she kicked underwater to the area where she last saw Rick, hit a wall, and surfaced.

"Over there," Ginger shouted pointing. "He came up over there." MJ went under again, this time with her arms outstretched, back and forth until she reached the wall again. She emerged and looked at Ginger. "Nothing. He hasn't come up again." On her third try, MJ used another tactic. She swam in circles.

Ginger looked on with fear. The water was pouring into the cave at a monumental rate. She looked at her watch. MJ had been under for more than a minute. Rick? At least two. With a splash, MJ came to the surface gasping for air with her arm wrapped around Rick's neck. She kicked her way toward the wall and pulled Rick's chest against her. With one foot braced against the rocky water's surface, she straddled his leg over hers. Blood from the gash on his head ran over his eyes and down his face. He was barely breathing. MJ put her arms around his chest and squeezed hard. Water projected from his mouth. She slapped his face. Nothing. The second slap was so hard it echoed off the walls. Rick opened his eyes with fear. She gripped the uneven ledge with one hand and held on to Rick with the other. The rising water worried her. She might lose him. Her fingers bled from the jagged rocks but she held on.

Ginger, sizing up the problem, disappeared. She was back in a flash with the rope, fashioned a bowline, and dropped it. MJ wrapped the rope securely around Rick's chest. As Ginger pulled Rick to the top he pushed himself away from the wall with his legs. MJ scurried up the rope behind Rick. "We've got to get out of here before the whole side of the cave blows!" she yelled to Ginger as they pulled him to the opening. Ginger and MJ placed their arms under Rick's shoulders and pushed him over the opening.

Gomes hovered above trying to keep the helicopter steady and close to the mountain. When he saw them appear he yelled to Ramon. "Drop the harness now."

The girls dragged Rick over to the harness and strapped him in. There was only room for one other person. "You go first," MJ said. Ginger knew better than to try to dissuade MJ and waste precious time. The harness was slowly pulled toward the helicopter. MJ headed up the trail trying to get as much distance as possible between her and the cave. She knew the eruption would happen at any moment. The pressure from the water tore through the cave with such force that the wall and everything in its path disintegrated. Rock, debris, and water flew down the side of the cliff. Gomes watched with horror as MJ ran further up the ledge trying to get away. Ginger and Rick were barely inside the helicopter when Gomes inched toward the cliff again. Ramon had lowered the harness less than two-thirds of the way down when the rest of ledge started to fall apart. MJ continued up the hill but she knew the gap that fell earlier was in front of her. Gomes could see her dilemma. He made the only decision possible. He moved the helicopter toward the ledge before the harness was fully extended hoping MJ could reach it.

The downdraft from the helicopter caused the harness to swing back and forth as he neared the cliff. Gomes hoped she could reach it. On the first swing around, MJ jumped but missed the harness. She fell headfirst and landed precariously close to the edge. Ginger gasped. MJ was momentarily stunned. Gomes could see the ledge disintegrating as he dropped the helicopter lower for a second try. He knew it was his last chance before he either crashed into the side or MJ disappeared down the hillside. When the harness swung around this time MJ jumped and caught the netting at the back of the seat. She clung to the seat as Gomes moved away from the mountain and let her body move in rhythm with the harness. Then she wrapped her legs over the chair, smiled, and gave Gomes a thumb up. He turned the helicopter around and headed out.

CHAPTER 43

Don Hernando felt his nose twitch at the same moment he heard buzzing around his head. Then he caught the vile smell in his nostrils. He opened his eyes and focused through the dawn light. Hundreds of insects swarmed at his left, around Wiley's dead body. They were maggots.

He struggled to his feet and tore off his bloody shirt. The maggots fled. How long had he been sleeping? Hours he guessed. He was starving. He found Wiley's small backpack, dug out a bag of pretzels, and drank a thermos of water. He chewed on pretzels, skirted around the burros, and approached the tree where the packs lay. The animals were hungry and whinnied, but they could wait. The packs were what he wanted. He smiled. Finally the Cortez dynasty would have its reward. He lifted the nearest pouch and immediately dropped it. The damn thing was heavy. He bent over, unbuckled the top, and dug in his hands. Cool, sharp objects touched his fingers. He pulled out his hand, now wrapped around an array of stunning jewelry. A topaz necklace was entwined with a gold tiara encrusted with diamonds, rubies, and sapphires. A large black pearl earring hung precariously on the edge. He held up the tiara for a better look. Wait till his mother saw this. He heard a ping on his shoe and realized the earring had fallen on the ground. He placed the tiara and necklace back in the pouch and looked around for the earring. Where was it? He crouched down and ran his fingers around the base until he found a hole. The earring must have dropped in there. He moved his fingers around the dirt in the cool damp opening but didn't feel an earring. He felt a sharp prick and jerked his hand out.

As he watched in horror, a rattlesnake slithered out, continued up his arm, slid across his chest, and wrapped itself around him. Don Hernando pulled at the snake but it wouldn't let go. When he yanked again, the snake bit him on the neck. Out of desperation he reached for his belt, found his knife, and cut at the snake until the bottom half fell to the dirt. He dropped the knife and laid down on the ground gasping for air. He waited for the snake on his chest to stop moving. After a few minutes the snake fell off his body, but he no longer cared. He gazed at the branches above him and saw a blur of green against the blue sky. His whole body tingled. Everything was quiet. Peaceful. He tried to feel his face, but couldn't lift his arm. Then a sudden intense pain radiated across his head and chest and his breathing became shallow. He was so tired. He closed his eyes and saw his mother walking toward him with outstretched arms. She had a smile on her face. She reached out, took his hand, and held him in her arms.

———

It was another cloudless, dry Baja day. And hot. Before the day was over the thermometer would reach one hundred degrees. MJ peered over the side of the helicopter. She was looking for burros, the easiest thing to spot. The plane cruised across the arroyo at two thousand feet, just below the threshold air control mandated.

Earlier today MJ visited Rick and was assured he was fine. She was free to coordinate the search with Mama for Wiley and Don Hernando. Neither man had surfaced. Antigua was frantic about her son after Alberto's body had arrived in Loreto yesterday afternoon. The medics found him in the overturned Hummer on the side of the mountain. There was no sign of Don Hernando. Mama convinced Antigua it was fruitless to send anyone to search for him except Gomes and MJ. They knew the area and had seen the Hummer. They promised to be back before sunset. It was now early afternoon and so far they hadn't seen any sign of Don Hernando or Wiley.

"The place where I picked you up off the plateau is straight ahead," Gomes said.

MJ focused on the mountain and tried to recall the last place she remembered seeing Wiley.

"Can we head in that direction?" MJ asked pointing to a thicket of elephant trees.

"Sure," Gomes said. He broke into a big smile exposing his silver crowns. "Anything special you're looking for?"

"Just a hunch."

The helicopter panned the hillside and eased into the valley, passed over a dry riverbed, and continued toward the next mesa. "Stop," MJ said.

Gomes momentarily frowned.

"I mean can you turn around? I think I saw something."

Gomes eased the helicopter left.

"Down there. See the buzzards flying around? Why, do you think that is? Let's take a better look."

Gomes was a pro. He could put a helicopter down almost anywhere. He neared an area. It was so thick with birds he was unable to see what they were eating. He dropped the helicopter and hovered. The downdraft and noise forced them to scatter.

MJ felt the bile rising in her throat. "Oh, God," MJ said as she gazed down on Wiley's ugly remains. She started to gag.

"You all right?" Gomes asked. MJ shook her head.

"There's another body, near the trees," he said.

CHAPTER 44

A month later

The sign on the door of Mama's restaurant said, *Closed for Renovations*. It aroused much speculation from the people passing by because so many Federale cars were parked around the building. Inside, laughter reverberated off the walls. Mama's girls carried a constant supply of food to the buffet table although no one was eating.

Everybody's attention was focused on the twenty tables lining the room. The treasure from the Lost Mission of Santa Isabel sat in magnificent display. The layout of the historical items closely resembled the arrangement that MJ and Rick found on the wagons. During the past month, MJ photographed, catalogued, and supervised the removal of every item in the cave. Then everything was relocated to a storage facility on the outskirts of Los Santos, except for the items in Mama Esrada's restaurant.

After all the guests had arrived, MJ handed out a brochure and waited for everyone to settle down. She tapped the side of a glass to get everybody's attention.

"Ladies and gentlemen, I'd like to thank all of you for coming," MJ said. "Everybody in this room is in some way responsible for the collection assembled before us today." She held up the pamphlet. "The brochure you are holding contains a photo of every item here, along with some information about its history."

MJ walked over to Mama and took her hand. "I would like to extend a special thank you to Mama." MJ looked directly into her eyes. "You had the foresight and determination to help us locate the Lost Mission of Santa Isabel." Everyone clapped.

"Now let's all have fun with the heirlooms." MJ panned her hand around the room. "The next time you'll see the objects that are on display here today, they'll be behind glass in the soon to be constructed Los Santos Museum. You'll never have an opportunity again to touch and feel them up close and personally." MJ paused trying to remember what else she needed to say. She clapped her hands and everyone turned. "I almost forgot. They tell me Mama's lobster tortilla will be out any minute."

Thirty minutes later the party was in full swing with people munching on tortillas and drinking wine. Father Leo leafed through the booklet looking at the photos that showed the contents on the wagons when they were found. Most of the others had scattered around the room holding whatever item had caught their eye. They used the brochure as a guide to find it's historical significance, date, and what it was used for.

Mama was seated on a high back chair and the center of attention. She wore a twelfth-century crown, three necklaces, and several bracelets. "Thank God I'm not hungry," she said. "I can't lift my arm to eat anything." Everybody laughed.

Across the room Rick and Ramon were sorting through ivory game boards with a catalogue from Oliver's library. The two men had formed a closer bond now than when they were boys. They seemed to genuinely enjoy each other. Ramon was leaving for Spain in a week but had promised to return for the holidays.

Johnny, with his arm still in a cast, wandered around wearing a silly smirk on his face. Ginger had tied a sword around his waist and put a breastplate over his shirt. She was heading in his direction with an armored head mask.

MJ was enthralled with the black pearls from La Paz Bay. They were first mentioned by Cortez when he landed in 1535, then shamelessly pillaged by the Spanish over the next three centuries. When the wagons from Santa Isabel were unloaded, bags of pearls were found hidden inside statues and pottery, under clothing, and beneath the cab of the wagons. MJ was astounded by the quality and quantity, and equally mystified about how she would display them in the new museum.

Antigua was invited to the private event but declined. She was in mourning for Don Hernando. The only bright spot in her life was the discovery that her son Don Miguel was now Father Hernan, a Carthusian monk living in Burgos, Spain. The monastery gave him a dispensation to come to Mexico and visit his mother.

Mama and Antigua jointly donated the collection from the mission to the state of Baja California with the understanding that it would be housed in a separate wing of the new museum. The project had the approval of the town fathers, and ground-breaking was scheduled for September.

MJ, lost in thought, felt a hand on her shoulder and a kiss on the back of her neck. She giggled and turned. "I was wondering when you'd finally tear yourself away from the game boards."

"And now that I have?" Rick said with a grin.

"Well, I have a plan," MJ said. "How 'bout I meet you outside by the truck in ten minutes." She nodded toward the room. "By the time they realize we're gone, we can be half way to Santa Juanico."

Rick winked. "You're on."

THE END

ACKNOWLEDGMENTS

I would like to thank several people who guided me in the publication of *The Lost Mission of Santa Isabel.* A thank you to Mark Acito, the first person to give credence to my writing; to Jennifer Springsteen, co-founder of PDX Writers, whose encouragement and tough editing pushed me along the process; to Patrick Coffman for his probing questions; to Guillermo Beron Prieto for his many facets of knowledge of Mexico; to Judy Flohr for proofreading extraordinaire; to Brock Taylor for insisting I do one more draft; and to Holly Lorincz whose wisdom and wit guided me through the final stages to publication.

A special thank you to Baja California for providing me with fascinating women with compelling stories as I traveled from the Sierra Lagunas to the Sea of Cortes.

Joan Candler